RULE BREAKER: ALTERNATE COVER

MM COLLEGE HOCKEY ROMANCE

BAR DOWN 1

AVA OLSEN

CHAPTER 1
MADDOX

THE FIRST WEEK OF SCHOOL

Fuck off was my favorite expression. One I used without hesitation. I didn't just say it to other people. Sometimes I aimed those words right back at myself. No matter how many times I'd repeated that I was strong enough, I never fully believed it. Self-doubt is a cagey bastard that keeps slithering back, even when you think you've kicked his ass to the curb.

At twenty, my life until this point could best be described as a shitshow. Part of it good, but the rest unquestionably bad. I was always on alert. On edge. Waiting for the next blow to knock me down. I was used to facing things head on and bracing myself for impact.

It's probably why I chose to be a goalie. It was always me against everyone else.

Eight months ago, at the urging of my former hockey coach, Daniel Toth, I'd applied to Sutton University. Three of the top goalies in the professional league had played there. Guarding the net was all I wanted, so I went for it. And with

Sutton's acceptance came a new start. I packed up my shit and found myself alone, as usual, but in a different country.

Going from Canada's largest city to a small town in the Green Mountains of Vermont was the biggest shock of all. I was used to the chaos and anonymity of Toronto. I didn't court attention. But sometimes I got it, whether I wanted it or not. Why? I was a surly asshole on the best of days. A loner and an introvert. And I planned on staying that way. College or not.

Case in point, today was the first official hockey practice with my new team, the Cougars.

While everyone was gathered at center ice, getting to know each other, I was in my net. My safety zone. I wasn't in the mood to talk to any of these guys. Nothing personal, it's just me.

I was grumpy as fuck after days of dealing with incoming paperwork and getting settled into my dorm. At least they'd accommodated my special request for a room to myself. There's no way I'd handle living with a roommate because only one of us would survive.

I was used to living in a house, or, rather, a basement apartment. By myself. The only people I interacted with were Daniel, who owned said house, occasionally his wife, and their kid. I'd been living with his family since I was sixteen, after I'd left a bad situation.

But I had hockey. I didn't need anything else.

Still, a new school, living quarters, classmates; it was a lot for me to take in. To say I was on edge was putting it mildly. There was a crap ton of students and being in close quarters with so many strangers—overly friendly ones, at that—had my hackles up.

So did the guy now skating toward me, wearing number ten.

He was the biggest defenseman I'd ever seen, never mind played with. The six-foot-five behemoth glided down the ice, talking with every player, and all with an over-the-top grin on his face that made me gag. He looked like he ate, slept, and shit literal sunshine. And I was a thunder and lightning kind of guy.

"I'm Kayden Melnyk," he announced when he skated up to me. He pulled off his glove, reaching his bare hand out. Just like his face, it was covered in golden freckles. "Welcome to the Cougars."

"Fuck off," I muttered, my voice muffled by my mask.

"Excuse me?" he asked, looming, his hazel eyes bearing down on me.

Despite his ginormous stature—I was six-one—I wasn't intimidated by him. Not by his size or that neon smile of his that was making me more irritable by the second.

"Look, it's simple," I snapped, pushing my mask up.

When Melnyk saw my expression, he took a step back. Score one point for me.

"I don't like people," I continued. "I don't care how you're doing, how much you love hockey, this college, or this team. And I don't want to be your fucking friend, got it? You have your job out here and I have mine. Now let's get on with the goddamn game."

Then I slammed my mask back down. End of discussion.

The only thing more satisfying than telling someone off was watching them walk away. Once that happened, they rarely came back. If they did, my lethal mouth ensured they didn't try again.

Melnyk—Kayden—took off down the ice and my nerves eased.

I didn't need friends; hockey teammates or otherwise. No thanks. I trusted two people in my life—Daniel and my therapist. That was it. Oh, and the guy who did my tattoos and piercing. Other than that, I didn't want to be engaged in any kind of conversation or, even worse, any attempt to be touched. Unless it was a tattoo needle. Pain I could handle. I understood. Anything else was foreign to me.

I skated in front of my net, side to side, tapping the bar while I hummed a favorite song. Getting my head prepped. It didn't matter if it was a practice game or a nail-biting season closer, my ritual was always the same. And I wasn't the odd person out. Every hockey player has their thing before, during, and after, a game. If no one interrupted my vibe, I didn't care what they did.

I glanced over and watched Kayden as he skated up to our captain, Dane St. Pierre, one of our forwards, Jace Rowland, and a defenseman, Silas Moss. Dane seemed like an okay guy, but again, way too fucking friendly for my liking. Jace too. Then there was Axel Lund. Another forward, and like me, a new addition to the team. I knew him by reputation, a guy who played fast and hard.

Silas skated around Axel and headed my way.

Fuck, not another one.

But unlike Kayden, Silas didn't smile at me.

"It's like a fucking frat party out here," he grumbled as he skated past me. "Jesus, can we get on with the playing already?"

Now, Silas, I could relate to. He looked older than the rest of the guys, with a thick blond beard. There was a quiet intensity about him. And his sarcastic outburst had me biting back a grin.

Hey, I'm an asshole, but not totally without a sense of humor.

More guys skated out onto the ice. Ethan Walker and Colin Goring, two forwards whose reputations I was also familiar with. Both guys were top scorers. Then I spotted more defensemen, Julian Hudak and Finn Baran, and finally, Sean Virtanen, another goalie. He'd had an injury or something at the end of last season. I'd looked up his stats. He was good. But I wasn't satisfied with being good. It was best or nothing.

Last up was our coach, Damien Banning. A former professional d-man who'd been coaching college hockey for the past four years. This was his second year at Sutton.

He joined us on the ice and whistled to get everyone's attention. I tapped the bar one last time and then I did my final stretches.

"Are we gonna stand around looking pretty for the freshman or get this game going?" Silas yelled out.

Coach Banning replied that he was in charge, not the other way around. When Silas rolled his eyes, I caught Coach's ensuing glare. Banning was a guy who didn't bullshit—he didn't give it and he didn't take it—and I could respect that.

He was especially blunt when it came to his expectations for me this season.

"Second place isn't an option," he said to me yesterday when we sat down in his office.

No shit.

Sutton U Cougars had ranked third in the college hockey standings last season, Banning's first coaching the team. The team ranked tenth the year before that. This year, the goal was to overtake Langston College for the top spot. If there was one thing I knew for certain, it was that I wanted to win. And, yeah, I had no choice but to work with my teammates. But, for the most part, I did my own thing.

My only concern was the hockey scouts that were starting to take notice of me. I knew my cranky attitude wouldn't mix well with my aspirations. Still, I did what I wanted—smoked, drank, and enjoyed the occasional spliff—and said whatever was on my mind. I didn't care to hear anyone's opinion about it. Or censor myself. I made my own rules.

Everyone else could, you guessed it, fuck off.

But, for real, I wasn't the only player with a smart mouth. There were plenty of those to go around.

And it wasn't just trash-talking on the ice. Most guys my age couldn't shut up about who they were banging and how often. Times like that, I realized how different, how odd I was compared to the norm. The only thing I didn't do was sex. I guess if I thought about it, that was its own kind of rebellion. Not by choice. Sure, I was curious. But I didn't think about sex the way other guys did. There was a disconnect inside me I didn't fully understand yet. And letting a stranger touch me was not in the cards. I wish I could screw all my frustration away, but for now, my fist would have to do.

Then again, I wondered, who'd want to be near me? On the outside, I'd pass for any college student. But on the inside, I had a lot of fissures. At this point, I had nothing but my hockey net holding me together.

Coach suddenly blew his whistle and the high-pitched sound startled me out of my head and back to the moment. Shoving my anxieties away, I focused on the players in front of me. Out here, I wasn't fucked up. I was in control.

Dane separated the team into two groups, and next thing I knew, he was facing off against Axel for possession. When the captain himself got hold of the puck and started barreling down the ice in my direction, everything clicked into place.

I was ready for this. College. Hockey. A new life. All of it.

Or, so I thought.

CHAPTER 2

KAYDEN

"What did you think of the game? And the new guys?"

Sitting in front of my stall, sweaty and padded up, I glanced up at my friend Dane and thought about his question. I was thrilled to be out on the ice again with my team. Even if it was a practice game.

But I wasn't so happy about meeting our new goalie, Maddox Rocher. Number two. Kind of an odd number for a goalie to pick. Usually, it was one. Whatever. Goalies were always strange. But this one was grumpy as hell. No, that word didn't even begin to describe him. When he told me to *fuck off,* I was stunned. I'd never experienced that kind of hostility from a teammate before. He didn't even know me, and already, he hated me?

Those smoky eyes of his sliced deep, like catching my skin on a freshly sharpened blade. And I was pretty sure I was still bleeding.

Dane had cautioned me about Maddox's acidic attitude, but as usual, I stumbled forward. Then I thought about the other guys that were new to the team; Silas and Axel—a defenseman with a smart mouth and a cocky forward with a wicked slapshot.

"The energy's fucking intense," I replied. "Pretty feral."

Dane nodded and yanked off his jersey. "I know what you mean. We've got a lot of talent, but high expectations. Everyone's out to prove themselves."

Coach Banning had given us a post-practice welcome speech. Getting us ready for the season. The pressure was on this year to reach the top college spot. Sutton had consistently ranked in the top ten, but last year, under his leadership, was the first time the school had broken the top five. Now, it was onwards and upwards.

And, despite my shitty start with our goalie, I was pumped. Like all the guys on our team, I was aiming for a spot in the professional league in the not-too-distant future. My dream job. And I wouldn't let anything or anyone affect that. Or change who I was.

I tried my best to make friends with everyone. It's the way I was raised, in a family of eight. You go along and get along or chaos erupts. Not only that, but when you're the odd one out—struggling to learn, well, anything—in a sea of high achievers, you find a way. A way to fit in. My two brothers and three sisters were smart as fuck; top of their class. Like my parents, who owned a successful real estate company. Me? What did I have? Size, strength, and a knack for hockey. Oh, and I had people skills. I could poke fun at myself and make others laugh. 'Goofy,' 'golden,' and 'adorkable' were tags I was used to. But it had taken me a long time to get here.

In high school, before I hit my growth spurt, I was picked on relentlessly. Every day I was told by other students that I was stupid or worse. Things got so bad that to this day, I still hear the echo of their taunts in my head.

"Dumb fuck, why don't you quit already?"

"Moron."

"Loser."

It's just words. I'd been told to move on. Get over it. Easier said than done. That shit replays in your head like earworms, and never leaves.

My phone buzzed, but I ignored it. It was probably another message from my academic advisor asking for a meeting. Unlike most students, I didn't get accepted at Sutton because of my outstanding grades. Thanks to hockey, I'd earned a full athletic scholarship. But there were conditions. I was supposed to maintain a minimum 2.0 GPA or a C average. Last semester I barely got there, even with tutors.

The thought of losing that scholarship, of having to go back home a total failure, suddenly loomed larger than any opponent I faced on the ice.

When I looked up at Dane again, he was already undressed, a white towel around his hips.

"Jackson and I are going to head in town for a bite. Come with?" Dane asked.

Jackson was Dane's new roommate, but his old friend. One that Dane knew from his high school days in Arkansas. Dane had been acting kinda strange the past week, but I figured he was still getting used to living with his former classmate. Jackson was also an athlete, but with the rowing crew. I liked him the moment I met him. He was quieter than Dane, but funny and kind. He'd even helped me and Dane organize the welcome week games and brought his crew to our practice today to watch us play.

I was about to reply to Dane's dinner suggestion when my phone buzzed again.

"Hold on."

Reluctantly, I tapped my phone, and sure enough, there was a message from my advisor. We had a meeting scheduled tomorrow at ten. I confirmed that I'd be there, my stomach now in a painful knot. I was always freaking hungry after practice, but suddenly food didn't seem like a great idea.

"Sorry, you said you're going into town?" I asked.

Dane nodded, reached for his water bottle, and took a long gulp.

"I'm happy to come with," I replied. "If you don't mind a third wheel."

My friend spewed his mouthful of water all over the bench, nearly dousing me.

"Bud, I know I need a shower, but I'd rather wait for one without your germs," I teased.

Dane wiped his mouth, grabbed a spare towel, and wiped down the bench. "Fuck, sorry about that."

"What's with you?" I asked. "You've been jumpy all week. And, let's be real, I'm usually the one who does clumsy shit like that."

It was true. The only time I was coordinated was on the ice. Off it, well, let's just say that my dorkiness was well known. It was the same when it came to everything, including sex. Not that I'd had any yet. Not that I'd tell anyone. Yup, still a virgin at soon-to-be twenty years old. Fuck me. Or, in my case, *not*.

Sure, I'd made out with a few girls at parties, but nothing more than that. It was fun, but I didn't feel anything more than mild interest. Maybe because I was always the last option. My female classmates preferred the slick, smart guys who had big plans. I was the friendly guy, the one who knew everyone, but no one really knew. The shoulder to cry on when they got dumped. The placeholder.

"I'm fine, I've just got lot on my mind. And you're not a third wheel. Jace is coming too, but he's gonna meet us there later," Dane muttered as he finished dressing. "See you out front?"

I nodded and grabbed my phone again. I added a reminder about my appointment tomorrow. If I didn't, I'd forget for sure. And speaking of which, one of my notifications pinged. I reached into my backpack and searched for my meds. I'd been diagnosed with ADHD in high school.

Meds helped to an extent, especially with my concentration when it came to tasks. But it wasn't a cure-all.

Once I downed the pills with electrolyte water, I shoved my hockey gear in the stall, grabbed my shampoo and body wash, and headed for the showers.

I didn't see any sign of Maddox around, and I was thankful for that. Thinking back to his reaction, a strange uneasiness took hold. Then I remembered he was bitchy like that with everyone on the team, including Coach. I had no reason to feel weird because it wasn't just me.

Ten minutes later, I headed out of the sports facility and looked for Dane and Jackson.

They were standing at the bottom of the stairs in some kind of intense conversation. But it was the way Dane leaned into Jackson that made me curious. Were they more than friends? Dane was cagey about his personal life, never talking about who he hooked up with. Assuming he did. Then again, he probably thought the same of me. Or maybe I was seeing things that weren't there thanks to my horny, frustrated brain.

I made it almost all the way down the stairs, but clearly, I was walking too fast (or I was lost in my head), and I tripped on the last one, crashing into my friends.

"Shit!" I blurted out.

"Oof," Jackson groaned as he pitched forward.

Luckily, Dane grabbed hold of Jackson and stopped his fall. Which was a miracle, given my size.

"Fuck, I'm so sorry," I explained when I finally caught my balance.

"No worries, Kay." Jackson smiled at me. "Dane caught me in those massive hockey hands of his. I've got no complaints."

Now, I wasn't the brightest guy around, but I knew flirting when I heard it.

"Really?" I looked at Dane with one eyebrow raised.

Was his face red from practice or something else?

"Dinner. Then we'll talk," Dane grumbled and started off without us.

"Ignore him," Jackson replied and patted my shoulder. "He's just hangry."

We soon caught up to our friend, but as we were walking, someone shouted our names. I turned to find Jace jogging up to us. He looked like your typical student, in jeans, a denim jacket, and a baseball cap turned backwards. Jace was an amazing forward and vying for the coveted center spot this year. I had no doubt he'd earn it.

"I thought you were meeting us later?" Dane commented.

"The call I had scheduled got pushed back to tomorrow," Jace explained with a smile, then nodded at me. "Everyone in one piece?"

I stared back at him, confused.

"I saw you take that tumble down the stairs, Kay. Poor Jackson was nearly crushed."

I rolled my eyes and gave him my best finger. Smart ass.

"Thank fuck Dane was there for Jackson to land on," Jace continued, his cocky smirk in full effect. "Right Dane? Was it good for you?"

Dane grunted and ignored Jace's comment. And his shit-eating grin.

Crossing the south lawn, we headed through the gates and into the town proper. The campus was crawling with students and the electricity of first-week nerves was in the air. I loved being here in Vermont. It reminded me of my home-town of Wells. Lots of friendly people, quiet streets, and plenty of outdoor activities. But I had to admit that while Lake Kinnear, the one that bordered campus, was beautiful, it wasn't the same as the ocean in Maine. I missed the briny air and the sand in between my toes. No matter what, the beach was home to me. But this place had its charm. There were green mountains—now turning to fall colors—cool shops, and plenty of places to eat. For any athlete, the last one mattered most.

"What do you guys feel like eating tonight?" Dane asked as we hit Main Street.

"How about Fried Up?" Jace replied. "With the picnic tables?"

My stomach rumbled loudly at the idea of fried chicken and mac 'n' cheese. Fuck, any food at this point would be welcome. And the place had heat lamps on its patio for the fall weather.

"Hey, is that Maddox standing over there?" Jackson asked.

I turned my head so quickly that my neck popped. Sure enough, standing in the darkened alleyway beside the pharmacy, was Maddox. He was leaning against the brick wall, smoking, and staring up at the sky like he was mesmerized.

Suddenly, he turned his head and spotted us. I got the same look he'd given me earlier. I wasn't cold, but I sure as fuck was shivering.

CHAPTER 3
MADDOX

The first official game of the season went like this: there was pre-game nausea, trash talk—other players, not me—and the chugging of a shit ton of electrolyte water. Then came the near-fatal anxiety when I stepped out of the locker room and stepped onto the rink. And finally, the rush of exhilaration when the puck dropped, the sudden hush of the crowd, and the loud crack of the rubber hitting the ice. That puck was hypnotizing, and it was the only thing I thought about for three periods, aka two and a half hours of play.

Today, we faced off against Wissick, a neighboring college from New Hampshire. Though, there was nothing friendly about them, us, *or* this game. The first period unleashed a torrent of pent-up nerves. And we hadn't completely settled by the end of it. Jace and Axel accidentally collided while chasing the puck, and Silas let one of Wissick's forwards get the drop on him.

By the second period, there were still no goals, so it was anyone's game. I glanced over at Kayden. He hadn't made any further move to talk to me since our first meeting. Just the usual nods of awareness that teammates shared on the ice.

That was fine by me. Stay the fuck away.

When the third period rolled around, I'd already stopped twenty-two shots on goal, and I was still holding strong. Despite my stormy expression, I was over the moon. This was where I belonged. This was where nothing could stop me. Well, as long as I had good defensemen to help me.

I begrudgingly admitted to myself that I was glad Kayden was on my team. For his size, he was quick to react, so attuned to where the puck was at all times. And being in the defensive zone, he took the hits necessary to protect me. Him and the other d-men too. Finn was smaller, but scrappy, Julian was lightning quick with a temper to match, and Silas? I hadn't quite figured him out yet. Sometimes, he moved with anticipation, and other times, he seemed bored. Or caught up in his head? I had no idea. It was early days yet.

Five and a half minutes left in the final period, and I watched as Jace tore off down the ice with the puck, leaving Wissick's team in his icy dust. Axel and Dane weren't far behind, heading into the fray. From my point of view, I could see almost everything, every play, and missed opportunities, too.

"Rowland! Rowland!" The crowd chanted Jace's name.

And with good reason. Jace was one of the best forwards on the college ice, weaving in and out of Wissick's players like a slippery eel. When he got his opportunity, he took the shot. The hometown crowd reacted, jumping up to their feet and hollering as loud as they could as the lamp lit up.

Holy shit. Suddenly, we were on the board. Our first goal of the season.

Jace glided around the net, hands in the air, and came back around to leap on Dane. The rest of our team followed, piling up around each other, shouting and cheering each other on. I tapped my stick on the ice, my version of acknowledging my teammate's success.

Suddenly, Kayden turned around and locked eyes with

me. I nodded, and he did the same before turning away. That was as friendly as we were gonna get.

The excitement of that goal stayed with me for the rest of the period.

Dane was just as eager as Jace, stick-handling the puck with a skill and an ease that impressed me. And he pulled off our second goal of the game. There was more cheering, more chanting, and another incredible high.

Until the minutes ticked down to seconds. Unfortunately, a timeout and line change for Wissick brought out their top forward, a guy named Lakeley, and he couldn't be stopped. The shot was so fast, I hardly believed it happened at all. It touched the edge of my blocker and bounced into my net. He scored on me with thirty seconds remaining, my earlier elation reduced to ash.

But we still finished strong, and when the final buzzer sounded, I gave a sigh of relief. Cougars 2-1.

Was it the best game I ever played? Unfortunately, no. But the thrill of winning consoled any disappointment I had with myself. That was the hardest part about being a goalie. Managing expectations. Not letting a goal get to you. Holding strong, not only physically, but mentally. All game, every game.

It was so fucking ironic. In my everyday life, most days, I was barely holding on.

Kayden

Dinner after the game was a team event with every player as giddy as me. Well, almost everyone. Silas left early without so much as a 'goodbye.' And our new goalie? Maddox had his ear pods in as he ate silently, ignoring everyone around him. I was going to tell him he was being rude as fuck, but it wasn't my place. I left that to Coach or Dane. Then again, not everyone was a talker like me. Still, we were going to be spending a lot of time together over the next season between practices, games, and workouts. There had to be a way to get through to him. He couldn't ignore us forever. It was bad for the team.

"You okay?" Dane nudged me.

"Yeah, more than good," I replied as I focused on my friend. "You?"

Dane shrugged his shoulders. "I'm great, but the post-game exhaustion is starting to hit."

I nodded. I'd probably be there in another hour or two.

"So, I wanted to ask you something," I said and took another sip of my soda. "Well, the entire team, actually."

Dane nodded. "What's up?"

"I've signed up to volunteer with a local sports charity that helps kids with disabilities. It's called All For Play. I'd like to see if some of the guys might want to help."

"That's awesome, Kay. How much time are we talking?"

"A couple of hours?"

"I'm in."

"Cool."

Dane got everyone's attention and raised his glass. "As Captain of the Cougars, I want to thank everyone for an amazing game today. We're starting out strong, so let's keep it going!"

There were cheers and glasses clinked.

"Kayden?" Dane motioned to me to go ahead.

I cleared my throat. "I know we've all got busy schedules, but I'm volunteering for a local children's charity and wondering if anyone wants to help. It's two hours, once a month. No pressure either way. You can text me if you're interested. Thanks."

There were nods around the table and I left it at that. Guys had a lot on their plate with hockey and classes. Then I thought about juggling everything I had on the go this year. And my struggle to maintain my grades. I was probably taking on too much, but I hated saying no. Especially when it came to volunteering. It was second only to hockey in terms of what I loved to do.

"Kayden!" Jace called out from the other end of the table. "Sign me up."

I nodded, appreciative of his enthusiasm.

Maddox suddenly stood up, walked around the table to talk to Coach, and then left the room.

"Was it something I said?" I quipped out loud when he was out of sight.

"More than likely," Ethan snarked. "But we gotta give the guy some slack. He's a goalie. They're all bizarro. Right, Sean?"

"No." Sean rolled his eyes. "We're the normal ones. It's the rest of you that are a pain in the a—"

Coach coughed and interrupted Sean's comment.

"I've got to get going, but great game today." Banning nodded. "I'll see you at practice in two days."

Coach paid the bill and headed out. Everyone filed out of the restaurant, with me, Dane, and Jace walking back to the dorm. When we got to the third floor, I said goodbye to my friends and headed for my room. I barely made it to my bed and it was lights out.

———

I would've loved to have slept in the next day, but there was no rest for this college student.

After heading to the cafeteria and scarfing down a questionable breakfast burrito, I hopped in a rideshare and arrived at All For Play. Once a month, they organized a designated game day for the kids. Today, it was adapted basketball.

I met with the activity coordinator, a woman named Keeley Truitt, helped her set up the space, and met all the kids before I refereed the game. Watching these nine- and ten-year-olds—many of them in wheelchairs—making friends and having fun was its own reward. It reminded me to never take what I had for granted. I always knew that hockey was it for me, but helping my community was just as important.

After the game, I was invited by Keeley and the kids to join their pizza lunch. Hey, I never said no to free food either.

"I'm organizing a sledge hockey series this winter," Keely announced when we were eating. "Are you familiar with it?"

"I've been to a few games back in Maine," I replied. "I could ask if the college would be willing to let us use the rink."

"The kids would love visiting Sutton U, but if not, there's a local rink we can book. I've already sourced the equipment we need."

"You mean the sleds?"

She nodded. "Our fundraiser this fall should cover it. Fingers crossed we hit our target and then I can start planning for the new year."

"I've already mentioned to my teammates about volunteering. I'm sure they'd be keen for sledge hockey."

"I'll keep you updated," Keeley replied.

Once lunch was done, I said my goodbyes to the kids, with promises to return.

When I arrived back on campus, I went straight to the gym for a light workout. Instead of waiting for the elevator, I took the stairs to the second floor. As usual, I was all up in my head, and not even noticing where I was going. Until I ran right into someone.

Not someone. Maddox.

"Oof, sorry," I blurted out, steadying myself.

"Watch it," Maddox snapped, grabbing onto the railing.

"I said, I'm sorry."

"Get out of my way," he hissed.

I stood aside with my hands up in the air and watched as Maddox ran down the rest of the stairs.

My good mood vanished along with our goalie.

CHAPTER 4

MADDOX

A WEEK LATER

hated college. Go on and tell me I'm being an ungrateful asshole. Whatever.

It was a lot for me to deal with and pushed my limited patience to the brink. Between the eager—and downright nosy—students in the dorm, meeting with my advisor, and actual classes, I was in a perpetual state of pissed.

And I was totally unsurprised. This was the reason I'd held off from applying after graduating from high school. I wasn't sure I could handle being in class again. Not the actual classwork, since no matter the subject, I always scored high marks. It was the in-person thing that always threw me. Especially in courses where the teacher paired people up for projects. Working with, and depending on, someone else to help me with my coursework was a no-go. The dreaded 'T' word. Teamwork. It was bad enough I had to deal with others when I played hockey. At least there, I had distance. Goalkeeping is its own thing.

But school? Ugh. The whole structure of college was stupid, anyway. Outdated. I was already deep into coding and programming. I worked online, part time, setting up websites, and making decent money. In fact, I probably didn't even need a computer science degree at this point. But still, if hockey didn't work out, I needed a plan, so I wasn't totally screwed. No way I'd ever be in a vulnerable position again. And getting a degree seemed like the logical thing to do.

My core classes were fine. But it was here, in my elective, Economics 201, where I was prepared to be bored out of my mind. It was either economics or a social sciences class. Which, of course, involved group work. Hard no. Programming, algorithms, calculus—those were my classes and it was all about individual achievement. No way was I depending on anyone but myself for my grades.

This elective, however, proved to be popular with a lot of students, probably for the same reason. There were at least sixty or so students in attendance. As usual, I sat at the back, in the last seat of the last row, on my phone, playing solitaire. Shut up. The game calmed me.

A door slammed, and I looked up to find a familiar figure entering the room. Aw, shit. Kayden was in the same class as me? Just fucking great. I'm sure my scowl could crack my face in half at this point.

Kyden was so huge he nearly hit the top of the doorframe. But he didn't walk so much as tumble into the room, tripping over something, and nearly face-planting into a row of students. The difference between his coordination on the ice and off it was startling. And concerning.

Kayden looked up, and when he spotted me, he jolted.

Oh my God. Please stay away.

He made his way to the front row, and I breathed a sigh of relief. Good. Perfect. One less annoyance for me to deal with.

But when Kayden sat down, and even though the rows were staggered, the people behind him couldn't see around. I bit back a chuckle as one classmate, then another, tapped on Kayden's shoulder to talk to him.

Unfortunately, my laughter was short-lived.

Kayden got up, red-faced, and headed up the stairs to the back of the room. Then I realized that there was only one other seat left up here, and it was right beside me.

Doing my best to look busy, I kept my eyes focused on my phone and absently tugged on my silver earring with my free hand. I didn't watch Kayden sit down, but I felt the ground underneath me vibrate when he did. When his knee hit mine, I nearly jumped out of my chair.

"Sorry," Kayden muttered.

I grunted and shifted away, my feet resting in the aisle. When I looked up, I noticed a few raised eyebrows from other students.

"What?" I snapped.

No one bothered me after that.

Kayden shifted, and the loud creak of his chair had me biting back another chuckle. Fuck, twice in one day. It was a miracle.

He was sitting way too close for comfort, but what could I do? At least Kayden didn't smell bad. I caught the scent of something woodsy, spicy. Anything was better than hockey sweat, and if I could survive that shit, I could survive anything.

"Damn," he whispered.

I glanced over and noticed that he had his laptop open, but the telltale buzz meant he was out of power. He shut his computer, and pulled out his phone, typing away.

A middle-aged man in a rumpled brown suit stepped into the class and walked up to the podium, tapping it once.

"I'm Professor Thomas H. Clarke and this is Economics 201. If you're registered for 101, 301, or 401, guess what? You're in the wrong class," he paused.

Five, no six students got up and quickly left the room.

"Now, our first lecture today is about common theories of macro—"

Boring.

I continued to play solitaire on my phone and half-listened to the teacher. Kayden was typing relentlessly. It sounded like he was either taking word-for-word notes or was texting someone a really long fucking message. Given that he kept muttering and swearing under his breath about 'talking too fast,' I assumed it was the former.

"You don't need to note every damn thing he says," I bit out.

"Uh, yeah, I do."

Weird, but okay.

After what seemed like an hour (it was six and a half minutes), Professor Monotone started asking the class questions. Pretty sure Kayden was taking notes on that, too.

"…And to see how much everyone was paying attention, we're going to have a pop quiz," he continued. "Open your email. You have fifteen minutes to complete."

"Shit," Kayden exclaimed.

Why was he so torn up about a stupid quiz? I pulled out my laptop, filled out the answers in under five minutes, then got back to my game. By the time the class ended, thirty minutes and another boring lecture later, I was dying for a smoke and some kind of mental stimulation. Any kind.

Thankfully, Kayden grabbed his stuff and lumbered off without saying a word. I thought for sure he'd try to talk to me again. But apparently, he'd learned his lesson the first time.

What can I say? I was a really good fucking teacher.

Kayden

I was never going to pass Economics 201. The professor talked too fast, I didn't understand half the concepts he rattled on about, and most of all, I was distracted by the warning from my advisor. Panic was setting in.

If I lost my scholarship. If I lost, if I lost…

I wouldn't. I couldn't. I needed to stay calm.

I'd already been granted extended time for my assignments. But I wasn't expecting that quiz today and it totally threw me off. Pretty sure I failed that. Not a great start.

How did I forget to charge my laptop? And why the fuck didn't I remember to bring my charger? I had reading and spelling apps on my phone, and normally they worked great. But when my laptop died and my app froze, I was fucked.

On the positive side, I had tutors lined up. Hopefully, between that and extra time for tests, I'd be okay. As long as I didn't have to sit beside Maddox again. He finished the quiz in half the time it took me. When I glanced over, I noticed he had his schedule open, and a computer programming class was next. The guy was probably a coding genius or something. Or a hacker. I could see that. He had that *'I'm angry with the world and I live in a dark basement,'* vibe.

I rushed back to my dorm, grabbed my laptop charger, and headed for my next class. Halfway across the campus, I spotted Dane and Jackson and headed over to say hi. It turned out, my hunch about the two of them was right. And Dane confirmed it that night in town, when me and Jace had dinner with them.

"Jackson and I are dating," Dane admitted as we sat on the outdoor patio. "We were together back in high school, but I wasn't ready to come out. But we're only telling a few of our close friends. I'm not ready to tell everyone. You guys know, obvi, and Coach. I'm still not sure about when I'm going to tell the rest of the team."

I was happy for them, but I understood.

Jace was bi and had gone through the same thing last year. He hadn't told the rest of the team either, only me, Dane, and Coach. I got it. There was enough pressure on us between hockey and classes. And fuck knows a lot of people weren't accepting. Not in the hockey world, and not in the world in general.

"I guess this means we'll see you at every home game?" I teased Jackson. "Are you gonna bring Mullet too?"

Mullet was Dane's leopard gecko and not my kind of pet. I preferred dogs. But Mullet was cute, if you liked scaly reptiles. And the other players thought he was cool, so he became our unofficial second mascot.

"I don't think the cold is good for him," Jackson replied, his eyes bright. "But I'll try to make every game. Or as many as my schedule allows. Unless I'm in a regatta."

Dane turned to his boyfriend and the heated look that passed between them had me suddenly envious. What would it be like for someone to want me like that?

"…Do you want to come?"

I stared at Dane and Jackson, totally lost at this point.

"What?" I said, shaking out of my daydream and back to the present.

Dane laughed. "I said, Jackson and I are going to grab some lunch at the Blackbird Café. Do you want to come with?"

"Sure."

After I'd scarfed down a chicken Caesar wrap and chips, I said goodbye to my friends and headed for my next class.

Halfway through my community development course, I got an email from Coach Banning about our team schedule. Our first away game with an overnight stay was taking place in Rochester in two weeks. Which meant traveling the night before. Last year, I got lucky and roomed with Dane for our road trips. I was hoping for the same this year. But it turned out, hope wasn't enough.

And when I saw the name of the person I was rooming with? Let's just say that my earlier panic hit an all-time high.

CHAPTER 5

KAYDEN

TWO WEEKS LATER (OCTOBER)

"Switch with me."

"No."

"Dane, come on," I pleaded.

I wasn't above begging to get what I wanted.

It was a cloudy afternoon, crisp but not cold, as we waited for our bus at the campus gates, along with the rest of the hockey team. Everyone had their bags by their feet, headphones on or around their neck, ready to roll.

Me? I wanted to run right back to my dorm.

Why the fuck had I gotten stuck with Maddox as a roommate? I'd approached Coach about it, but he told me that barring an emergency, there were no changes. Suck it up and deal.

"I sympathize, bud, but you know how Coach sets this up," Dane replied. "It's done. And someone has to room with Rocher. You're probably the best choice."

"What? Why me?" I asked.

"Come on, you're the nicest guy on the team. If anyone has patience for assholes, it's you."

I sighed. Dane wasn't wrong about the patience part. I was training to be a social worker, so empathy and patience were mandatory, but I wouldn't go so far as to say I was the nicest guy on the team. That was Jace. Not me. And, yeah, usually I could always find something good in everyone. But my exposure to Maddox so far left me with a restless twinge in my gut. Like the kind I get when a game is going downhill real fast, and the clock is running out. Despite all the practices to date, I still couldn't get past that mask of his. I was starting to think it was permanently attached to his face, and his personality.

"He hates me," I added.

"Maddox hates everyone," Dane lowered his voice and leaned in closer. "I heard he had it out with Coach. Demanded his own room on the road. Said he'd pay out of pocket, but the request got denied. And Maddox was pissed."

I shoved a hand through my messy hair and tugged. "Great. Now he's gonna be extra snarky, and I have to sleep in the same room. I'll be lucky if I wake up at all."

"Ignore him. Wear your headphones all the time. Do your own thing. Chances are, he's not gonna talk to you, anyway. It's not that big of a deal."

"Says the person *not* rooming with him," I replied.

"Sorry."

I glanced behind us and counted heads, and the entire team was lined up. Everyone except Maddox.

When our bus pulled up a few minutes later, I was still pacing like I was hopped up on too much sugar. Still, no sign of our snide goalie. Maybe he wouldn't show up at all. Maybe the Coach's rules were gonna push him over the edge, and he'd quit.

Nah. No one dropped their team over something like that. The hockey world isn't that big. If you get saddled with a difficult reputation, it can have consequences. I couldn't afford to fuck up, but maybe Maddox didn't give a shit. Still, I found it odd that a guy like that played a team sport.

"Maybe I'll ask Silas." I looked around and spotted the defenseman with his ear pods in, ignoring everyone around him. "I'm sure he won't mind sharing with Maddox."

"The answer to that is a hard no."

I turned at the sound of Coach's voice. Shit.

"You know the rules, Kayden. Rooms are set," Coach muttered before he stepped onto the bus.

Fuck.

Ignoring my nerves, I shoved my bag into the underbelly of the bus and stepped on board. At least I could sit beside whoever I wanted. Same thing when we went out for a team dinner.

Dane and I took the seats behind Coach, with Jace and Sean on the opposite aisle, and everyone else filing on behind us. I pulled out my phone and checked my messages. We were leaving in five minutes, Maddox or not. The bigger part of me hoped he wouldn't show up. I felt a bit guilty about that, but it was short-lived.

The bus driver talked to Coach, then got back to his seat, readying us to go.

Suddenly, the door opened, and Maddox finally stepped onto the bus, resting asshole face in place. His undercut was slicked back, with a few stray pieces of black hair falling into his eyes. He didn't look at me, though. Didn't even glance my way. Maybe Dane was right. Maddox would ignore me. Fine. The room situation wasn't going to be a problem, right?

When he walked past me, I smelled tobacco and the musk-iness of his leather jacket. That unsettled feeling in the pit of my gut hit me again. Or maybe it was motion sickness. Oh, wait, we were still in the parking lot...

Five minutes later, we pulled out of campus and headed for the highway. It was a six-hour drive to Rochester, and since I hardly slept last night, I crashed hard.

When I woke up, three hours later, I was starving and had the drool-crust on my mouth to prove it. I glanced around to find Dane typing on his phone. Jace and Sean were asleep, their heads back, mouths open, snores abundant.

I looked back and it was the same thing. The bus was quiet, except for the chainsaw that was Ethan's nose, and the hum of someone singing with their headphones on. We'd be stopping for a bathroom break soon, thank fuck, and hopefully, a decent fast-food chain while we were at it. I needed carbs and fat.

Then I smelled it.

A cigarette. Not stale, like the day after a party. Actual smoke drifted over me.

I stood up and turned around to find Maddox, ear pods in, smoking a cig, relaxed as can be. When he glanced up, instead of his usual glare, I got a smirk, the corners of his lips curled up. I didn't know which was scarier, his angry face or this one.

Coach was still asleep, but probably not for long. Without thinking, I got up and stalked to the back of the bus, not pausing until I reached Maddox.

"Put that out."

He yanked out his ear pods. "What?"

"I said, put that out."

"No."

"No smoking on the bus, or didn't you see the sign?" I hissed. "Coach catches you, and you're fucked."

Maddox shrugged and took another drag, then blew the smoke in my face. "He's gotta have two goalies for the game. I'm not worried."

"No one's impressed by this so-called rebel routine you're trying to pull off. It's just annoying," I snapped. "Now put that thing out before we all get kicked off the freaking bus."

"You heard him."

Thank you, Captain. I turned to find Dane standing behind me, giving as good a glare as Maddox.

Our goalie had one foot resting on the opposite knee, so he pushed the lit stub of the cigarette into the sole of his running shoe.

"Happy now, Cap?"

"You don't have to like us, and we don't have to like you. But you do need to have respect. That includes road trips and any group event where we represent the school—on or off the ice," Dane continued. "Unless, of course, you prefer to find another team to play with."

Maddox shoved his ear pods back in and closed his eyes. Was he agreeing with Dane or being a brat? At this point, who knew? Who cared?

"Come on," Dane encouraged me with a pat on my shoulder. "We're about to make a pit stop."

"Thank fuck," I muttered as I turned around, and we headed back to our seats. "Can we leave him there?"

Dane stared at me. "Really, Kay? That's so not you."

I would never. But...

"He's pushing my nice limit," I admitted.

When we got back to our seats, Coach was talking on his phone. Once he was done with his call, he turned to us. "Is there a fire I should know about?"

Dane and I both shook our heads.

"It's taken care of," Dane confirmed.

I didn't say anything, but I was half tempted to ask Coach to let me switch rooms. Again. But the stressed look on his face told me not to push my luck.

When the bus finally came to a stop, there was practically a stampede to get off. Every damn time. There's nothing hockey players hate more than sitting still for any length of time.

The service center was busier than I'd expected, with lineups at the burger place and the sub shop. After using the restroom, I got in line with Dane. Thankfully, I was familiar with the sub chain and their menu. Otherwise, I'd have to pull out my phone to read what was on display. Only a few of my teammates knew about my learning disability. Not sure why, but if it didn't come up, I didn't bother saying anything. It didn't affect my ability on the ice, so most guys probably wouldn't give a shit about it. I worried, though, that they'd see me differently. And treat me the same. I'd had enough of that in high school.

After I paid for my sub, I sat down with Jace, Dane, and Sean, and scarfed down my meal. Silas, Axel, and Ethan were sitting at the table beside us, with the rest of the guys beside them. Everyone was eating as fast as they could so we could get back on the road.

I spotted Maddox sitting alone at the very end, an unwrapped burger and a pile of fries in front of him. He'd barely eaten any of his meal. Instead, he sipped on a soda and was looking at his phone.

It hit me all at once. I flashed back to myself at age fourteen, sitting in the cafeteria. By myself.

My turkey sub sat like a rock in my stomach as I remembered how shitty that feeling was. Not fitting in. Everyone around me laughing, caught up in their conversations.

This is different. He wants to be alone.

It still didn't sit right.

Maddox had a prickly outer layer. But acting the way he did, the anger, the snarky vibe, I was pretty sure his attitude was all about defense. He was protecting himself. From what, I had no idea. And given that he didn't want anyone near him, it'd be hard as hell to suss out what the issue was.

On the ice, it was my job to protect him. But off the ice? I had a feeling I'd need more than my pads to protect *myself* from him.

CHAPTER 6
MADDOX

Fuck this.

I wrapped what was left of my meal and shoved it in my bag, then headed out of the service center for another smoke. My nerves were ratcheting higher the closer we got to our destination.

You should've told Coach why you didn't want to share a room.

Yeah, no fucking way. Bad enough I had to send a confidential note to the school about my dorm arrangements. No way in hell I wanted the whole hockey team knowing my business. Not that I thought Coach Banning would narc or anything. But teams were the same, whether it was high school, college, or beyond. Secrets had a way of getting out. And I didn't want to risk anyone overhearing my reasons for wanting to be alone. The last thing I needed was pity.

I could do this. I'd had plenty of therapy for the past four years, so it wasn't like I hadn't dealt with my issues. But still, sharing the same room with anyone, especially someone I didn't know, made me edgy.

I lit up, taking a deep drag, letting the heat fill my lungs. Pot would be even better, but I didn't want to do that the night before a game. It made me fuzzy, and I needed to stay sharp. Speaking of that, would I even sleep tonight? I had emergency sleeping pills, but again, I didn't like the way they made me feel the next day. Groggy as fuck. And, I didn't like taking anything that might leave me vulnerable.

From everything I'd overheard so far, Kayden was a stand-up guy. Someone everyone liked and trusted. There were no worries. I'd be fine. I'd had to share a room with a guy from my last team in Toronto and I managed okay. It was only one night. Okay, more than that, a couple in the next few months. Nothing I couldn't handle.

"That's a filthy habit."

I turned around to find Axel standing behind me, leaning against the wall. The cocky forward had a smug grin on his face that I hated as much as Kayden's. Wait. No. Axel's was slightly less annoying.

"I didn't ask for your opinion," I snapped and took another drag.

"Look, I get that you wanna do your own thing. You're a goalie. Most of you are weird as shit. That's fine. Just don't piss *everyone* off. Especially the guys playing defense. Otherwise, it fucks with the team dynamic."

I shook my head. "Stick to scoring goals, not sports psychology."

Axel pushed off the wall and walked up to me. "This is my year. I'm getting that center spot. Nothing, and no one, is going to get in my way. You read me?"

"Why don't you save your ego for the ice, Lund?"

Suddenly, Jace stepped forward and gave Axel a dirty look.

"You're another one," Axel sneered. "Too much talk and not enough action."

"Really? Who scored more in their last season? Me or you?"

Axel gave him the middle finger and stalked off towards the bus.

"Ignore him. He's a douchebag," Jace muttered and then motioned at me.

"What?" I asked.

"Give me a freaking smoke, man."

I scoffed. "Get your own cigs."

"One."

I sighed, pulled the pack out of my bag along with the lighter, and threw it at him. After he pulled out a cig and lit it up, he threw the pack back to me.

"Happy?" I snarked. "And I don't give a shit what Axel has to say. Or you, for that matter. And I don't need anyone to come to my defense. Now leave me the fuck alone."

"What's going on here?"

Kayden's sudden, deep voice startled me, and I nearly dropped my bag.

"What does it look like?" I asked him as I rolled my eyes. "We're smoking."

"Jace?" Kayden asked him.

Jace took a drag, then threw his cigarette on the ground. "Axel was running his mouth, so I told him to get lost. No biggie."

Kayden stared at me, and, for once, he wasn't smiling. I was pretty sure he heard the whole damn conversation with Axel and Jace. His eyes looked worried. Tough shit. I wasn't any of his concern.

"If there's a problem with a teammate, you—" Kayden started.

"There's no problem," I spat out. So much for trying to relax. I'd need a whole fucking pack of cigs for that. Why couldn't everyone leave me alone? "Axel is a cocky shit who thinks the world, and the team, revolves around him. Same as most guys who play this game, myself included. We all have our own agendas. And I don't care what he says to me. It doesn't. Fucking. Matter."

Kayden's face flushed, but he stood there, silent. Unmoving.

"I'm heading back to the bus," Jace announced and walked off.

"What?" I asked Kayden. "If you have something to say, say it. If not, leave."

Kayden shook his head and wandered off after Jace. I let out a breath I didn't realize I'd been holding. If my scathing comments didn't put Kayden off for good, nothing would.

I took one last drag, dropped the cig, and ground it under my shoe. As I stalked off to the bus, all I could think about was how badly I wanted this day to be over with. I wanted to close my eyes and wake up on the ice, in my gear, in my net. Where I was supposed to be. Where I belonged. I was looking forward to the game tomorrow more than anything else.

But afterward? Fuck no. There was always a team dinner. More bonding bullshit that I had no patience for. Still, I had to eat, and Coach informed me that the team dinner was mandatory—no exceptions. Banning had a lot of fucking rules like that. It chafed, but I could deal.

Instead of my pods, I searched my bag for my headphones. With those on, no one would bother me. I slid them over my ears, blasted the music as loud as I could stand, then hopped on the bus. Axel, Jace, and Kayden were already seated. Kayden and Jace were talking. Axel had his ear pods in and his eyes closed.

Over the next ten minutes, the rest of the team piled back on board, and we were off again.

It was another four hours before we made it to Rochester. And it was late. So late that all we did was collect our hotel card keys and shuffle aimlessly to our rooms. Kayden didn't speak to me. Or me to him. Not that I'd notice. I kept my headphones on, so even if he tried to talk to me, I'd have no way of hearing him. He seemed to have finally gotten the message.

He used the bathroom first while I took my meds and stripped down to my briefs. I checked my phone, but there were no notifications. Not that I expected any. The only people I ever texted were my therapist and Daniel. I had a private profile on several social media accounts, but I never posted. I perused stuff about hockey. Goaltending, of course.

I walked over to the window and closed the drapes, then sauntered back and flopped down on my bed, staring up at the popcorn ceiling. Instead of music, I grabbed my phone and tapped on one of my favorite podcasts.

Obviously, I didn't hear Kayden walk into the room. But I saw his shadow on the ceiling, and I sure as hell felt the bed vibrate when he walked closer. The man did not step lightly. I glanced over and watched him bending over his bed, his Sutton U sweatpants clinging to his ass. For some reason, I was unable to tear my eyes away.

WTF was wrong with me?

Kayden slid under the covers and I nearly laughed out loud when I saw his feet hanging over the end of the bed. Hotel rooms, beds especially, were not made for six-five giants like him. I'd been staring too long, though, and he looked over, catching my gaze.

He mouthed words, but of course, I couldn't hear him. Yanking off my headphones, I sat up.

"What?" I snapped.

"What are you listening to?" he asked quietly.

"A podcast."

"About?"

I sighed. Might as well answer his questions, and then maybe he'd leave me alone for the rest of the night. "It's called Below the Depths. It's about oceanography."

Kayden lifted an arm up and scratched his head. "Sounds intense."

"It is. Humans are acting like idiots, polluting the very thing we need to survive."

"Truth. You wouldn't believe the amount of plastic we've had to clean up on the beaches at home. Is that why you have that fish tattoo on your arm?"

That was my limit for conversation for the day. I placed my right hand protectively over my left shoulder. I couldn't talk about my tattoos. Not with a stranger. Not with anyone.

"No," I replied, turned away, and put my headphones back on.

There was no way I was telling Kayden the meaning behind my tattoos. That was for me, and me alone.

Next thing I knew, he turned off his lamp, leaving me with the glare of my phone screen. Oddly enough, my earlier nerves calmed. Which was really fucking weird because I wasn't comfortable with strangers. And that's what Kayden was. I still didn't know anything about him. Except that he seemed extra sensitive to others around him. He was too big for every room he entered. And he lived near the ocean. Wherever that was.

An hour later, my eyes grew heavy. And with the sound of the waves in my ears, I slid into my dreams.

CHAPTER 7

KAYDEN

I was up before my alarm. Unusual, and it only happened on game days. I was pumped, wired, and ready to hit the ice. And that was all before I even got out of bed.

Speaking of bed, I glanced over and looked at Maddox, who was lying curled up in a ball on the farthest corner of his bed. I couldn't believe he'd actually answered one of my questions last night without completely ripping my head off. There was a human being in there somewhere. I was pretty sure. Or maybe a vampire, given his dark blue eyes and the whole angry look he had going on.

One thing I was known for—when it came to hockey and everything else—was persistence. And even though my head was telling me to stay away from Maddox, my gut was telling me to keep digging. He wasn't like most college students. Hell, he wasn't like any other person that I'd ever met. There was a story there for sure. I'd spied those tattoos last night and those alone had to have some kind of meaning. A detailed fish surrounded by sea creatures on one arm, a skull biting a snake on the other. The designs were as intriguing as the guy sporting them.

"You're staring," Maddox grumbled.

How the fuck did he know that?

"Am not."

"Are too."

We sounded like were nine instead of nineteen. Instead of lying there feeling embarrassed, I got up and headed for the bathroom. After taking a much-needed piss, I washed my hands, brushed my teeth, and slathered on antiperspirant. Twice. Hey, it was game day, and I was already sweating a shit ton.

By the time I walked back out into the bedroom, Maddox was up, dressed, with the headphones on again.

"You're giving me a complex," I muttered.

He pivoted suddenly, stalked past me, and slammed the bathroom door.

"Okay, you're not a morning person either," I said out loud to myself. "Got it."

I texted Dane. He and most of the guys were already down in the restaurant, having breakfast. My stomach was pitching a fit, growling louder than my roommate. But I wasn't a total dick like Maddox. I got dressed and waited for him.

"Seriously? You're still here?" Maddox snapped when he emerged from the bathroom five minutes later. "Go down to breakfast already."

The guy's attitude was as pissy as ever. Man, he was uptight. Or, just tight. Like the ripped jeans and the long-sleeved Henley he was wearing. I'd thrown on baggy jeans and an extra-extra-extra-large T-shirt that had seen better days. Okay, so I was kind of a slob in the morning. What college student wasn't? Oh yeah, Mr. Model over here, with his trendy earring and slicked-back hair.

Rolling my eyes, I grabbed my room card and headed for the door. Until my phone beeped.

Shit, my medication. I turned around and grabbed my backpack, searching for my pill container.

Maddox walked past me and left the room. Nice.

I pulled out my water bottle, chugged my med, and was out the door not thirty seconds after him.

"Can you at least hold the elevator for me?" I shouted after him.

Maddox was halfway down the hallway and stopped short. But he didn't turn around. He paused, shook his head, and then kept walking, until he reached the elevators. Since my legs were so long, I had no problem catching up to him.

"Can't we just be normal teammates?" I asked. "We don't need to be friends, but we are sharing a room. The least you could do is—"

"I don't *have* to do anything," he snarked and rolled his eyes. "And I'm not normal. Or haven't you figured that out by now?"

He slammed the elevator button and then crossed his arms. Jesus Christ, dealing with Maddox was like trying to calm an angry toddler. Time out.

The elevator doors opened, and I let Maddox go in first. I followed, standing beside him, silent.

Don't say anything. Don't say anything. Don't say…

I couldn't help it. I wasn't one for the silent treatment and not talking was just plain weird for me.

"Did you study the videos of Rochester's last season?" I asked.

No response.

"Or maybe Coach didn't send you the link?" I continued. "No, wait. We reviewed one of them after last week's practice, so of course you saw them. Maybe we can re-watch them together? I'd like to hear a goalie's perspective on their strengths and weaknesses."

No reply again. A total shutout. Damn.

The ride was thankfully short, and we exited on the main floor, following the signs to the restaurant. When I spotted the team sitting at the back of room, I nearly ran over to them in relief. Dane and Jace waved at me and pointed to an empty seat. I was so fucking grateful there were people who actually wanted me around.

Maddox stalked away and sat down near Silas. For sure, those two should have roomed together.

"You survived the night?" Dane teased. "I thought maybe you would've been injured by now. Or worse."

"Not before a game," I replied. "Maddox is scary, not stupid. He'd wait until afterward."

"Did he talk to you at all?" Jace asked as he glanced down the row of tables.

"Well, I tried talking to him. You know I can't be silent for long."

"No shit," Dane chuckled. "You talk in your sleep, Kay."

I waved off my friend. "No way."

"It's self-serve here," Jace replied as he pointed to the far end of the dining room. "Go grab a plate, or two, and hit the buffet."

Without delay, I got up and headed over to the breakfast station. And yes, I loaded up two plates. Ten eggs, ten pancakes, and ten slices of bacon. And yes, I was that superstitious. It was game day after all…

With both hands full, I'd have to come back for juice. I whirled around and nearly crashed into Coach Banning.

"Kayden."

"Coach."

"Things okay with Rocher?" he asked me.

I nodded. What was there to say? I wanted to switch rooms, but I wasn't going to ask Coach today.

"Good." He nodded and looked at my plates. "Fuel up. We have a game to win."

Then he stalked off, and I headed back to join my friends. I looked around for Maddox, but he was nowhere in sight.

After a half hour, with my plates empty and my belly full, I was ready to roll out of here. I rode back up the elevator with Jace and Dane, then got off on my floor and headed for my room.

When I entered, I spotted my roommates' headphones on his bed. Then I heard the shower running in the bathroom. I grabbed my earplugs off the nightstand and swept the area for any items I might have missed. Of course, my phone charger was still plugged into the wall. I bent over to yank it out when the bathroom door opened.

I glanced up to find Maddox standing there, his black hair wet, a small towel around his hips. Now, I've been in a lot of locker rooms with a lot of guys, so seeing him like this was no biggie.

So, why was I staring? And why couldn't I remember what I was doing bent over my bed? Dirty, dirty thoughts popped into my head when I thought about *beds* and *bending over*. My hormones suddenly came out to play, and it was the worst fucking timing. Ever.

"I need to grab my—"

Fuck, I couldn't remember the words.

"My...my thing that plugs into the wall...the charger thingy. So, did you have a good breakfast? I mean, not that I care if you eat well, that's your business. Of course, you eat well, look at you. Not that I'm looking at your shape or size or any part of your body. I mean—"

My face grew hotter with every word that vomited out of my mouth.

Shut up, Kayden.

And then it happened. Like a tornado out of nowhere or a bolt of lightning. Maddox laughed. And holy fuck, the resting dick face was gone and, in its place, a smile that would make anyone look twice. Me included.

But, as quickly as it appeared, it was gone. Maybe I'd imagined it?

"Stop talking," Maddox growled.

Yup, it never happened. I must've had way too much sugar at breakfast or something.

"I'm going to grab my shit and wait for you in the hallway," I replied.

"Or, better yet, go to the fucking bus already!" Maddox snapped and slammed the bathroom door.

Shaking my head, I grabbed my stuff, checked the bed again, and then headed for the door. But I didn't leave. I didn't want Maddox to have to walk onto the bus alone. Not on game day. We always paired up, so no one had a chance to get in their heads and psych themselves out.

Despite his angry words, I was pretty sure Maddox had laughed. At me, but still. As much as I didn't love feeling like an ass, I'd take that over the silent treatment any day. And, if I could make him chuckle once, I could do it again. There had to be a kernel of something good inside him, something that would be worth the pain of dealing with his prickly thorns. I reminded myself that people lashed out hardest when they were hurting.

I waited in the hallway, bag at my feet, perusing my phone. Five minutes later, he stepped out.

"Fuck off," Maddox grumbled as he slammed the door shut.

If I had to room with him over the whole season, I was going to lose part of my hearing for sure.

"Your mouth says fuck off, but your eyes say—" I paused dramatically, and he walked right past me, heading for the elevator.

"The exact same thing!" he finished, yelling over his shoulder.

"No! You laughed in there. I heard you. And I saw your mouth curl up in a smile. Don't deny it."

"And?" He turned around, his steely blues locked on me. "You were acting like an ass; of course I laughed. Who wouldn't? I'm pissy, not dead."

"Woah," I held my hands up in the air. "You realize this is the most you've said to me since we've met, right? Are we, like, starting to become actual friends now or something?"

Oh man, I couldn't wait to see his reaction to that statement.

Maddox gave me two middle fingers and turned on his heel. He speed-walked down the hallway, his ass cheeks bouncing with every step. I'm surprised his jeans didn't bust wide open. And why I couldn't stop staring at his ass was beyond me.

What the fuck was in those pancakes this morning? Did I get roofied and not know it?

"You like me," I teased as I caught up to him. "I knew it. It's just a matter of time."

"Are you sure you're okay to play today? 'Cause it seems like you might have injured your head this morning," he returned.

We stepped into the elevator. And I did what I usually did when I felt awkward. I kept on blabbing.

"How did you sleep last night? Did I wake you? Sometimes I snore like a fucking freight train, and—"

Ping. Ground floor.

The doors opened and Maddox stepped out first.

"—It drives my siblings crazy when I fall asleep in the car on road trips. I'm one of six kids," I continued. "What about you, Mad?"

"My name is Maddox. Maddox, Rocher, or Rock. *Do not* call me Mad. And please, shut up already."

"I like Mad. Not Mads with an 's.' That's too cute for you. But Mad is like, perfect."

He grunted and stalked out of the hotel, but I was right behind him.

As we headed for the bus, Maddox pulled out his sunglasses and shoved them on his face. His expression was still sour, but I could've sworn I saw his lip twitch.

CHAPTER 8

MADDOX

I didn't need adrenaline to get worked up for the game. Just being around Kayden sent my blood pressure sky high. If I had my blocker with me, I would've been tempted to put it over his face. Not that I was a violent person. The total opposite, despite my surly temperament. If anything, when there was a fight on the ice, I broke out in a cold sweat, no lie. Some guys loved that shit. Guess they thought it made them feel powerful. It made me want to puke.

Kayden followed me onto the bus, my constant shadow, chattering away about fuck knows what. The snickers of our teammates got louder as we passed each row of seats.

"Button it, Kayden. Save your energy for the game!" Axel shouted.

Laughter surrounded us.

I whirled around. "Take your own advice, Lund. You gonna score today or skate around looking at your reflection?"

More chuckles, snorts, and hollers.

Axel stood up, but I didn't move an inch. If he wanted to come after me, he could go for it. I hated fighting, but I would defend myself. Then I realized he hadn't been making fun of me but Kayden. Why didn't I ignore the stupid taunt? I was damn good at that. Still, Axel's attitude pissed me off.

Let's be honest, for me, it didn't take much.

Dane, who was sitting across the aisle from Axel, got up, holding his hand in front of the forward.

"Hey! We're on the same team, remember? Can we put aside our egos and think about what we need to do today to win?" Dane asked. "Now, Coach is gonna be here any minute. Chill."

I turned around and headed to the seats at the back of the bus.

My roommate sat, or rather flopped, onto the seat beside me. Swear to fuck, the bus swayed when Kayden sat down. Instead of acknowledging him, I pulled on my headphones and drew back into my world.

But I was rudely interrupted by a nudge to my side. I yanked off my headphones.

"Don't touch me," I warned him.

Of course, the retriever ignored me.

"Thanks for sticking up for me back there."

"I didn't," I scoffed. "I just wanted Axel to shut up."

"Sure, you did. He made a joke about me and you were all protective," Kayden smiled. "That means a lot, Mad. And I'm so fucking happy that we're friends now."

What kind of bizarro world had I stepped into at this school? With this roommate?

"Seriously, did you hit your head in the shower or something?" I asked.

Kayden leaned in close, and I thought for sure I'd get up and leave. But I didn't. I just sat there, trapped in his hazel gaze. He was too close, and I could smell cinnamon on his breath. And another scent that was spicy. Soap? Deodorant? Whatever it was, it was damn good. Not that I should've noticed or anything, but hey, a nice-smelling person, and a hockey player to boot, is rare.

"You and me?" he pointed between us. "BFFs in no time."

Rolling my eyes and biting my lip so hard I tasted blood, I shoved my headphones back on and prayed for teleportation to the rink.

I'm pretty sure Kayden kept talking, but I closed my eyes and ignored him.

When I felt the bus move five minutes later, the relief was palpable. But by the time we got to the venue, I was all but jumping out of my skin again. All I wanted was to get on the ice. The cold air in my lungs, the weight of the pads on my body, and the familiar swoosh of my blades on the ice. When I was in my net, I wasn't angry, or sad, or filled with *'what ifs.'* The chaos of a game gave me something I rarely had and treasured above anything else—peace.

Everyone filed out of the bus, and I waited for Kayden to leave. But he shook his head and motioned for me to go first. Jesus. The sooner I got away from this guy, the better.

I followed the rest of the team as we headed into the rink. The tension in the locker room was as heavy as it was on the bus. Kayden and Dane joked around, but the rest of the guys looked like they were about to throw up. There was no home ice advantage so nerves were high. And no wonder. Rochester had a solid reputation.

I was the first one suited up in green and gold, and headed for the ice. With the opposing team's hometown crowd packed in every seat, the atmosphere was amped all the way up. The guys from Rochester were warming up, and only paused to give me the stink eye. Good luck with that. I didn't need a talisman to ward off any bad juju. I *was* the evil eye.

Ignoring the dickheads in blue and white, I went through my motions, my stretches. There was no rushing this part for a goalie. First arms, legs, hip flexors, repeat. Until I was satisfied that I was ready.

One by one, the rest of the Sutton Cougars filed out onto the ice, including Kayden. He skated past me and winked. Winked, that fucker. I bit my lip, hard, to keep from reacting. Thank fuck he couldn't see my face. I almost cracked another smile. I gave him the finger, but it wasn't effective with my blocker on. Still, I'm pretty sure my hand gesture told him everything he needed to know.

The air filled with the smell of junk food and sport sweat; the crowd getting noisier the closer we got to game time. It was all white noise to me at this point, until Coach Banning called us over to the bench for the usual pre-game scuttle. I ignored most of the hurrah speech and kept moving around on the ice to stay limber.

"… and remember, there's no second place in hockey. Rocher, Rowland, Ethan, St. Pierre, Melnyk, Moss, you're up."

We lined up, waited for the national anthem to play, and afterward, passed the other team in greeting. There were lots of '*fuck you*'s' and '*kiss my ass*' whispered low enough for the refs not to hear. I didn't make eye contact with any of the opposing team. I tuned it all out.

Pulse-pounding rock music blared from the speakers as I skated down the ice, heading for home. When I turned around, Kayden and Silas were in position. At that moment, I didn't care if Kayden annoyed me. If he protected me here, now, I was good. Strangely enough, though, I had a weird sense that it should be the other way around. There was something naïve about Kayden. His friendliness was something that other people could, and probably would, exploit. Why that should bother me, I had no idea. My brain didn't always work in a logical way, so I let those thoughts go. Not that I needed to be thinking about him at all.

I tapped the bar one last time and got into position.

Axel faced off against Rochester's Grant Healey for the

puck. When Healey got possession, I knew this was going to be one hell of a game.

Kayden

Rochester had a kick-ass team, and that's how the first period went. We got our asses kicked.

Their best forwards—Healey, Louis, and Rokick, were hungry as hell and all over us, every play. Thank fuck Maddox was as good a goalie now as he was in practice, otherwise, we'd be down 5-0. Healey's faster than I anticipated, faster than last year, that's for sure. He's only gotten bigger and better. And he's already scored the first goal of the game.

I couldn't deny it, the shot was beautiful, bar down, over Maddox's left shoulder. The shot was so fast that there was nothing Mad could have done to save it. Nothing that I could tell, anyway.

When Coach called for a line change, Maddox kept pacing, tapping his bar, and ignoring everyone else. He was probably spitting fire under that mask of his, and I didn't dare go near him. As much as I was teasing him earlier, I knew that when the game started, there's no fucking around. I wanted to win as much as him.

I skated towards the box and passed Julian and Finn. I wished I was on the same line as one of them. Silas was doing alright, but he barely spoke to me, and he hesitated on a few plays, which got me wondering. He'd been off for a year—no idea why—and it seemed like he was still finding his groove.

So far, we were down 1-0 and even though there was plenty of time left to play, the pressure kept ramping up. The hometown crowd roared for their team and booed anytime we so much as got close to Rochester's net.

"Come on, Rowland! Lund! Let's get numbers on the board!" Coach yelled.

Jace got control of the puck, flying down the ice with an aggression that surprised me. He blew past Rochester's offense with speed and skill. And Axel wasn't far behind. But Rochester's defense wasn't to be fucked with. Until Jace pivoted, surprising them. He passed to Axel, and Axel took it the rest of the way.

The shot was low, but a beaut, sneaking right through the five hole. When the buzzer sounded and the ref signaled *goal*, everyone in our box popped up, yelling and screaming.

"Yes! Did you see that?" I shouted at Ethan. "Holy fuck, what a goal!"

"Axel delivered!"

I was happy for Axel, even if he did talk out of his ass half of the time. Most of all, I was happy for our team. At least some of the pressure was off Maddox. Not that he seemed bothered by the weight of anyone else's opinion. Not what I've seen so far.

I looked across the ice as Julian skated by Maddox. Words were exchanged as Julian bent over, hands and stick resting on his knees, his mouth running a mile a minute. I loved to talk, but my teammate wasn't far behind me.

But of course, I was too far away to know what Maddox was saying in return.

Then, I heard it. Julian's laughter. So loud that it echoed over the din of the crowd. For a reason I couldn't explain, the sound irritated me. What the hell were he and Maddox talking about?

So much for our goalie hating everyone. Turned out, it was only me.

CHAPTER 9

KAYDEN

Third period and Rochester was up 2-1.

We've lost momentum, a shift in energy. Frustration weighed us down, on the ice, in the box. Like Maddox, who skated back and forth, shaking his head.

Coach called for a line change and I was hungry to get back out there. Healey barreled down the ice, but I was ready for him. Him and his teammates.

The hits got aggressive, the crowd chanted louder, and the tension soared. An away game always hits hard. That win can make you feel like you're gonna take on the world. That loss? It gets in your head. But if it stays there? Then you're fucked.

Rochester doesn't score on us, but we don't score either. And it ends 2-1.

Our first loss of the season and it fucking hurt. We do the usual lineup after the game and shake hands with Rochester, but everyone on our team is skating like a zombie, their faces unreadable, their shoulders slumped.

"It's nerves," Dane muttered as we stepped off the rink. "It'll settle. It's one game. We got this."

"I fucking hope so. We were so damn close."

Everyone's left the ice, or, so I thought. When I glanced

back, my eyes caught on Maddox standing in his net, hands on the bar, head down, holding on. I'm tempted to go back out there, but I don't need his backlash.

Instead, I turned away and kept walking beside Dane.

"We lost by one freaking goal," I sighed. "I hate that. And the whole game it felt like we were playing more defense than offense. No offence."

Dane laughed and patted my shoulder. "None taken. And yeah, I know what you mean. With so many new players, I guess it's going to take time to find our groove. But we'll get there."

"Hopefully before the end of the season."

I was a glass-half-full guy, but my anxieties were cresting. Even when I was struggling with schoolwork, I could always count on hockey.

"Truth? It wasn't just our offense that needs improving," Dane replied. "Silas was tense, and so were you."

"I'm having a hard time anticipating his moves," I admitted to my friend.

"You gotta find a way to communicate," Dane paused. "And, speaking of that, don't let Maddox get to you."

"What? What's he got to do with anything?"

Dane stared at me.

"Okay," I shrugged. "Maybe I'm also stressing about my roommate."

"I know you. Maddox isn't an approachable guy, so your best bet is to ignore his attitude and just do you. Not everyone is going to want to be your friend, and that's okay. It's better to let him be. Don't stress over him."

Maybe Dane was right. I tended to overthink things, and I wanted to get along with everybody. Why was I so hell-bent on getting to know our goalie? Why couldn't I leave things be?

We headed for the locker room and I knew what was coming next. Coach was standing at the entrance, arms crossed, face expressionless. He didn't give a nod or a say a word. Unlike other coaches I'd worked with, Banning didn't need to yell. His silent glare was just as effective.

Until all my teammates gathered around, and then Coach let loose.

"I don't need to tell you guys that today was disappointing as hell. I felt it, I saw it, you experienced it. That's not the kind of teamwork I expect and demand from you. Be prepared for our upcoming practices to be long ones. We're going to do drills until the rink closes or you can't move, whichever comes first," he barked. "Clean up and head for the bus. We'll talk more at dinner."

Coach stalked off and most of the guys sat there, too numb to move or talk. I started undressing, whipping off my jersey and then my pads. Glancing around, I noticed Maddox sitting on the last bench, mask off, head in hand. This time, however, I listened to Dane's advice and instead of walking by Maddox and teasing him, I headed in the opposite direction, towards the showers.

Once I was scrubbed up, I quickly changed, grabbed my bag, and followed Jace and Dane out the door.

"I can't believe I'm saying this, but I don't know if I can eat. That loss has my stomach in knots," I admitted.

Jace elbowed me. "It's only one game."

"Yeah, but it's still a big-ass bummer."

"Don't wallow in it. It's done. We'll watch the tape and learn from it," Jace reassured me. "Next game, we'll be the ones kicking ass."

We got on the bus, and I grabbed the seat next to Dane. Slowly, the rest of the team filed on. No sign of Maddox. I was tempted to get off the bus and go look for him.

Let it go.

A few minutes later, Coach got on, then our driver. Maddox was the last one on, again. He ignored me (I know, shocking), and headed for the back of the bus.

"Hey Coach, is Sean going to be in goal next game?" Axel asked.

Oh fuck. Why was Axel deliberately trying to be an asshole?

Coach got up and turned around.

"Focus on your playmaking, Lund," he bit out. "And remember, this is a team sport. We win or lose not because of one person, but because of everyone. If you don't like hockey, there's always speed skating."

Ooh, burn.

Coach sat back down and signaled for our driver to get going. We hit the road and by the time we arrived at our destination, my raging appetite had returned. It probably helped that I wasn't sitting next to Maddox. Dane was right. I had to stop being such a retriever and let the guy go do whatever the hell he wanted. After all, I had plenty of friends. And Maddox made it clear he wasn't interested in making any.

Of course, all those intentions fell out the window as soon as we got inside the restaurant. Maddox was sitting at the end of the row again, by himself. He wasn't talking to anyone, and no one was talking to him.

Shutting off Dane's advice—and my better judgment—I got up and walked over to the end of the table and sat down across from my snarly roommate.

He looked up briefly, and for once, his expression wasn't angry. He was upset. Holy shit. I guess he *was* like the rest of us.

"There was nothing you could have done differently," I blurted out. "Healy was insane today; no one could touch him. And I'll take the blame for part of it. Our defense wasn't what it should have been. We let you down."

Maddox reached up and gripped the headphones that sat around his neck. I waited for the inevitable 'fuck off.'

But it never came.

"Why are you talking to me?" he bit out.

"Why are *you* talking to *me*?" I countered.

We stared at each other in a showdown, neither of us wanting to give in. After having our asses handed to us by Rochester, the last thing I wanted was to lose. Even if it came to a stupid staring contest. Hockey players; we're weird.

"I wasn't." Maddox broke first. "You came to me."

"Yeah, I did. You keep claiming that you want to be left alone, but I don't buy it. Why pick a team sport if you're anti-everyone?"

Maddox licked his lips and why my eyes were now locked in on his mouth, I had no fucking idea.

"I have good reason for being the way I am and that's all I'm gonna say. Now, you can accept it, and go back to your friends at the other end of the table, or you can sit here and talk to yourself. Your choice. And as to why hockey, well, to start, I'm Canadian, so duh. And I picked goaltending for a reason. I'm introverted and it suits. Does that answer your question?"

"No. If anything, I have more of them." I leaned forward. "Like, what do your tattoos mean? Where in Canada did you grow up? Tell me more about being introverted."

"Fuck me. I've never met anyone so goddamn nosy in all my life," Maddox snapped and ran an agitated hand through his hair.

I was about to reply to his comment, but our server arrived and started taking orders. Flustered, I volunteered to go last. I pulled out my phone and tapped my reading app so I could review the restaurant's menu. There was no mistaking that Maddox was staring at me, but when I looked up, his gaze was more confused than angry.

Say it. Tell him.

I looked down at my phone, figured out what they had to offer, and what I wanted to eat. "I'll have the ribeye with mushrooms, medium, fries, and a Diet Coke. Thanks."

Oddly enough, Maddox ordered the same thing.

"You know, after a loss like the one today, I don't feel like talking much either," I admitted. "But inevitably, my mouth won't stop moving."

Maddox bit his lower lip. Whether in frustration or trying to hide a smile, I didn't know. But I was going to find out.

"What were you listening to?" I asked, pushing ahead. "Another podcast?"

"No." He shook his head. "Music."

He barely got the words out, like they were painful for him to speak. I don't think his jaw moved either.

"What kind?" I prodded, curious.

"The kind you listen to."

"Can't you just answer a simple question?" I asked.

"If you're gonna insist on annoying me with your presence, I need to make it entertaining," he snarked.

"For you."

"Obvi."

I stared at Mad until he rolled his eyes and sighed.

"I like grunge music from the '90s, okay?" he muttered.

"That figures."

That got me a choice finger in response. I'd take it.

"I like pop," I admitted. "Taylor, Sabrina—"

Maddox scoffed. "Don't you dare give me a fucking bracelet."

"Oh man, what a great idea! I could make them for the entire team. Why didn't I think of that sooner? We should've done that for Welcome Week."

I looked down the table and motioned to Dane, who was talking with Jace, Colin, and Julian.

"What's up, Kay?" Dane shouted over the din.

"Friendship bracelets for the entire team, D! I'm on it!"

Dane chuckled and shrugged. "Why not?"

I turned to Mad again. "See, the captain thinks it's a great idea."

"He said *'why not?'* not *'do it.'* That's not a ringing endorsement."

I waved Maddox off. "It's gonna be so much fun. You want to help me?"

"Do I look like I want to make fucking bracelets?"

"Don't be so rigid. Guys like making jewelry too."

"I didn't mean it like that," Maddox hissed. "I'm not into arts and crafts, alright? I left that behind in kindergarten, along with face painting and puppet shows."

I laughed at his comment.

"College is all about new experiences. Come on, don't be so freaking uptight," I urged him. I was pushing my luck for sure, but I was already all in. "Make bracelets with me, Mad."

Of course, our server returned at that exact moment and started snickering. Until Maddox turned his glare from me to the waitstaff. Then there was total silence. Well, except for the sound of our plates hitting the table.

"No," Maddox replied when the server walked away. "But if you're going to insist on making them, I get a say in the message I want on mine. Any message. Got it?"

"I'll hand out warning bracelets first."

CHAPTER 10

MADDOX

Thank fuck we were driving back tonight and not staying over. I didn't know how much more of Kayden I could take. His constant chatter was frying my patience and my brain cells.

So, why then did I keep talking to him at the restaurant? Maybe it was the shock of the loss. The fact I'd let not one, but two goals in net. Disappointment reverberated in my head like the worst kind of regret. And I wanted something, anything else, to take the place of those memories. I was so fucking pissed at myself. Disappointed didn't even come close.

But I couldn't let it fester. Strong goalies don't give up and they don't give in.

And I was sure that with practice, with more time on the ice, our team would find a way. If we got our synchronicity right. It might require an attitude adjustment on my part. And, you know, me actually talking to my teammates.

Admittedly, I hadn't made a friend in years. Didn't want to. Didn't need to. So, I was out of practice for sure. Not that Kayden and I would be friends. But it was entertaining to listen to him. And to meet someone who, despite repeated warnings to stay away, kept popping up like an eager groundhog. Or, like an addiction you couldn't quit.

I honestly didn't know what to make of him. The guy needed a fucking keeper. He was so goofy and naïve. Maybe I didn't like him. Or, I didn't want to like him. I wasn't sure which. What I did know was that I didn't like it when Axel made fun of him. I was strangely protective. Which was not like me. I learned the hard way to protect myself first.

For the first time in years, I was curious about another person. And I had no clue as to why. Why him? Why now? Was it the whole being in a different country, and a new school thing? That had to be it. I was out of my element and still finding my footing. On the ice and off.

"Hey, roomie. Thanks for saving me a seat," Kayden announced as he sat beside me.

I didn't, but I couldn't be bothered correcting him. So much for being at the back of the bus, where it was dark and quiet. *Was.* But instead of letting him get to me, I decided to turn the tables.

"What was that app you were using in the restaurant?" I asked.

I'd noticed how carefully he'd scanned the menu, holding his phone close to him, like he didn't want anyone else to see what he was doing.

Kayden's mouth opened, but no words came out.

"Is this how I get you to stop talking? Ask *you* a question? Holy fuck. Thank God, I figured you out."

Kayden nudged me with his elbow and for once, I didn't jolt.

"Shut up."

"That's ready fucking ironic coming from you," I replied.

"It's—" Kayden bit his lower lip and whispered. "It's a reading app. I'm dyslexic."

Oh. I wasn't expecting that.

"Why are you whispering?" I asked. "Is it a secret?"

"No. I mean, yes. Sort of," he sighed and ran a hand through his messy hair. "I don't tell everyone. Not that I'm ashamed, but some people treat me differently when they find out. Like I'm stupid. Or it's contagious or something. Or I'm not worth their time. I got bullied a lot in high school. Until I hit my growth spurt."

If there was one thing I couldn't stand, it was bullies. Sure, I was bitchy, and I kept people at arm's length—further, even —but I did it to protect myself. And them.

Something else about Kayden's admission made my stomach twinge. No. I'd probably just eaten too much at dinner. That had to be it, right?

"Wait, is that why you were freaking out that first day in economics class? Cause something happened to your app?"

Kayden nodded.

"Yeah, it froze. And I have software on my laptop too, but sometimes I forget to charge it. Or I forget my charger," he sighed. "I've also got ADHD, so school can be a hot mess for me a lot of the time. Despite meds and tutors."

"So, your brain works differently," I offered. "College is one way of learning stuff. Not the only way. I've learned more online, in my own time, than school could ever teach me. Don't let others get in your head. It's like when we're on the ice. You don't think about all the fucking noise around you. Focus on what you can control. And fuck everyone else's rules."

"Tell *that* to my parents. And future employers."

"Your goal is the league, right?"

"For sure." Kayden nodded. "All I want to do is to play hockey. But, I need a plan for after. Still working on that."

"What's your major?"

What were all these questions coming out of my mouth? I didn't even recognize myself.

"Social work. I want to advocate for people with disabilities. Differing abilities," Kayden replied. "That is, if I can manage to get my degree."

I nodded. "That's cool. At least you're gonna do something useful. Not become one of those faceless corporate assholes."

"Mad, did you compliment me?"

"Fuck off."

"Your mouth says fuck off, but your body language says —" Kayden gave me a long once over and and I started sweating. "No, it still says fuck off."

"Remember that."

"At least I know what your bracelet is going to say."

"Exactly. I'll hold my arm up and everyone will back away."

The bus started moving, rolling out of Rochester. Maybe, once I was back on campus, I'd stop talking and revert to my usual grunts and glares. Today was a weird fucking trip. And I didn't even get high.

"Well, that's enough human interaction for me for today. For a lifetime," I admitted as I reached for my laptop. "I've gotta work on my economics essay."

"There's an essay?!" Kayden shouted.

Heads turned in our direction and I gave my teammates my favorite sign.

I gave Kayden the side eye. "It's due on Wednesday."

"Shit!" Kayden blurted and reached for his bag. He pulled out his tablet and started typing. "Oh yeah, phew. I have a note in my calendar to work on it tomorrow. Jesus, Mad, don't scare me like that."

I rolled my eyes. "Be quiet and let me work. Can you do that? One hour?"

"One hour? I don't know if I can do it for one minute."

Placing my headphones on, I glared at Kayden and made a zipping motion over my mouth. His face turned bright red.

He started working on his tablet, but his knee was jumping, the seats were vibrating, and there was no way I was going to be able to concentrate.

Do it. Write.

Could I? Not with Kayden staring at me. I was barely into my first paragraph and I couldn't take it anymore.

I whipped off my headphones. "What?"

"Do you have a girlfriend? Or boyfriend? I shouldn't assume." He paused. "Are you dating?"

"What the fuck is it to you?" I snapped.

"I'm just curious," he shrugged. "You said you don't like people. So, does that mean you're not into sex? I mean, I think about it. A lot. Not you. I mean, sex. Not with you. Just sex. In general."

Kayden's face was near purple. And he wasn't the only one. I swallowed hard, not prepared for this conversation. For Kayden, for this conversation, for anything that happened today. I wanted to go home. Maybe if I slipped our driver a fifty he could run me across the border to Canada…

"I get it," I bit out. "And the answer is none of your business."

"Okay, but—"

"Kayden, don't. Talk my ear off about anything else, just not that, alright?"

Kayden nodded. "I'm sorry. You're right. I don't know why I asked that. Ignore me."

"Ignore you? What do you think I've been trying to do since I met you?"

"Will you two shut up!" Axel interrupted. He got up out of his seat, two rows in front of us, and turned around. "Some of us are trying to sleep. Isn't it bad enough we sucked ass today? Now we have to listen to you two argue?"

I placed my laptop aside and stood up. "Watch it, Axel."

"Or what?" he bit back.

"Take it easy," Kayden added. "Maddox and I were just talking."

Axel scoffed. "Whatever. Keep it down."

The testy forward turned around and sat down again. I waited for Coach Banning to intervene, but there was silence. He was probably sound asleep like everyone else.

Except me. And Kayden.

My head fell back against the seat, and I stared at the ceiling.

"Can I ask you something?" Kayden whispered.

No fucking kidding. I bit back an unexpected—and unwanted—laugh. That was how many times today? More than I'd laughed in…years.

I will not be charmed. I will not be charmed. Stay pissy, stay pissy…

"What?"

"Could you help me with the economics essay this week? If you have time. If you want to. Well, you probably don't want to, but I figured, now that we're gonna be bracelet besties—"

Bracelet what?

I turned my head to snark at him, but I didn't realize he'd leaned over, so close that I could count every golden freckle on his face. A full-on shiver wracked my body. Did the driver have the A/C cranked up?

Against my better judgment, common sense, logic, and sanity, I opened my mouth.

"Sure."

What the fuck was I doing?

"Awesome. Give me your phone." Kayden held out his hand.

Reluctantly, I passed it over and watched as Kayden typed in his phone number.

"This is going to be great," he gushed.

"No," I bit out and snatched my phone back. "Only contact me if it's about the course. You start texting me about anything else, and I'll block you."

Kayden sat there and gave me a shit-eating grin.

Fuck. I'd been outplayed.

CHAPTER 11
KAYDEN

finally fell asleep an hour after we left Rochester. And I woke up five hours later to find Dane standing in front of me.

"We're home. Time to get off the bus, bud."

I glanced around and sure enough, the bus was empty, save for the two of us.

Maddox was probably the first one off. And hey, maybe he didn't want to listen to me, but at least he was talking now. I knew he couldn't stay silent forever. Sooner or later, I got everyone to talk. Wait. That sounded like I was a mafia don or something. I snickered at that image. Me, as an enforcer? Man, I was sleep-drunk.

"Kayden, are you okay?" Dane asked.

"Yeah." I grabbed my bag and stood up, still groggy. "I crashed hard and now I feel loopy."

"No kidding, and after that game?" Dane ran a hand over his face. "I'll probably sleep all day tomorrow."

"Maddox is gone."

Duh, Kayden, state the obvi.

Dane nodded. "He hightailed it outta here as soon as we came to a stop."

"Figures."

Dane started down the aisle, and I followed.

"You guys were talking at dinner," Dane said over his shoulder. "How'd that miracle happen?"

"I have no freaking clue. I kept talking and asking him question after question. And he finally cracked."

"Maybe you should consider a job as an interrogator with the CIA instead of playing professional hockey."

"Hilarious, D."

We stepped off the bus and into the crisp night air. I glanced at my phone, 12:30 a.m. I was tired, but now that I was awake again, wired. Then I remembered I'd exchanged numbers with Maddox.

> Kayden: Hey bestie! Did you get back to your room safely? TTYT

I didn't expect Maddox to reply. If anything, he was probably going to block me.

By the time we made it back to the dorm, I was more than ready for my bed. I said goodbye to Dane and headed to my room down the hall. My dorm roommate, Darby, was already asleep. I tried to be as quiet as possible, though it was never the case. But since Darby was a pothead, he never woke up when I stumbled around. It was a good match.

I glanced at my phone again. No reply from Maddox. I'd expected something. A 'fuck off' for sure. But, nope.

My head hit the pillow, but my brain was running a hundred miles an hour. Thinking about the loss today, the next game, whether I was going to hit my GPA goal…

To distract myself, I put in my ear pods and pulled up a music app. But instead of my usual tunes, I searched for '90s grunge.

Maddox was still a mystery, but at least I finally had one clue.

. . .

The next day

I was in the gym, doing a workout, when my phone pinged.

> Maddox: Meet at the library at 3. Second floor, near the elevators.

It was 2:50. *Thanks for the heads up, Mad.* Shaking my head, I slowed the treadmill to the lowest setting, hopped off, and headed off to change. There was no way I'd have time to shower. Whatever. I quickly got dressed and ran like hell across campus, arriving at the library at 3:05. When I headed up to the second floor, I looked around. No sign of Maddox. What the fuck?

"You're late."

I startled, whirling around. How was it that this guy could sneak up on me like that? Was my hearing going or something? And then, I could hardly breathe. Probably because I ran like a track star to get here.

Maddox wore a tight denim button down, sleeves rolled up, ripped jeans, and chucks. He hadn't shaved, and the scruff really suited him. No matter what he wore, he was always effortlessly cool. Strands of his black hair fell into his eyes, and I had the strange urge to reach out and push them off his face.

Uh, no. I was overtired. Or lightheaded from that run. What was wrong with me?

Maddox glared at me like he was about to ask the same question. Then I remembered that I'd come from the gym. I was hot, sweaty, and probably not smelling my best. Or looking my best. Not that I should care what I looked or smelled like. Not with him.

"Where'd you come from?" I asked.

He pointed to the far end of the floor.

"I booked us a room," he replied. "Come on."

He started off, and I quickly caught up to him.

"Just the two of us?" I teased. "Aw, Mad."

"It's because I know you won't shut up and I don't want to have everyone in the library staring and telling us to be quiet."

I couldn't argue with that.

We walked past several study rooms, and when we arrived at the last door to the right, Maddox opened it and ushered me in. There was one large desk, two chairs, and the unwelcome glare of florescent lighting.

Maddox dropped his backpack on the table and pulled out his laptop.

"You could've given me more warning, you know," I added. "I was working out. I had to run from the gym, no shower, and I'm sweaty as hell."

Maddox eyed me up and stepped closer. At least one of us smelled good. He leaned in and for a second, I thought he was going to touch me. My heart pounded so fast, I was dizzy. Maybe I'd run too much at the gym? And why was I blushing again?

When Maddox closed the door behind me, I realized I'd panicked for nothing.

Calm down Kay. This is a study session, not the start of a porn scene.

Not that I should be thinking about porn, or sex, or Maddox touching me. Or touching him. Or anything like that. I wasn't into guys. That I knew of. But Maddox was definitely hot. And why I noticed was beyond me. Holy fuck, never mind a workout; I was sweating more now than I was at the gym. I really should've jerked off when I woke up this morning. Being backed up was fucking with my head.

"I'm used to hockey sweat." Maddox smirked. "Now, sit. Let's get to it."

"So bossy."

Not gonna lie, I was kind of into it.

"You don't like it, you're free to leave," he quipped.

Nope. I'd take bossy Maddox over the silent one any day. I obediently sat down in the chair beside him and pulled out my tablet with sweaty hands. Hands that were shaking. Shit.

"Okay, so, the essay assignment requires us to provide real-world examples of scarcity in microeconomics, including demand, supply, and structural," Maddox stated.

"So, a paragraph on each?" I asked.

"More like two or three. The entire essay has to be seven hundred words minimum."

"I get the concepts," I replied. "The problem is writing my thoughts down. It's all ends up looking like a jumble."

"Do you dictate?"

"Sometimes. But my learning advisor told me not to rely on it."

Maddox shrugged. "Maybe they're right. In theory. But it's your class and your grade. Do what you need to in order to get the best mark you can."

I nodded. He was right.

"Let's work on our own essay for fifteen minutes, then we'll switch and give our feedback," Maddox offered.

"Okay. But you're going to put your headphones on, right?"

"Why?"

"Because I'm going to dictate. And it's weird to have you listen to me as I speak."

Maddox rolled his eyes. "Hello? You don't have a problem talking my ear off."

"That's different."

Maddox grabbed his headphones and put them on. "Happy?"

I nodded, and he turned to his laptop, typing away. Fuck, he was fast.

And I was, well, I was too busy staring at him to focus on my essay. Until Maddox turned his head and mouthed '*work.*'

I searched my backpack for my ear pods, shoved them in, and opened my writing software. I started dictating, but it took getting used to. The software didn't catch all my words, and some weren't correct, but I could go back later and edit. Still, it was much easier for me to express my thoughts this way. I didn't have to stare at a blank screen for ages.

I was already two paragraphs in when Maddox stopped typing, and turned to me.

"Okay, let me see what you've got."

We switched, but I had a difficult time reading Maddox's text.

"I'm going to scan this into my app, if that's okay?"

"Do it," Maddox replied.

Once I scanned it, I started reading. And, man, his essay was good. Not good, incredible. He sounded like our teacher. My essay was so simple in comparison. Too simple. Oh God, this was embarrassing. The study session was my idea, and it was turning out to be a bad one. Now Maddox would know just how dumb I really was.

Suddenly, *I* was the one who wanted to be left alone.

"I'm not feeling good," I muttered. "I have to go."

Maddox silently handed over my tablet, and I shoved it in my bag, not making eye contact. The sooner I got out of here, the better.

Once I was out the door, I hauled ass for the elevator.

I looked over my shoulder, but Maddox hadn't followed me. Good. What a relief. He didn't want to be around me, anyway. He was probably thankful I left. And it made me wonder why he'd said yes to helping me in the first place. I was teasing him yesterday. I didn't think he'd actually go through with it.

Maybe this was all a joke to him? Maybe *I* was the joke.

My stomach clenched tight as I headed out of the library and back to my dorm.

Forget about Maddox. Forget about trying to be his friend. Ignore him. Like he wanted you to.

Why did I feel this intense need to be around him, anyway? What was going on with me?

Hours later, as I lay on my bed, alone, listening to music, I replayed every moment since we'd met. And the answers I was searching for? The ones about why I was so determined to figure out Maddox?

They never came.

CHAPTER 12

MADDOX

I hadn't heard from—or seen—Kayden for days. I should be ecstatic, grateful, so fucking relieved that the guy was no longer hounding me. There were no annoying text messages or sudden pop-ups at the gym. I had time to myself. Alone. It was perfect, great. Sort of.

Sunday was still bothering me. The way Kayden suddenly up and left the library, out of nowhere. I didn't know what was wrong, but it was something. I hadn't been my usual pissy self. But that wouldn't have deterred Kayden anyway.

So, what had happened? Why did he take off like that?

Kayden shouldn't have been preoccupying any of my thoughts, but he was. And I didn't like it. I didn't angst over other people and their problems. Selfish bastard 101; I worry about myself and that's pretty much it. That, and hockey.

And now I was nervous as hell going into our next practice. Me.

Fuck it.

I wanted Kayden to get lost, and he did. Why should I care how it happened, only that it did?

Don't go asking for trouble.

I headed for the locker room and got into my gear. I'd

arrived a half hour early so I wouldn't chance meeting anyone else. But Dane was already here, and Jace too. I nodded at them, and they gave me a wide berth.

No sign of Kayden yet. Not that I was looking for him or anything.

I headed for the rink, and spotted Silas. Another player looking for early ice time. But then I realized that he wasn't alone. Coach was standing on the other side of the boards, gesturing at him. Silas said something that had Banning throwing his hands up in the air before stalking off. I was too far away to hear the exchange. When Silas slid onto the rink and skated away, he slammed his stick on the ice.

Tempers were running hot, so this was going to be an interesting fucking practice.

Soon, the rest of the team joined us, including Kayden. He looked like his usual self, smiling and joking with Dane, Ethan, Julian, Finn, and Sean. The other goalie started laughing at something Kayden said, and Kayden playfully shoved him. Fine. He could bug Sean from now on.

Suddenly, Axel skated by and nearly collided with Jace.

"Watch it, Rowland," Axel grumbled. "Maybe if you pay more attention to what you're doing, we'll win next time."

"I've had enough of your shit attitude and your stupid comments," Jace snapped back. "Back off and leave me alone."

"You're good at that, right? Using people and then leaving," Axel bit out and took off down the ice.

What the hell was that about?

Coach Banning re-appeared and skated to center ice. "Okay, let's go! Get warmed up and then get ready for new drills!"

Kayden completely ignored me, skating past without saying a word. I should've been elated. This was what I wanted. I asked him to leave me alone and now he finally was. So why did I feel like total shit? And why was I thinking about him at all?

"Melnyk, Moss, Hudak, Baran," Banning shouted. "Over here."

I watched as Kayden skated away, and a strange lump lodged in my throat. I reached for my water bottle and took a sip, but that didn't help matters at all.

"You think we're going to work out the kinks by the next game?" Sean asked me.

"We better."

The next two hours were nothing but drills, more drills, and sweat. Lots and lots of sweat. I was exhausted by the end of it. Probably because I forced myself *not* to be snarky for once. I made eye contact with the guys, I said a few encouraging words, and I kept my resting bitch face to a minimum. Much as I loved to do my own thing, Kayden was right. This was a team sport and if I wanted to succeed, I had to be all in.

We'd all loosened up, and it looked to me like Silas and Kayden finally found a rhythm together. And the rest of the guys, like Axel and Jace, put their attitudes and tension aside and worked hard.

Once practice was called to an end, I watched as player after player left the ice. Kayden was hanging with Dane, joking around. But the defenseman still hadn't acknowledged me. I didn't know what burned worse, that, or his overeager friendliness.

Enough.

I couldn't take it anymore. When Dane took off down the ice, and Kayden skated around my net, I caved.

"Why did you leave the library?" I asked him.

"What's it to you? I thought you wanted me to leave you alone."

"I did," I replied. "I do."

"And?" Kayden asked without looking at me.

"And, nothing. Fine," I bit back. "Fuck off."

"Why don't you save your breath and get *that* printed on your jersey instead of your number?" Kayden snapped and skated away.

Normally, I don't leave my net until I'm good and ready, but my temper ran hot. I needed an answer and not a bullshit runaround.

Not one to let anyone have the last word, I followed him.

"Hey!" I called out. "I want to know what's going on. Are you playing a game with me?"

Kayden turned around and this time, he was the one with angry fire in his eyes. I was shocked, my heart racing, my pulse pounding in my ears, drowning out any other noise around me.

He shook his head. "The real question is, are you?"

"The only game I play is hockey, so the answer to your question is no. Now stop talking in circles, and say what you mean. One moment we were reading each other's essay, the next—"

Kayden scoffed and looked away. "*You* wrote an essay. Like a PhD thesis. And I wrote... I wrote shit."

"What?"

Wait. This is all about that econ essay?

"I'm sure you had a good laugh about it," he continued. "Stupid Kayden who can't write. Were you gonna tell everyone on the team about how dumb I am?"

His assumption hit me like a two hundred pound skater at full speed. He thought I was going to do that to him? Then again, he didn't know me at all.

"I don't think it and I would never say it. You're making an accusation that has no basis in fact. I offered to help you. Now you're accusing me of what? Making fun of you? I didn't fucking do that. And I wouldn't."

Kayden looked up and finally met my gaze. "It hit me in the library that maybe you were, you know, getting close to me just to turn around and—"

"And what, bully you?"

Kayden nodded, biting his lower lip. "It's happened before. I start to trust someone, and then they do a one-eighty and blindside me. It's like getting cross-checked from behind. It hurts worse because you're not prepared."

I yanked off my mask, finally able to breathe.

"You don't know me, and I don't know you. But I'll tell you something; what you see is what you get. If I have an opinion about you, I'll say it. Flat out. I don't evade, I don't play mind games, and I don't fucking bully."

Kayden said nothing. He stared at me for a moment and… skated away.

Whatever. I had no more talk left in me. *This.* This was why I didn't bother making friends. What a fucking headache. And it stung. Given my sharp mouth, it wasn't surprising that Kayden thought the worst of me. Who was I kidding? I wasn't good for anyone, not as a friend, and least of all for someone like him.

I slowly made my way down the ice, back to my net. I waited there for a while, alone, letting the cold and the quiet calm me.

Once I was ready, I headed for the boards. The locker room had to be empty by now. And when I got there, thankfully, it was. I undressed and headed for the showers.

Only, I was wrong. There *was* a player here. And, since it was an open shower room, I could clearly see that the player in question was Kayden.

Hot water sluiced down his broad back, between his shoulder blades and lower, over his taut ass. I stopped short because I couldn't stop staring at him, my mouth suddenly dry.

Kayden was…fuck, I couldn't deny it. The guy was hot as hell. There. I'd said it. I could admit when a guy was fit. It's not like I was immune to good-looking people. And he was. Nothing but hard muscles and smooth skin that was marred only by hockey bruises and sprinkled with golden hair. And freckles. Everywhere.

He lifted his head back and the water poured down over him. The scene reminded me of a Greek statue coming to life. Then I imagined Kayden trying to sit still long enough to pose for an artist and I bit back a laugh. Man, I had to stop doing that. Laughing. And staring at my teammate's body. Especially that big, round hockey ass.

But it was his posture—hands on the wall, shoulders slumped—that had me concerned.

Before I could think about it, I wandered into the room and turned on the shower across from him. I could've sworn I felt his eyes on me. And my cock—wayward bastard that he was—started to get hard. Okay, it chubbed up when I walked in here and saw Kayden naked, but now my dick was getting to full mast and there was nothing I could do to stop it.

Think of something, anything, to calm down.

With my back to him, I scrubbed up and ignored my dick. Which was painfully hard, curled up against my abs.

Flashes of someone touching me, jerking me off, flooded my mind and I couldn't shut it off. But the hand that was touching me wasn't a woman's. It was big and calloused, the rough grip teasing my skin. Worst of all? The hand was covered in freckles.

Stop it.

Despite deep breaths and repeated attempts to calm down, my erection didn't flag. Neither did the images of me and Kayden.

I heard Kayden's shower shut off and prayed that he was going to leave and leave now. Why the fuck had I wandered in here? To clean up, duh. But as soon as I saw him, I should've waited. Why couldn't I just wait until he was done?

When his footsteps got farther and farther away, I breathed a sigh of relief. Glancing around, and now that I was alone, I poured more soap into my hand and tugged on my cock, jerking off hard and fast. I shouldn't be doing this, not here, not now, but I didn't care. I needed to come so badly. I closed my eyes, and all I could see was Kayden kneeling at my feet, his big hand stroking my dick.

Oh fuck.

My hand moved faster and faster, caught up in the fantasy of fucking Kayden's fist. He was moaning, and I was panting, ready to come.

"Suck me off," I bit out and imagined those plump lips of his wrapped around my dick. This part was oh-so-satisfying because finally, *finally*, I got to shut Kayden up. And get off while doing it.

The vision of me fucking his face totally did me in. I jolted, trembled, the intense pleasure snaking up my spine and sparking every nerve ending in my body. My balls pulled up tight, and with one more stroke, I came hard, lashing the wet tile with my load.

Holy shit. I hadn't come that hard in a long time. And I hadn't jerked off to fantasies of myself with a guy. That was a first. But hot. Like the hottest damn jerk off, ever. Did this mean I was gay or bi? I'd been numb for so long that I didn't think I could feel anything for anyone. I'd hardly taken any interest in sex.

But I guess things were changing.

It was all Kayden's fault. My teammate. My classmate. My roommate on the road. The guy who was driving me nuts and making me feel things I had no desire to feel.

It was one wank session, let it go.

Easier said than done.

CHAPTER 13

KAYDEN

didn't walk back to my dorm. I ran like a goddamn sprinter. Like I hadn't spent two hours on the ice skating my ass off.

My cock was hard and leaking, making a mess of my briefs. I needed to jerk off, and I had to do it now. My roommate better not be around. Or, if he was, he better be prepared to hear my loud concert of moaning and groaning in the bathroom. I couldn't care less who heard or saw me at this point; I needed to come.

But why Maddox and why now? It's not like guys are shy about walking around naked in the open shower room, or the locker room in general, and I never got turned on by the sight before. But suddenly, Maddox's naked swagger was seared in my brain. I couldn't unsee it. I was a total ass man, but I couldn't remember the last time a woman's butt got me going like this. And Mad's? It was high and tight, two handfuls of sweet perfection. Then I noticed more details about his tattoos, the veins in his forearms, and his sculpted thighs. What would it feel like to touch him? To have those arms and legs wrapped around me?

Fuck, I'd never noticed my teammates this way. Or any

guys, for that matter. Well, I noticed hot guys before. Sure. But it was always in appreciation, not outright lust. And I had a moment, a second, where I was about to call out to Maddox. To get him to turn all the way around so I could see the rest of him up close. The brief glimpse I got when I walked out was just a tease. Was that semi he was rocking about me or was that wishful thinking? What was even more surprising? This new obsession of mine wasn't only about his dick or that spectacular ass of his. I wanted to look into his stormy blue eyes. I wanted to lean in and taste his lips.

Then I remembered how I'd acted on the ice. Maddox probably never wanted to speak to me again, never mind look at me. And so what if he was half hard? We're young, it's normal. No way he was thinking about me. Right?

Even that did nothing to calm my dick down. I got to my dorm in record time and when I passed through the front entrance, I rudely ignored people, and ran for the elevator. All while holding my backpack in front of me. Strategically.

I power walked once I got off the elevator. Down the hall-way, a few more steps, almost there… and finally, I was back in my room. Which was, thankfully, unoccupied.

I didn't waste any time, throwing my backpack on the floor and reaching for my jeans. I unzipped and delved my hand inside my briefs, but then I realized.

Lube, I need lube.

With my jeans around my hips, I shuffled to my night-stand, frantically searching for my lube.

"Yes!" I called out when I found it.

My hands were shaking, and I nearly squirted half the tube on the floor. Shit. Finally, I managed to get some in my hand, thank fuck, and got busy.

"Oh yeah," I moaned as I tugged on my dick, imagining that it was Maddox's hand.

Oh God, why was that the hottest thing ever? Would he be a total control freak? Demanding? I bet he would. Would he tell me what to do? I'd never touched a guy before, except for bro hugs, or swats on the ass. I was clumsy at the best of times, so I'd need guidance in the bedroom for sure. And I really loved that image of him taking over, showing me exactly what he wanted.

"You come when I tell you to come, Kayden."

Yes. This. Fuck, I needed this.

"Fuck my fist," Maddox commanded. "Do it."

I could almost feel Maddox's hot breath in my ear as he jerked me harder, faster, his rhythm never letting up, his other hand cupping my balls, rolling them. When his hand slid from my balls to my hip, I let out a loud whimper.

"No. Don't stop."

But his hand kept moving, sliding back around my ass, teasing the crease. Fuck yes, I wanted him to touch me like this.

When his finger slid over my hole, I pushed back, wanting more. I didn't know what was better, the finger on my hole or the rough grip on my dick. I pumped my hips back and forth, and held on tight to his shoulders, letting him touch me however he wanted.

"You want this?" he growled, teasing my rim. "You want my finger in your ass? What about my dick?"

"Yes. Fuck, yes."

Fantasy me had no hesitation in saying yes, virgin or not.

"Let's see if you can take my finger first."

When he pushed his slick finger inside my hole, slow and steady, I fucking keened. There was so much pleasure mixed with pain, and I wanted more. I needed it. Maddox drilled his finger deeper, and I couldn't hold on anymore.

"I'm gonna come," I moaned loudly.

Maddox's dark chuckle made me shiver. "Next time it's going to be my cock. I'm going to show you who this ass belongs to."

"Yes!" I shouted, my body jerking hard as I came in a heated rush.

In real life—and in my fantasy—shockwaves of pleasure rippled through my body. I crested higher, one incredible wave after another, until I crashed hard and finally calmed enough to take a breath. Opening my eyes, I looked down to find I'd spilled my load in my hand, on the floor, and on my backpack.

"Fucking hell," I panted. "Jesus."

That was the most intense orgasm I'd ever had, and as a horny, almost twenty-year-old, I'd had a lot of them. But an orgasm that started and ended with Maddox? I wasn't prepared for *that*. What did it mean? Or, did it have to mean anything? I'd heard other guys brag about threesomes with a girl and a guy. Guys that were emphatic about claiming they were straight. Was I just curious? Or was I was bi? Or gay? Was this why the limited experience I had with women was less than what I expected? Or was it because I was a virgin and nervous as fuck about having sex with anyone?

Whatever was going on with me, now that I was seeing Maddox like this, I didn't know if I could unsee it. But that didn't mean I was ready to accept it.

Dane and Jace were queer, but they weren't out to everyone, only their inner circle. They had fears about coming out to the rest of the team. Not a surprise when you consider that the hockey world is still ridiculously behind on stuff like inclusivity.

"What do I do now?" I asked myself out loud.

I could only imagine Maddox's reaction if he found out about me. Then again, I wasn't the only one sporting a hard-on in that shower. He'd turned away, and I thought that would be the end of my curiosity.

But no, it wasn't. I wanted to know what his skin tasted like, especially those lips of his that were always pursed in an angry pout. Would he kiss the same way? Aggressive? Would he maul my mouth and then maul the rest of me?

I had to stop thinking about sex. Sex with Maddox. In the shower, in my bed…and, what do you know? More cum leaked out of my cock.

Suddenly, I knew what I had to do. Talk to Dane. Well, I had to clean up first…

Catching my breath, I stripped off my shirt, and wiped the floor before heading for my shower. Another one.

Then I threw on clean jeans and a sweatshirt, and grabbed my phone.

> Kayden: In your room?

> Dane: Yup. Jackson and I are studying

> Kayden: Does that mean you're actually studying or having sex LOL

> Dane: Studying. For now. What's up?

> Kayden: I need to talk. It's personal.

> Dane: Just me?

> Kayden: Jackson too

> Dane: Come on over

I headed for the door and sauntered down the hallway to the other end of the floor. As always, I knocked on Dane's door before entering. There were no sex noises, so I assumed it was safe to enter, but still, you never know. It was a college dorm, after all.

"Come on in!" Dane yelled out.

I pushed open the door to find my friends, side by side, sitting on the floor, laptops open, Jackson's dark, curly head leaning on Dane's shoulder. I glanced around, relieved to see that Mullet the gecko was in his tank, and not roaming around Dane's room.

"Hey guys."

My face heated. Jesus. There was no way I was going to make it through this conversation without turning ten shades of red. Then again, what was I embarrassed about? This was sex. No biggie.

Right. Said the virgin.

"Have a seat," Dane motioned to the chair in the corner, put his laptop aside, and got up. "You want anything to drink?"

"Uh, Coke if you have it."

"Diet?"

"Is there any other kind?" I chuckled, my nerves easing.

Dane headed over to his mini fridge while I sat down.

"Sorry about the loss on Saturday, Kay. But I heard you had a good practice today," Jackson offered.

"The team's still finding its rhythm. We'll be ready to grab the next one," I paused. "And practice was, well, interesting."

"You still having issues with Maddox?" Jackson asked. "Dane told me all about your road roomie."

Dane offered me the can of soda, and another to Jackson, then sat back down. I gratefully popped the top and took a long sip. I needed that after a long-ass practice. And a mind-blowing orgasm. *Shit, don't think of orgasms.* The blush spread down my neck and chest like a rash.

What had Jackson asked me? Oh yeah. Practice. Maddox. Which brought me back to orgasms again.

Focus, Kay.

"It was a misunderstanding," I started. "See, we're in the same economics class. So, I asked Maddox to help me with an essay. We met up Sunday at the library."

"Whoa, you got him to talk to you, *and* work with you?" Dane asked. "How did you manage that?"

I shrugged. "I guess my annoying persistence paid off.

Anyway, when it came time to read each other's essays, I freaked out and took off. Mine sounded so lame and his was like something a PhD student would write. I figured he was gonna make fun of me after that. And then I thought maybe he was helping me as a kind of setup, you know? To use against me later on, like a cruel joke, to tell the team how stupid I am."

"Did he?" Dane asked, his glare immediate.

Jackson looked at me with the same fierce expression.

"No. He said that even though we don't know each other, he'd never do that. And that if he had an opinion about me, he'd tell me to my face. Which, from what I've seen and heard so far, is true. He's blunt about everything," I paused. "Anyway, I guess I overreacted. High school bullshit that I can't seem to shake off."

"Does he know about your learning disorder?" Jackson asked.

I nodded. "He saw me using my reading app in the restaurant on Saturday. It's weird, because normally I don't like to tell people. I know I should own it. It's the way my brain works and I shouldn't be ashamed, but that doesn't make it easier to say. So yeah, I told him. Also about my ADHD. He seemed cool about it. Which is why I was totally off base on Sunday. Leaving like that. And ignoring him in practice."

"I thought he wanted to be ignored," Dane replied.

"Yes and no. He was really pissed that I thought he might be the type of person to make fun of someone like that. And I didn't say anything else. I skated away. But I don't know what to do. I'd finally started to get through to him when we were in Rochester, and now, everything's fucked up again," I paused. "Then there was the shower room incident."

"Incident?" Jackson asked, leaning forward. "What happened in the shower?"

"I was in there, alone. I thought for sure Maddox would

wait until I left. But suddenly he was there. And that's not all
—" I paused, my body heating as I thought about the way I'd
eyed up Maddox's naked body.

Could I tell them? Fuck it. I took a deep breath and went
for it.

"I got a boner while watching him and I think he had one
too and I can't stop thinking about his ass and what it would
be like to touch him or kiss him and then I ran home and I
jerked off and now I think I might be bi or gay and I don't
know what to do."

CHAPTER 14

KAYDEN

had no oxygen left after spewing out that mouthful without pause.

Jackson and Dane stared at me, eyes wide, mouths open.

"Hello?" I asked. "Did you hear me? Please don't make me repeat all that."

Jackson ran a hand through his hair and looked at his boyfriend. Dane shook his head and turned to me.

"I was *not* expecting that," Dane muttered as he took a sip of his drink. "Um. I need a moment to process."

"I can't blame you, Kay." Jackson smiled at me. "The guy's smoking hot. Even with that angry attitude. Or maybe that's it. Yeah. The bad boy vibes are so—"

"So what?" Dane bit out.

Jackson laughed and leaned over, kissing Dane. "Intriguing."

"Intriguing?"

"But not as much as you, babe."

Dane cupped Jackson's face and kissed him back. It was brief but hell, they were hot together. Why hadn't I noticed that before? I pulled at my shirt and took another sip of my soda.

"Uh, guys?" I asked.

"Sorry." Dane turned to me. "Okay. First off, it's not unusual to get a hard on after a workout, right?"

"Yeah, but I was thinking about him before he got there. And then he *was* there, and I couldn't stop staring at his bite-able ass, and—" Shit. "Did I say *'biteable ass'* out loud?"

Jackson and Dane nodded.

"And then when I got home, I was, you know, thinking about him when I jerked off. Like, imagining stuff we were doing. Together. In detail."

"And this is the first time you've reacted like that to a guy?" Jackson asked.

"Yes. No. I mean, yes. I think. Okay, I've noticed hot guys, but I didn't imagine myself with them. And I've got limited experience with sex in general. I've only made out with a handful of women."

"It sounds like it's time for research," Dane offered.

"Research?" I asked.

"He means porn," Jackson added.

"Like you and your first day here?" I teased. "When we caught you mid-jerk?"

"Yes. But be smarter than me and use your ear pods and, most important, lock the door," Jackson chuckled. "I can send you the link to my and Dane's favorite site. See what you like, don't like, what turns you on. *If* it turns you on. After that, you'll know if you're ready for more…personal exploration."

Like touching an actual guy? But the only guy I wanted to touch was Maddox, and he'd probably bite my hand off.

"I guess that's a good plan. But I'm worried. It's a lot to deal with. Like, I've got enough on my plate with hockey, classes, and volunteering. And now my sexuality, too?"

"You don't need to figure out it right this second, Kay.

This week, this month, or even this year. Take your time," Dane encouraged.

I nodded, slightly less panicked. "True. And maybe I'm concerned about nothing. Maybe I'm having a reaction to stress? I've never felt so frustrated before. I've also never met anyone who's as prickly as Maddox. But also, I want to know why. He's dealing with something big. I don't know what, but something. The guy needs a hug, or a shoulder, or a friend? I don't fucking know. Why do I need to know?"

Jackson reached out and patted my leg. "Because you're sweet, Kay. You want to help people. But be careful. If you're right about Maddox, he might be more trouble than you can handle."

My mind was running so fast that I didn't know what to think. But Jackson had a point. One thing at a time.

"Well, I'll let you guys get back to studying," I replied and got up. "Thanks for the Coke, and the talk. I feel better. First, I have an apology to make to Maddox."

My phone buzzed, and I pulled it out. It was an email notification. The results of my essay were in. Sixty-five, barely a passing grade.

"Shit."

"What's wrong?" Dane asked.

"I got sixty-five on that economics essay. I'm so fucked."

Dane got up and gripped my shoulder. "The semester's not over. How much does it count toward your final grade?"

"Only ten percent, but still."

"Maybe if you clear things up with Maddox, he can help you out?" Jackson added.

"Maybe. Anyway, thanks again. I'll catch you guys later."

I headed for the door and made my way back to my room.

My phone pinged again. And again. One was a message from Jackson with the porn link. Oh man, I had to leave that until later or I'd get no studying done at all. The second was a reminder from Coach about Thursday practice and our home game on Saturday. The third was a confirmation for my official tutoring session on Friday. More work.

My mind wouldn't settle, and I didn't know what to do first. That was always a challenge for me. Starting ten things and finishing none of them.

But there was one thing I wanted done.

Kayden: Can we meet up?

I didn't count on Maddox replying to me, but I hoped. And surprisingly, a minute later, he responded.

Maddox: If I say no, are you going to keep hounding me?

Kayden: Yes

Maddox: When and where?

Kayden: Library, second floor, one hour

Maddox: K

Maddox

I was only here for Kayden's apology. At least, I assumed that's what he was up to. Once that was done, I was gone.

Bad enough I couldn't stop thinking about that wank session in the shower, or what had inspired it. For the first time in a long time, I needed someone to talk to. But not my therapist. I didn't feel like getting analyzed. I just wanted another opinion about this situation. So, I texted Daniel. My former coach was the only person I trusted. Outside of my mom. But I could only talk to her in my dreams.

Daniel was the reason I was here, and yet I'd barely called or texted since I arrived. Guilt gnawed at my gut. Another example of me being a shit person. A shit friend. Which is why it was better that I had none.

> Maddox: Something's come up at school and I'm not sure what to make of it.

A few seconds later, Daniel replied.

> Daniel: About class or the hockey team?

> Maddox: It's about one of the players, a guy I room with on the road. Kayden.

> Daniel: Did you tell him to fuck off? LOL

> Maddox: Of course. But it didn't take. He's persistent.

> Daniel: And that's it? He annoys you?

> Maddox: Yes. No. Sort of. We had a misunderstanding on Sunday and then we were arguing at practice today. He drives me nuts. But that's not all. Fuck, I don't even know if I can say it.

> Daniel: Whatever it is, you know you can tell me. When you're ready.

I typed out a response, deleted it. Typed it again. And finally sent it.

> Maddox: I'm feeling things. More than I should. Like, in a way I haven't about anyone else.

> Daniel: What do you think it means?

> Maddox: I don't know. I shut off that part of myself because I can't imagine getting close to anyone.

Daniel: You've come a long way in the past
four years. Maybe this is the next step. A
new friendship?

Friendship? Or, more? My hormones were messing up my head and I couldn't think clearly.

Maddox: Maybe

Daniel: Tell him the truth. If you think Kayden
is trustworthy, tell him. That's the only way to
bridge a gap. Like you and me, right? Once
you told me, things changed. Things got
better.

Maddox: I'll think about it. This could be all
for nothing. I should ignore him and focus on
my game, my studies.

Daniel: Follow your gut

Maddox: TTYS

I shoved my phone in my pocket and waited by the elevator. As the minutes ticked by, my nerves kicked up. Until finally, I heard the telltale ping. Somehow, even though the doors were still closed, I knew who was on the other side of it.

Sure enough, when they opened, there was Kayden. My body primed like fight or flight. And when he walked in my direction, I realized the shower fantasy was *not* a one off. Because I sure as fuck noticed him now. Which ticked me off. I didn't want this. I didn't want to feel anything.

"I'm here. What do you want?" I bit out.

Kayden ran a hand through his tawny hair. "I wanted to apologize for Sunday. For thinking that you were going to make fun of me."

"Noted," I replied and started to walk away.

"I'm not done yet!" Kayden called out.

"Surprise," I snapped and turned around. "What is it?"

"I wanted to know if you'll, you know, still help me with the economics class? I got a sixty-five on the essay and if I'd stayed and worked on it with you, that probably wouldn't be the case."

Fuck, why was I suddenly soft for this guy? I was pissed. At him, and at myself. Goddamn empathy had picked a fine time to show up.

"Once a week, we meet here for two hours," I replied. "Fridays at noon. Take it or leave it."

"I have my regular tutor ten to eleven thirty, so that works perfect," he whispered, looking relieved. "Thanks."

The big guy grinned, and it looked damn good on him. It shouldn't. But it did. Staring at his smiling face was like staring into the sun. Or a solar eclipse. Either way, I was sure to get burned, or worse. I couldn't even believe the thoughts running through my head…

"Anything else?" I asked.

There had to be. Kayden couldn't say one thing and leave it at that.

"Well, I—"

His comment was interrupted by my phone ringing. *Unknown number*. Who'd be calling me? Maybe it was something to do with school?

"I have to take this," I replied and turned my back on Kayden.

I tapped *accept* and brought the phone to my ear. "Hello."

"Is this Maddox Grange?"

The echo of my former last name gave me instant chills.

"It's Maddox Rocher," I bit out. "Who are you and why are you calling me?"

"My name is Wallace McKenzie. I represent Corey Grange's estate. I'm reaching out with an update and—"

I tapped *end* and cut off any further words. Jesus Christ.

The mention of my father's name had my stomach roiling. The snack I'd eaten after practice was about to make its way back up. I ran to find a bathroom, and I made it just in time. Heaving, I puked into the toilet, and blinked away the tears that threatened.

No. Fuck him.

A loud knock on the door startled me.

"Mad? Are you okay?"

Fucking Kayden.

"Go away!" I shouted. "Leave me alone."

My stomach flipped again, but this time, thankfully, I didn't throw up. Once I was sure I wasn't going to heave again, I washed up and headed back into the hallway. Of course, Kayden was standing there waiting. At first glance, with his arms crossed over his chest, he looked like a guy you'd want to avoid. But he wasn't. And I fucking knew that this goddamn teddy bear was gonna follow me home. I knew it.

"What happened?" he asked me.

"Don't you ever take a hint and leave people alone?"

"No. Are you all right?"

His golden eyes pinned me in place.

"I don't know," I muttered. "That call was about someone I never want to think about."

"That bad?"

"I ran off and puked my guts out. Yes, that bad," I snapped.

"Tell me."

Jesus Christ. "No."

Fuck the elevator. I needed to walk. I headed for the stairs, Kayden following. When I made it outside the building, I took a deep breath of clean, cold air. It was okay.

I'm here in Vermont. I'm safe. He's gone and I'm safe.

"Mad," Kayden whispered as he stood beside me.

Fuck this.

"The call was from an attorney, okay? One who represents my father," I admitted as I leaned up against the brick facade of the building. "His estate."

"Oh," Kayden paused, biting his lower lip. "What happened?"

I shook my head. "Trust me, you really don't want to know."

CHAPTER 15

KAYDEN

Standing outside the library, Maddox was pale, sweating, and visibly shaking. My first instinct was to reach out to him, but when I made to step closer, he backed away.

"I need to be alone. I mean it, Kay. Just go."

It was the first time he'd called me that. I nodded, ignoring my gut. I let up. For once.

"I'll see you at practice Thursday, yeah?" I asked.

Maddox nodded and leaned forward, hands on his thighs, head down.

"Text if you need to talk or anything," I said.

No reply.

I was still unsure about leaving him alone like this, but I did.

Two weeks later, and I was still thinking about that day. Had I made the wrong decision by leaving Maddox alone like that?

I'd been working my courage up to text him, but every time I started typing out a message, I stopped. But I thought about him. Every fucking day. To the point where I was distracted in class—not that it took much—and at night. It took forever for me to fall asleep.

The only time I saw Maddox was at practice, but he

ignored me. I was ready for the sharp replies, but instead I got nothing. And I didn't know what was worse.

Last week I'd arrived at the library for our study session. I waited half an hour before realizing he wasn't going to show.

And here I was, another week later, waiting again. Hoping this time he'd make good on his promise. I'd booked the same room and waited until 12:10 hit. This was ridiculous. He wasn't coming.

I was about to grab my stuff and leave when there was a knock at the door. When Maddox appeared, I got up so fast I nearly toppled my chair.

Smooth, Kay.

He was dressed in his usual jeans and leather jacket.

"Hey." He nodded and sat down.

I did the same and opened my laptop.

"You didn't show up last week," I stated. "I was gonna text you but—"

"I'm here now, aren't I?" he snapped.

Thank fuck that Mad was, well, mad. He was back. And I'd never been so happy at having a grump around.

"Yes, you are."

I wanted to ask him if he was feeling better, but I didn't want to poke the bear. Not too hard, anyway.

He reached into his bag and pulled out what looked like a journal, a set of pens, and… stickers?

"Here." He placed them in front of me. "Okay, let's start with reviewing chapter five and six on macro—"

"Wait, what's all this?" I asked him, confused as hell.

"It's a type of journal designed for people with dyslexia. And apparently, color coding things, with pens or stuff like stickers, is like a visual prompt that makes it more engaging."

Wait. He'd bought this stuff for *me*?

"So, chapter five deals with three concepts," he continued. "We're going to get quizzed on this next week and—"

"Thank you," I interrupted, nudging him with my shoulder.

This was totally unexpected. No one, not even my closest friends, had done anything like this.

Maddox refused to make eye contact and began typing away on his laptop. He was wearing a couple of silver rings and a rolo bracelet that rattled with every movement. As I glanced at his hands, it struck me that they were as beautiful as the rest of him. It got me thinking about what those hands would feel like on my body. And what my body would feel like next to his.

Then I remembered our practice, and watching him do his warmup stretches for his hip flexors. His knees spread wide, then wider still, until he was all but humping the ice. Fuck. Goalies had great flexibility, and I wondered how agile Maddox really was.

"Kayden?"

My mind veered off the dirty track and back to the present.

"Yeah?"

"We've already lost almost fifteen minutes of study time. You ready?"

"Sure."

I didn't want to study economics. Just Maddox.

"I want you to tell me about the concept of deflation."

"You mean, like, after you come?" I snickered.

"Jesus Christ." Maddox looked up at the ceiling and then turned to me, his steely blues as intense as ever. "Do you want to ace this course or not?"

"Yes. Okay, sorry. Sorry."

Focus, Kay.

We went back and forth about the concepts, and then Maddox quizzed me. I got eight out of fifteen. Not great. Another hour of study. More questions, more quizzes. But at least, Maddox let me explain stuff in my own time. And he didn't get frustrated or annoyed when I fucked up an answer.

After two hours, I was fried. But at least I had a better handle on the subject.

No, not Mad. That one I was still working out.

Maddox

What had possessed me to buy all that shit for Kayden? No freaking clue. Call it distraction.

After that disturbing phone call from my father's attorney, and the panic attack that followed, I called my therapist. Then I contacted Daniel and asked for his advice. I knew what was coming, but I still wasn't prepared.

I didn't want to hear anything about my father ever again. Thinking about him gave me full-on chills and made my stomach clench hard.

There was only one thing that kept me from spiraling, and it was hockey. Okay, two things. Hockey and my study session with Kayden. I'd been a dick and didn't show up last week but I wasn't going to go back on my word. And, like always, getting into the game—or the study session—and getting out of my head was necessary. But I wasn't ready to talk to Kayden about what had happened. Not at practice, anyway, and not with everyone around.

And whatever this was between me and Kayden? I still had no idea. I found myself reaching for my phone several times. But I didn't text him. Instead, I bought him that fucking journal. It was purely a selfish move on my part. If it helped him pass this course, then he'd be out of my hair. That was a good enough reason. Well, not totally because there was still hockey. But next semester would be different. We'd only see each other at practice and games. Okay, we'd see each other every week. But not up close and personal. Not that study sessions were personal, but being in close contact with Kayden was making me want things. And it had me noticing stuff I'd prefer to ignore.

Like the way Kayden worried his full lower lip when he was working out an idea in his head. And the way his eyes changed color, from light gold to the darkest honey, and back again. Not to mention the messy hair that I wanted to fix. My hand itched to reach up and tuck the unruly strands behind his ears. Not that I wanted to touch his hair or anything. That would be weird, right?

Thank fuck he hadn't made a big deal out of my gift. I was grumpy enough at myself for even purchasing the journal to begin with. Whatever. He could take it or leave it. It didn't matter to me either way. I didn't care.

With two hours of study done, Kayden suggested we grab a bite in town. I wanted to tell him to get lost, but I had to eat, anyway. And he'd probably follow me back to the dorm if I said no.

Then I remembered it was Friday.

"Don't you have a party to go to?" I asked as we headed across campus and down the south lawn.

"What?"

"It's Friday. Aren't you partying with Dane and Jace?"

"Uh, it's two in the afternoon, Mad," Kayden chuckled. "And, hello, we have a game tomorrow."

Jesus, I'd totally forgotten. Two hours with Kayden and look what happened to me. I was completely out of it.

"Right," I replied. "So, partying comes Saturday night?"

"Fuck yes." Kayden nodded. "One of the fraternities has a party planned. Ethan's frat. Everyone on the hockey team's invited."

"Are you going?" I asked.

"Oh yeah. You want to come with?"

"Me? At a frat party?" I scoffed. "Hell to the fucking no."

"Why?"

"Do I need a reason?"

"Yup."

I sighed. "I'd rather eat edibles and listen to music."

"You can do that at the party."

"Yeah, but there are people there. I'd rather do it alone," I paused. "Do you…hook up at these things?"

My God, I sounded so lame. What did I care if Kayden got laid? I glanced at his face, his cheeks ruddy.

"Uh, not really," he muttered. "Sort of. Well, no."

"I have no idea what that any of that means, but whatever. It's not my biz."

We walked in silence as we passed the campus gates. Small-town Sutton was starting to grow on me. Being away from the big city congestion and chaos wasn't something I thought I'd like, but did. And the quiet here had a way of calming me.

"So, edibles. Care to share tomorrow?" Kayden asked.

"Maybe," I replied.

Man, I wish I had one now. I was fucking nervous all of a sudden, so I pulled out my pack of smokes. And I didn't miss Kayden's side-eye.

"Don't give me that look," I snapped.

"What?"

"Judgment. I saw it," I replied as I pulled a cig out.

"I'd never. But those are gonna ruin your teeth and your breath."

I shrugged. "Then it's a good thing I don't kiss anyone."

Kayden stopped short. Shit. I shoved the cig in my mouth as my comment sat like a bomb between us.

"Not at all? Like, ever?" Kayden asked, eyes wide.

I fumbled for my lighter and lit up, taking a long, *long* drag.

"Fuck off," I mumbled and walked faster.

"If you did want to, you know, kiss someone, who would it be?" he asked.

"We're not in high school, Kay. Drop it."

"Sure. Fine," he sighed. "I've made out with a few women. But that's pretty much it. Still got my big v-card."

I inhaled too fast and choked on the smoke.

"I really didn't need to know that."

Okay, maybe I was curious. There was that damn word again. Why? Why did I want to know about him? I mean, I didn't. But I did.

Then I realized Kayden said women. He was straight. That meant whatever I saw in the shower that day was him thinking about a hot girl. That made my grumpy demeanor turn even more sour. I took another drag and waited for my nerves to settle.

"I haven't told anyone. Well, except you. And Dane. It's not like bragging about being a virgin is a thing, right? And not on the hockey team. A lot of the guys are always talking about how much they get laid. Especially Ethan, Sean, and Finn."

"They're probably bullshitting. As most guys do."

"But not you?"

I shrugged. "No one's ever asked me."

"Big surprise there," Kayden teased.

I offered him my best finger.

CHAPTER 16

KAYDEN

Maddox didn't kiss anyone. Ever? Did that mean he was asexual? Or anti-kissing? He said he didn't kiss, not that he didn't fuck. Of course, now I had even more questions.

"You should come to the party with me tomorrow."

"Nope," Maddox replied and threw his cig on the ground.

"Why not?"

"I don't like crowds."

"It'll be fun," I urged. "Stay for an hour."

"No."

I shook my head. Stubborn pain in the ass.

We walked down main street and headed for Boots & Burgers. The place had huge servings, cool music, and a relaxed vibe that drew in students and locals alike.

"How about I come by your room instead and we can hang out?" I offered.

"No."

"Do you know any other words?"

"No," Maddox repeated.

But then, I heard it. I could've sworn he was laughing. But

when I looked at him, he had his usual stern expression in place. Maybe I was having a low blood sugar episode…

I opened the door to the restaurant and motioned for Maddox to go first. Man, the way he glared at me, you'd think I'd spat on him.

"What?" I asked, confused.

"If I can manage to block dozens of shots on goal, I think I can open my own damn door," he snarled as he walked past me.

I rolled my eyes and followed him into the restaurant, which was surprisingly crowded for a Friday afternoon. "There's no pleasing you, is there?"

"No."

"OMG, Mad, stop saying that!" I chuckled.

A few patrons in the restaurant turned to stare at us. Oops. Thankfully, Phoenix, the owner of the place, recognized me and walked up to greet us.

"Kayden, how's it going?" he asked.

"Great." I nodded. "Phoenix, this is Maddox Rocher; he's one of my teammates."

"Nice to meet you." Phoenix smiled at him. Maddox nodded, but offered nothing but his scowl. No surprise.

"Uh, table for two?" Phoenix asked.

I nodded, trying to ignore the sudden rush of heat in my cheeks. Why did it suddenly feel like I was on a date? I went out with Dane all the time and it never occurred to me it was anything other than two friends hanging out. Ignoring the strange urge I had to place my hand on Maddox's back, I waited for him to follow Phoenix first.

We were led to a corner booth near the back of the restaurant. Maddox slid in first, his back to the crowd and I eased in beside him. I was waiting for him to tell me to move farther away, but when he didn't say anything, I relaxed. Our knees touched, but Maddox didn't budge or tell me to fuck off. Progress.

"You guys need a minute with the menu?" Phoenix asked.

"I'll have a double cheeseburger, onion rings, and a Diet Coke," Maddox replied. "Thanks."

"Same, but with fries, please."

Phoenix nodded and took off towards the kitchen.

"So, about tomorrow night—" I started.

"Okay. One hour. That's it. Now will you let it go?"

Side by side, he was so close, and I fought the urge to move closer. My mouth was dry, and I was in desperate need of water. Something. Anything.

"Cool."

I was anything but.

Suddenly, I heard a voice calling my name. I turned around to find Ethan, Axel, and Finn heading our way. I waved them over.

"Come sit with us!" I shouted across the din.

When they got to our table, Finn slid in on the other side of the booth, then Ethan and Axel.

"What's going on, guys?" Finn asked.

"We finished a study session. Gotta fuel up for tomorrow," I replied.

"I thought you didn't want to be around this guy," Finn teased Maddox.

Maddox rolled his eyes and grunted. "I don't want to be around any of you. But I'm on the team, so I don't really have a choice. And we're both in the same economics class. Like Kayden said, we were studying."

"That's not Kayden's area of expertise," Ethan smirked. "He's just a pretty face."

"Prettier than you," I shot back.

I didn't like the dig, but I managed to make light of it. Ethan always said he was teasing, and he did it to everyone. But, as always, I took it personally.

"Did Kayden tell you about the party tomorrow?" Ethan

motioned to Maddox. "You should come. Maybe with a couple of drinks in you, you'll actually crack a smile."

"Unlikely. The smile, I mean," Maddox snarked. "But I'll be there. I'm looking forward to watching you crash and burn."

"Crash and burn?" Ethan asked.

"Yeah, like when all the hot students hit on Kayden and not you."

I couldn't help laughing at that. Maddox's scenario was highly unlikely, but funny all the same.

"Score one for the goalie," Axel quipped.

Ethan gave us all a choice finger.

"I'm starving," Ethan announced. "Let's get food, already."

Phoenix returned with our burger plates, and the rest of the guys put in their orders. Of course, Ethan ate my fries while he waited for his meal to arrive. Maddox finished his burger, and pushed his plate towards me. His pile of onion rings sat untouched.

"Take it," he insisted.

Ethan reached out and Maddox shook his head. "Did I offer it to you?"

I gratefully grabbed his plate and finished off the greasy goodness in no time. Damn, I was still hungry as fuck. I probably should've ordered two burgers.

"I can't wait until tomorrow. I need a fucking win so bad I can taste it," Axel muttered as he sipped on his water.

"Boston sucks. They're like, third to last in the standings," Finn scoffed. "We got this."

Phoenix returned with more food, and I reached for Ethan's fries.

"Hey!" Ethan tapped my hand.

"What? You took most of mine. Fair's fair," I replied. "Besides, you need to stay leaner than me. Forwards gotta have speed."

Ethan shrugged and I gratefully took his fries.

"What do you guys think about Silas?" Ethan asked. "I heard a rumor that Banning wants to cut him from the team."

I didn't like to see anyone go, but Silas played hot, then not. He didn't make much of an effort to interact with the rest of the team. Not that Maddox did either, but his goaltending skills couldn't be denied. Silas was getting better with each practice, but to me, he was still holding back.

"It's only been a couple of weeks," I offered. "Give the guy a chance."

"If he's not top tier, he needs to go," Axel said between bites. "He's big, he's got skills, but he's in his own world out on the ice."

"Has anyone talked to him outside of practice?" I asked.

Everyone shook their heads.

"Did you invite him tomorrow?" I turned to Ethan.

"I did, but he said he had family stuff afterward. No clue what that means," Ethan replied with a shrug. "But who turns down a party after a home game on a Saturday night? This is college. It's time to let loose and fucking live. Family shit can wait."

"What does it matter to you?" Maddox bit out. "And FYI, it's not cool to spread rumors about teammates getting cut. I don't want to hear about it unless it actually happens."

Maddox pulled out his wallet, threw cash on the table, and motioned for me to move out of his way. I got up and Maddox slid out from the booth.

"I've got more studying to do," Maddox added and stalked off.

Without thinking, I grabbed my backpack, threw a twenty on the table, and got up.

"I'll see you guys tomorrow."

Finn, Axel, and Ethan stared at me like I'd lost my mind. I probably had, following Maddox outside, instead of staying with them. It wasn't like me to up and leave like that, but

Maddox had a point. I didn't like hearing rumours about players being cut either. And talking about it before a game was bad juju.

I hurried outside and found Maddox reaching into his bag again. Pulling out another cigarette.

"Not the night before a game," I said to him. "You already had one. Your lung capacity will be fucked."

"Says who?"

"Me."

"And you're a doctor?"

I chuckled. "Obviously not."

Maddox ignored me, lighting up as we walked down the street.

"Plus, they pollute," I added.

Maddox paused. Score one for me.

"I know," he muttered, shaking his head. "Truth? I've been trying to quit. But sometimes, I need a crutch. One. And smoking is it."

I nodded, and let it go.

"I need more calories," I confessed. "That burger wasn't enough."

"Pizza?" Maddox offered and motioned to the end of the block. "There's a place at the corner. Go grab a slice."

"You want?"

"I'm good. I don't have two stomachs like you."

"Funny."

"Given the size of you, it's not funny. It's true."

"I am a big boy," I quipped, holding my arms out.

"I've seen."

I stopped short. Was Maddox talking about my dick or was that a general comment on my size? He coughed, threw the cig away, and started walking faster, nearly sprinting past me.

He meant in general, right? He wasn't referring to my cock. That was just my horny brain playing tricks on me.

"Are you hungry for it?" I asked.

Maddox stumbled, but I couldn't grab his arm in time. He managed to right himself all on his own and slowly turned around.

"What does that mean?"

I pointed to the pizza place. "Pizza? Are you hungry for it?"

Maddox cleared his throat and shook his head, then ran a hand through his hair, shoving the loose strands back from his face. "No. No, I'm fine."

"Are you gonna leave as soon as I go in there, or will you wait for me?"

"I think you can manage to walk back to the dorm by yourself," he snarked.

I reached for the door and called out over my shoulder. "Admit you like me."

"Admit you're a pain in the ass."

It wasn't a statement of friendship, but I'd take it.

CHAPTER 17

KAYDEN

Dane and I walked to the rink together, game day nerves riding high, as well as our expectations. Students were filing into the venue along with us. The anticipation of playing for a home crowd pumped my adrenaline fast and wicked hot.

"Is Jackson on his way?" I asked him.

Dane chuckled. "He's already here. He wanted to get the best seat."

"How're things going with you two? I mean, you look happy as fuck."

Dane's wide grin said it all. "We are. I'm starting to feel like I'm ready to tell more people, but I've still got concerns. You and Jace support me, but what about the rest of the guys? And what does it mean for my future in hockey? There are a lot of unknowns."

I thought about my own recent revelation that I might not be straight, so I couldn't blame Dane at all. There were a ton of what-ifs. Every new question brought about more of the same.

"What about you?" Dane whispered. "Any more thoughts on, you know, what we talked about the other day?"

I bit my lower lip and looked around. If only Dane knew. After parting ways with Maddox, I'd raced back to my dorm, determined to jerk my intense feelings away. Only, it was the night before a game, so I took a cold shower instead. Gotta save the energy for the ice.

"I can't stop thinking about…that person. Or staring at them. Or wondering what it would be like to, you know, be with them. Not just kiss them, but more. A lot more. I mean, what the hell is this? A stupid crush?"

"So, you think you might be—"

"Bi? I really don't know," I sighed. "I'm saying that a lot lately."

"I'm all for exploration, but be careful. He's a teammate. That's asking for a shitload of trouble."

"It's pointless to talk about it. Why would he even look at me that way?" I scoffed. "He's gorgeous and smart."

"Hey, you are too."

"Come on, Dane."

"I mean it. Don't talk yourself down. Anyone would be lucky to be with you."

Dane gave my shoulder a reassuring pat.

"Thanks, bud."

We were the last players to arrive on-site, which surprised me. I looked around for my study buddy and spotted Maddox getting his gear on, head down, ear pods in, ignoring everyone as usual. Silas was next to him. Same damn thing. I was about to go over and talk to them when I glanced at my stall and noticed a black drawstring bag sitting in front of it. A bag I didn't recognize, but one that had my name on it.

"What's this?" I asked, pointing at the bag and looking around. "Who put this here?"

My teammates shrugged and shook their heads.

"No idea," Jace called out. "The bag was here when we arrived. We figured you were expecting it."

"Nope."

"Is there a tag on it?" Dane asked.

"Yeah, just my name."

Picking up the bag, I wondered why it felt like a sack of peas but lighter. I slowly untied it and looked inside. When I realized what it was, I couldn't contain my laughter.

"What?" Dane asked me as teammates crowded around me to look. "What is it? What's so funny?"

"This is awesome," I snickered as I pulled out a massive bag of beads. "It's a kit to make bracelets. Did you do this?"

Dane looked as surprised as I did. Either he had a great poker face or he was in the dark like me. "Nope. Jace?"

"Not me," Jace replied.

"Ethan?" I asked.

"I got better things to do than buy you beads, Kay."

"Well, someone from our team bought this," I added. "I mentioned making the bracelets when we were having dinner in Rochester. Fess up, now, come on! Who did this?"

No one volunteered an answer.

"Okay then. Play it that way, that's cool," I quipped and looked around. "Thank you to whoever bought this! Bracelets for everyone next practice!"

"Are you taking orders?" Finn asked.

"Fuck yes," I exclaimed. "Whatever message you want, colors, let me know."

"Team colors only," Finn insisted.

"Can I get six?" Jace asked. Typical superstitious hockey player, he wanted the number of bracelets to match his jersey. "Or twelve. Six for each arm. I like to stack 'em."

"Sure, I—"

"Enough already," Axel interrupted and got up in Jace's face. "In case you forgot, princess, we've got a game to play."

"In case you forgot, your hockey stick should remain in

your hands, not up your ass," Jace bit back, offering Axel two fingers in response.

Then Jace turned to me and smiled. "Six and six."

"You got it," I chuckled.

I was so fucking stoked. Maybe a few of the guys thought it was ridiculous, but I loved the idea of making bracelets for the team. It was fun. Something that everyone needed. A bit of lightness to ease the pressure we were under.

Glancing across the room, I noticed that Maddox was almost done suiting up. But it seemed like he hadn't even noticed the conversation going on around him. Since no one needed fun more than our grumpy-ass goalie, he'd be the first person to get a bracelet.

I placed the bag on the shelf in my stall, which was smelling ripe AF, and pulled out my equipment. The ritual of getting geared up was always comforting to me, priming me for the game. I put things on in the same order and when I was done, plunked down on the bench to put on my skates.

Jace ambled over and sat down beside me.

"So," he whispered as he nudged me. "Who do you think bought you the kit?"

"It's gotta be Dane," I insisted. "Remember last season and the T-shirt he gave me for my birthday? The one he made me wear to that freshmen party?"

"Oh yeah. The one that said *'Kiss me, I'm Irish. No wait, I'm a hockey player. Even better.'*?"

"Exactly. He loves funny shit like that. It's gotta be him."

"Did it work?" Jace asked.

"Did what work?"

Jace rolled his eyes. "The T-shirt. Did you get kissed?"

"I did, once. But she gave me a peck on the mouth. Followed by a friendly, *'Hey Kayden, cute shirt.'* No tongue," I sighed. "Just my fucking luck."

"Maybe tonight your luck will change? I hear the party's going to be massive."

There was only one set of lips I was thinking about. Not that I'd ever get the chance to kiss Maddox—or that I should want to. Maybe Jace was right. There were plenty of hot women on campus and I'm sure there would be plenty at the party tonight. I needed to get out of this weird headspace when it came to my feelings for Maddox.

"Looking forward to it."

Jace nodded and stood up. I finished lacing up and followed him and the rest of my teammates as we lined up in the gallery.

I looked over my shoulder and spotted Maddox at the back of the line. When his gaze hit mine, I quickly looked away. I paced in place, shifting from one foot to the other, keeping warm, listening to the boom of music that filtered through the rink. Then the reverberation of the crowd chanting, "Cougars! Cougars! Cougars!"

When we finally got called out to the ice, the game was the only thing I was thinking about. Maddox was only a teammate.

Out here, there was no room for distractions. The only thing I wanted was to win.

Maddox

Yes, it was me. I'd bought Kayden that fucking bracelet making kit. I'd ordered it along with the journal I gave him. But I kept the kit under my bed until today, second guessing myself.

Why had I done it? That part, I was still figuring out.

But there was no way in hell I'd ever admit it. And no one would ever find out. If they did, I'd never hear the end of it. I could only imagine the razzing from my teammates. Not that I gave a shit what they thought of me, but still. It was none of their fucking business.

I'd been careful to arrive extra early, hiding the kit in my backpack, and then dropping it quickly in front of Kayden's stall before anyone could see me.

Then when Kayden arrived, I had a sudden moment of panic. What if he was embarrassed by the gift and everyone on the team started making fun of him? Fuck, I didn't intend for that. Not after what he told me about being bullied. Thankfully, my worries were laid to rest. I was so relieved to see him laughing when he opened the gift, proudly telling everyone what it was. I had my ear pods in, so it looked like I was listening to music. But I wasn't.

And I had to give him props. Kayden didn't temper his enthusiasm for anyone.

Maybe that's why I bristled so hard when he came at me with that sunny aura of his. His attitude reminded me of things I'd lost, of feelings that were out of reach. It also got me thinking about my mom, who was, in fact, very similar in nature to Kayden. Thinking about her was always bittersweet —there were memories I clung to when I had nothing else, and lonely wishes that she was still here for me to talk to.

I swear, sometimes the skin of my shoulders grew hot, like she was holding me, healing me, telling me everything was gonna be okay.

"Rocher! Moss!" Coach yelled. "Let's go!"

Time to get my head in the game. Now wasn't the time to think about personal shit. It was time for the left side of my brain to get fucking moving.

When I shuffled into the hallway, I was hit by the blast of roaring students.

"Cougars! Cougars! Cougars!"

Mask on and lined up, I was ready to go.

Coach waved us on, and we took to the ice for our pregame warmup. I expected a big turnout for our home game, but nothing prepared me for the sight and sound of this college crowd. It was heady, energizing, and terrifying all at the same time.

I glanced over at the box and spotted Sean sitting beside Axel, Finn, and the rest of the guys. I wondered how Sean was dealing with being the backup. He'd had surgery on his achilles tendon near the end of last season. He'd recuperated well enough, but Coach kept putting me in net. I'm sure Sean was frustrated as hell. Watching and waiting when all you wanted to do was play was the worse.

Kayden and Silas were on the first line, along with Dane, Jace, and Ethan. Kayden skated in my direction, and I braced myself for whatever he was about to say to me, willing him to go away. Fucking up my concentration was the last thing I needed right now.

But he surprised me. Kayden tapped the bar twice and skated back to his position. Then, there was no time for me to think about other players, or silly gifts, or a defenseman who was taking up way too much of my headspace.

Out here, there was only me facing off against that puck.

CHAPTER 18

KAYDEN

This game was brutal. Boston was aggressive as fuck —tripping, shoving, high sticking—and these guys were nasty. There was always trash talk on the ice, but this was next level. Anytime there was a line change or a penalty called, they'd start in, and we gave it right back.

Axel looked like he was about to have a stroke. Dane too. Our captain was known for keeping his cool, but his patience was being tested. In fact, everyone on our team looked as pissy as Maddox on a good day.

By the time we hit the second period, it was still 0-0. Without a goal on the board, we were frustrated as fuck.

"Kayden, Moss, Lund, St. Pierre, Rowland, let's go!" Banning barked.

I rushed out onto the ice, bracing myself for battle.

Axel faced off against Blaine Reswell, Boston's center. The guy was fast, but with a nasty habit of playing dirty. He'd gotten away with a tripping call against Axel in the first period that everyone, especially Coach, was still seething over. Axel hit the ice hard and was shaken up. Plus, he got a nasty cut on his chin that had to be superglued. He'd be bruised as hell tomorrow, for sure. But the hit didn't stop Axel; he was adamant about staying in the game.

"Let's shut these fucking losers down," Axel bit out as he skated by me.

I couldn't agree more.

Another puck drop, another possession for Reswell. Goddamn it. I blinked and he was already taking off down the ice. Was there any stopping this guy? He deke'd around Dane, but Axel and Jace were hot on his trail.

Suddenly Reswell's elbow snapped up, and Jace got rammed in the shoulder, pushing him into the boards. Coach was screaming, but it was white noise at this point. Jace recovered and took off down the ice. Reswell wasn't slowing down. If anything, he'd picked up speed.

I staked out the blue line, ready for him.

Until Reswell passed to his teammate, Mika Lasler. Lasler took the shot, the puck whizzing past Silas and right into Maddox's glove.

Holy shit, no goal...

The whistle blew, but Reswell kept coming. The forward slammed into Silas, who, in turn, collided with Maddox. It all happened so fast I could hardly believe my eyes.

"You fucker!" Silas shouted and shoved Reswell back.

Reswell threw the first punch and all hell broke loose. I skated over to intervene, but I got a hit to the side of my helmet. Motherfucker. Both teams jumped into the fray, crowding around Silas and Reswell, whistles blowing, refs yelling, fans screaming, and chaos erupting.

Someone grabbed the back of my jersey. I whirled around, readying to defend myself, when I realized it was Jace.

"You gotta get him off the ice!" Jace shouted and pointed to the net.

Maddox was lying in his net, face down, shaking.

What the fuck? How badly was he hurt?

"Mad! Mad!" I yelled as I skated over to him, stopping short and getting down on my knees. "Are you okay?"

"Don't touch me!" he screamed back.

"It's me. It's Kayden."

"Leave me the fuck alone!" he snapped.

"Let me help you get up."

"No!" he shouted and finally rolled over, face up.

The only thing I could see were his eyes. He was terrified. How badly was he hurt? I didn't notice any obvious signs, but maybe he was in shock? Getting injured was a horrifying reality for any player.

"Come on. Let's get you up," I offered.

Maddox hesitated for a moment and then lifted his right arm. I hoisted him up, but with all his gear, it was awkward. He shook his head, continuing to swear up a storm.

When I looked around, the fight was breaking up, refs and coaches were on the ice, but everyone was still yelling. What a fucking disaster.

"I'm fine," Maddox snapped and pulled his arm away. "I got hit hard, but I'm okay. It's over. Get lost."

No way was I leaving him alone. He didn't look okay at all. In fact, I thought he might puke and suggested he take his mask off.

"Don't tell me what to do," he bit out.

Then he shoved his mask off his face, his skin sweaty and pale, almost grey. He was breathing fast and hard. Was it the adrenaline or was he hyperventilating?

"You don't look good. Get to the box, and have Johnston check you out," I demanded.

"I know what to do, alright? I don't need you or anyone else helping me!" he snarled and skated away.

"You're welcome!" I yelled out.

I rested my hands on my thighs and shook my head. There were helmets and sticks lying on the ice. There was blood, too. Fuck, I hoped like hell we weren't all going to get suspended for the rest of the season. There'd go our hockey careers…

A ref yelled about a five-minute major and game disqualification. That better be Reswell he was talking about.

I watched Maddox skate away. He made it as far as the boards and bent over, throwing up. Shit, did he hit his head? A concussion? Since the coaches were still arguing with the refs, I followed Maddox, not caring if he'd yell at me again. No matter what he said, he was obviously *not* okay.

The medic, Johnston, stepped forward and guided Maddox off the ice and into the gallery. Without thinking, I followed them.

"Is he all right?" I asked Johnston.

"I'm right fucking here," Maddox hissed. "I'm fine."

"You're not a doctor," I bit back and looked expectantly at Johnston.

"I need to check him over," Johnston replied, then motioned for Maddox to sit on one of the benches. "Did you hit your head? Any dizziness?"

"I don't think so. I don't know. It happened so fast," Maddox replied. He was still shaking. "One of the guys slammed into me, I hit the net, and that's all I remember."

Johnston took out a small penlight and checked Maddox's eyes and asked him question after question.

"Are we done here? I'm fine. I threw up. I feel better."

Maddox didn't look better. He was trembling. Still pale. Still breathing fast.

Johnston looked at me. "You better get back out there."

Reluctantly, I nodded.

"Is he out for the rest of the game?" I asked.

"Hey!" Maddox bit out. "'*He*' is right here. And I'm fine to go back and play. I'm good."

Johnston raised one eyebrow at me. Maddox bent forward again, his head between his knees. The medic looked at me and mouthed '*No.*'

"Sorry, Maddox, but the answer is no," Johnston announced. "We should get you to the hospital."

"No way!"

"Johnston!" Coach called out. I turned to find him jogging towards us. "What's going on?"

"I think Maddox may have a concussion. He was hit pretty hard, threw up, and he's still shaky."

"I had my mask on. My head doesn't hurt," Maddox muttered. "I'll be fine."

"Kayden, head back out," Banning replied. "I'll put Sean in for the rest of the game. Johnston, get Maddox to the hospital."

"I'll text Groeling to see if he can stand in for me for the rest of the game," Johnston added as he pulled out his phone and started typing.

"Is everyone else okay?" I asked Coach, then glanced at Maddox. His hands were shaking.

"Bruises and scrapes. Reswell's out of the game. But honestly, what the hell was Silas thinking by getting up in Reswell's face? The last thing we needed was a goddamn bench brawl. We're lucky he only got a five-minute penalty."

There was nothing I could say. If I was Silas, I'd probably react the same way. Being hit hard like that, and after the whistle, was uncalled for.

"Call me when you're done at the hospital," I said to Maddox.

He still had his head down. No response.

"Move it, Kayden. We still have the rest of the game to play," Coach warned.

I headed back out to the box, where all my teammates were gathered.

"Where's Maddox?" Axel asked.

"He's going to the hospital with Johnston," I replied. "Possible concussion."

"Fucking hell!" Ethan shouted. "Reswell gets a game misconduct, and that's it?"

I glanced across the ice at Boston. They were like us, gathered around in their box, and giving *us* the stink eye. Fucking assholes.

"We still got one period left," Dane added. "Let's stay calm and focus on what we need to do to win. Then we can rub their faces in it."

"Dickheads," Finn snapped.

"Like Dane said, let's do this," I called out. "The best revenge is winning."

At that moment, though, I was thinking more about Maddox than the game.

Maybe it was the frustration from that clusterfuck of a period, or maybe it was knowing one of our own was injured, but when the intermission was over, the guys went all out.

Dane scored within the first three minutes of play. Cougars 1, Boston 0.

It was still anyone's game, but we hung on. And when the final buzzer sounded off, there was relief and pure exhilaration. But I hardly felt like celebrating. I wanted to get out of here and go to the hospital to see Maddox.

Everyone was joking around as usual, but I wasn't in the mood. After I'd showered and changed, I was ready to haul ass.

"I'm out. See you later, maybe?" I said to Dane and Jace.

"You coming to the party?" Jace asked.

"Not sure. Probably. I want to see how Maddox is doing first."

Dane nodded. "I'll go with."

"Thanks, Dane."

I pulled out my phone and texted Maddox, but I didn't get a response. My stomach clenched hard. Then I spotted Johnston entering the building as we were leaving.

"Where's Maddox?" I asked him. "Is he okay?"

Johnston nodded. "They checked him over. CT scan. No concussion. He'll be discharged soon if he isn't already."

Kayden: Where are u?

Maddox: Back at the dorm

Kayden: Me and Dane are coming over

Maddox: Don't

Kayden: I want to make sure you're okay

Maddox: I'm responding to your message, aren't I?

"Ugh, he's driving me crazy," I grumbled as I showed Dane the texts. He rolled his eyes.

"Let's go. He's on the second floor, right?"

I nodded. I'd ferreted out Maddox's room number. Or, he'd given it to me after I asked a bazillion times.

When we arrived at room 222, I knocked twice.

Waited. Knocked again.

Dane's phone buzzed. "It's Jackson calling. I'll be back in a sec."

Dane answered his phone and walked down the hallway.

When the door finally opened, Maddox looked like his usual self, in worn jeans and a t-shirt with the sleeves cut off. But when I glanced at his face, I knew he was anything *but* okay. His eyes were red and swollen, and he was still pale. Something was really fucking wrong.

"Just you," he mumbled and opened the door wider.

I nodded, texting Dane to let him know, and entered Maddox's room.

"What really happened out there?" I asked him.

Maddox sighed and ran an agitated hand through his hair. "The past caught up to me."

CHAPTER 19

MADDOX

Physically, I was fine. Mentally, I wasn't great.

The logical part of me knew that getting hit in a game was inevitable. And an accident. One of those things. It's hockey after all. It'd happened to me before. And when six-foot guys weighing over two hundred pounds are barreling down the ice at full speed, it's expected. Not so much for goalies, but yeah, it happens.

Probably another reason why I gravitated toward the net.

But it wasn't just being hit. It was witnessing the fight that ensued. I had a visceral reaction to watching someone get punched. Immediate panic. Sickness, dread. Flashbacks. Horrible memories that never faded.

Brawls didn't happen often at this level, but fights weren't unheard of. And I wasn't as prepared as I thought I was.

"Can I sit down?"

Kayden's question snapped me back into the present, and I stepped aside, motioning for him to take a seat. My room was a standard one, with a twin bed, a desk and chair. That was pretty much it. Thankfully, Kayden took the chair, and I stretched out on my bed.

"You asked me about my tattoos," I started, crossing my arms, rubbing my hands over my shoulders, then gripping them as tight as I could.

Say it. I didn't know that I could. Not all of it.

"Some of them symbolize remembrance," I paused, swallowing past the lump in my throat. "My mom passed away seven years ago. The other tattoos represent vigilance. A reminder to never let my guard down. Not on the ice, not anywhere."

For once, Kayden sat still and didn't say anything. He leaned forward and stared at me.

"And that's all I'm gonna say."

"Why's your guard up? Who hurt you?" Kayden asked. "Wait, it was the fight that triggered your reaction?"

"I've already said enough. I don't want to talk about it," I snapped.

Kayden sighed. "I'm sorry. I just—"

"Sorry doesn't change things," I bit out. But for once, I regretted my sharp mouth. What was I doing? This wasn't Kayden's fault. Not what happened and not my reaction on the ice. "But, thanks. I'm fine, okay? I panicked, but, it's over. I'm good."

Kayden sat back, and the chair creaked.

Then I remembered. "The game. What happened?"

I desperately needed a change in subject.

"Cougars one, Boston a big fat zero."

"And Sean?"

Kayden shrugged. "He did alright. But he's not nearly as good as you."

That made me feel better. It shouldn't, but it did.

"Well, you can see that I'm fine now," I announced as I stood up and headed for the door. "You should go."

"Why don't we hang out for a bit? Order food? Play video games?" Kayden offered.

I turned around and leaned back against the door.

Tell him to go. You don't need him. You don't need anyone.

"And maybe, with that beautiful mind of yours, you can help me track down whoever bought me that bracelet kit."

The goddamn bracelets. What was wrong with me? And *beautiful mind*? Only Kayden.

"What about the party?" I asked.

"It doesn't start until ten. We've got a couple of hours."

"No."

Kayden's face fell, and he made to stand up. His head nearly hit the ceiling.

"I mean, no to the party. I think."

It wasn't like me to be indecisive. Kayden glanced at my bed and suddenly, I went from ice cold to burning hot. What the hell was wrong with me? He walked over and sat down on the end of the bed, and I swallowed hard at the sight.

"This okay?" he asked. "That chair's not my favorite. I'm afraid I'm gonna break it."

I barked out a laugh. Shit.

"Do that again," he demanded.

"What?"

"Smile. Laugh."

"Fuck, no. Bad enough it happened once," I replied, my face heating. I distracted myself by pulling out my phone. "What do you want to eat? And *don't* say food."

"*Lots* of food."

I gave Kayden my best finger. He smirked and patted the spot beside him. No fucking way was I getting on that bed right now. I was still struggling with getting the image of his naked body in the shower out of my head—with no luck. Now this?

"Wings? Fries?" I asked.

"Yes."

I placed the order, then plunked myself down on my chair.

Reaching across my desk, I grabbed the gaming consoles and passed one to Kayden.

"How about a friendly wager?" Kayden asked.

"No."

"If I win, you come to the party with me. If I lose, you come to the party with me."

I bit my lower lip to keep that annoying fucking smile off my face. "You know that doesn't make sense, right?"

"Just trying to cheer up my hockey roomie."

"Well, don't. I don't need cheering up. I told you, I'm fine."

Kayden stared at me and shook his head. He didn't believe me. And what was scarier? He already knew me more than I was comfortable thinking about.

Kayden

Maddox appeared to be okay, but I knew he was still shaken up. There was a lot of fidgeting, which wasn't like him. He'd had a panic attack because of the fight. It triggered him and that could only mean one thing. Jesus Christ. The thought of anyone hurting Mad like that pissed me off. I was dying to ask more questions, but I backed away. A good defenseman always knows how to read the players and the play. And pushing right now was not going to help.

Maybe normal was what Maddox needed now, anyway.

Not surprisingly, he was as fiercely competitive playing video games as he was on the ice. He won, I pouted, then we ate a shitload of wings.

An hour later, I was lying on his bed, and he was sitting on the floor while we listened to music. All the while, my phone kept vibrating.

"Will you reply to whoever that is, already?" Maddox finally snapped.

"It's Ethan. And Finn. And Jace. They want us to get our asses over the party. Now."

"Have fun," Maddox replied.

"Come with me. You told them you'd go," I reminded him. "Have a drink, let the guys know you're okay, and get out of your head."

Maddox looked back at me. "One hour. That's it."

Yes.

I watched as Maddox stood up and walked over to his nightstand. He pulled out a bag of candy and threw it at me.

"Take a few edibles. You're welcome."

"Sweet. Where'd you get these?"

"Back home," he replied. "Pot's legal for anyone nineteen and over."

"Lucky you. We can't even drink here, technically."

Maddox nodded, ambled over to his closet, and came back holding a bottle of tequila.

"What else have you got in there? Oh, probably more cigarettes?" I made a face.

Maddox uncapped the bottle, and took a long swig. "Just for that, I'm not sharing my booze."

I popped two gummies in my mouth and chewed. "Don't leave me like that. I need liquid courage, too."

"Why?"

"Because a hot person might say hi to me and I don't want to freak out and act like the dork that I am," I chuckled.

"You're not a dork," Maddox replied. "You're annoyingly persistent."

"Thanks so much," I replied sarcastically.

Maddox walked up to me and handed over the bottle. I took a grateful sip.

"So, are you hoping to hook up tonight?" he muttered.

I choked on the tequila and coughed. Man, that hurt. "Um, I don't know."

"Ready to change your virgin status?"

"Shut up."

"Have another drink. Or two. I'm gonna use the head and then we'll go."

Maddox took the bag from me, popped three edibles in his mouth, and headed for the bathroom. My eyes caught on his ass and one particularly tempting rip in his jeans that sat right below his right cheek.

One good tug and…

Fuck. I swallowed another mouthful of liquor. But I needed more than pot and a few drinks to relax. I really did want to hookup.

Too bad the only person I wanted was Maddox.

As I lay on his bed, I thought about what he'd look like spread out naked. Under me, over me. A minute passed, maybe two. I was buzzed and so freaking horny. Unfortunately, getting high had unwanted slide effects. I mean, side effects. Shit, I was already fucking up my words.

What was I saying?

Oh yeah, side effects. I tended to get touchy-feely when I was drinking. Not that anyone wanted to get that way with me. But still, I wanted to hug everyone. That was weird, right?

Maddox stepped out of the bathroom, and I nearly dropped the bottle of tequila.

I didn't want to hug him. I wanted to strip him down and lick him, from his gorgeous head to his sexy bare feet.

He'd put on a button-down shirt, but I wasn't sure why. He'd undone nearly all the freaking buttons. I could see his smooth chest and part of the tattoos that hit his collarbone. Why was that so fucking sexy? And then I noticed his hair was in that cool, messy style again. I wanted to run my hands through it, tilt his head back, and stare into those dark blues of his.

When he caught me staring, his scowl deepened.

"What?" he snapped.

"You look hot."

Me, pot, and tequila, was a bad, bad idea.

"How many edibles did you eat?"

I stood up on shaky legs.

"Not enough. And I speak only the truth. You are undoubtedly…wow, I can say a big word, but I don't think I can spell it—" I paused and shook my head. "Uh, yeah, you're handsomely hot. That doesn't sound right. Handsome. Hot. Hot AF. You know what I mean."

Maddox said nothing. He took the bottle from my hand, capped the top, and placed it under his bed. And fuck, when he bent over, that rip in his jeans opened right up. I spotted the curve of his ass cheek and…wait. Was he commando? The thought of sliding that denim down to reveal his bare ass had my dick chubbing up, hard and heavy in my jeans.

"Let's go already," he grumbled as he pulled on motor-cycle boots.

I turned around too fast, stumbling, and nearly slamming into the door.

Way to act chill, Kay.

After I grabbed my coat, I wrenched the door open, and headed out into the hallway. I needed distance. A lot of it.

Maddox joined me in the hallway, locked his door, and headed for the stairs. He'd thrown on his leather jacket and I was trying not to drool at the sight. I took my time following him. I wanted to enjoy the view of his ass in those jeans while I could. While no one else noticed.

Maddox stuffed his cigarette pack in his back pocket and all I could think of was, *damn, lucky cigs.*

Suddenly, he glanced over his shoulder, his gaze pinning me in place.

"You coming?" he asked.

Oh, yeah. As soon as I got back to my dorm tonight.

"Yeah." My voice cracked. "Yes. Coming. I'm coming with

you. I mean, walking with you. Not coming, as in, you know—"

Maddox shook his head and turned away. I could've sworn I heard the husky peal of laughter, but then I remembered who I was talking to. Still, I wanted to hear it. Not just that. I needed to.

I should've only had one edible instead of two. But it was too damn late.

CHAPTER 20

MADDOX

Was Kayden flirting with me? Was I reading that right? Or was he having a weird reaction to the pot he'd consumed?

When I turned around, his eyes were practically lasered to my ass. Any harder and they'd burn a hole through my jeans. And why was that so fucking hot? I'd never had anyone look at me like that before. And watching him fumble around me had my nerves hitting high again. I was dangerously close to being addicted to his attention. I didn't like the fact that I'd been taken in by his charm to begin with, but now this?

Cute, I could ignore. But chemistry?

My body was telling me things I was not prepared to hear. And whatever this was between me and Kayden, it was totally out of my wheelhouse. I'd avoided any kind of relationship for years. I didn't know what I should do, if anything.

And the worst part? I was teasing Kayden earlier, but the thought of him actually hooking up with someone at the party tonight sat like a weight on my chest. Which was all kinds of screwed up. He was my teammate. And sort of friend. Nothing else. It shouldn't matter to me at all.

Fuck, I should've had another drink before we left the dorm.

We walked across the south lawn, then headed east. The frat house was two blocks away from campus. Even if Kayden hadn't told me where it was, all I'd have to do was follow the trail of noisy students and the blaring sound of house music.

When we finally arrived at the three-story brick house, it was crawling with people. This was a mistake. I didn't socialize. I barely spoke to anyone, unless it was to snarl at them. Three edibles weren't enough to calm the anxiety that swirled in my gut.

As we headed up the steps, I spotted Ethan on the landing, chatting up Finn, Axel, and two other students.

"Hey guys!" Kayden shouted out.

"You made it!" Ethan smiled, his eyes glassy. "I thought I'd have to send Finn over to drag your asses out."

"After that win this afternoon, nothing could keep me away," Kayden replied. "Where's Dane and Jace?"

"Inside." Axel motioned to the door. "Go grab a drink."

"You go," I said to Kayden and pulled out my pack of cigs, leaning up against the wall.

"No way, you need to come in and say hi to everyone."

"It's me, Kay. Go already," I snapped and lit up my cig.

Oh yeah, I needed that drag. Smoking—it's the introvert's excuse when you don't want to people.

"I'll wait," Kayden insisted.

"You're such a pain in the ass, you know that?"

"I live to please."

Fuck it. Might as well get it over with. I threw the cigarette on the ground and motioned to the door.

Kayden opened it and gave me a wink. A freaking wink.

"What's with you?" I snarled.

"What?"

"Don't what me."

"You're the one that gave me the edibles. Now, stop grumbling and get your hot hockey ass inside."

Hot hockey ass?

Ethan and Finn's chuckles echoed behind me as Kayden and I stepped inside the house. And yeah, it was a huge-ass party. Wall-to-wall packed, with loud, crappy (in my opinion) music, and a shit-ton of pheromones in the air. A lot of students were playing drinking games and quite a few were sucking face. I glanced around and spotted Dane and Jace talking with another guy I recognized. Jack? Jake? Kayden mentioned him a few times, but I couldn't remember the guy's name. All I knew was that he was one of Dane's friends.

I ambled through the crowd, but I got jostled, and nearly freaked out again.

Until Kayden did something that I was not expecting. Something that, if anyone else tried it, would have me backing right out the door.

What did he do? He put his hands on my shoulders and guided me through the room. To him, it was probably nothing. To me? It was major. I hadn't allowed anyone to touch me in years. What was more shocking? I really fucking liked it. My heart was pounding louder than the music. Kayden smelled so damned good; and with his body at my back? I was protected. Safe. Not that I needed his protection, but still.

What was in those edibles?

When we cut through the packed room, people moved out of the way. And when we finally caught up to Dane and Jace, they turned and stared at us, shit-eating grins on their faces. Great. I shrugged off Kayden's hands. No point in getting used to that. He was trying to be helpful; he wasn't touching me because he wanted to. And I didn't enjoy it. I was high.

"Salty and Sweet have finally arrived!" Jace called out.

I gave my honest reaction to that comment via my finger while Dane and his friend tried, unsuccessfully, not to laugh.

"I am definitely making bracelets that say that!" Kayden laughed.

I gave him my best glare. "Don't you dare."

"Before you get into the bickering, Maddox, this is Jackson West," Dane announced. "Jackie's my...best friend. He's not a hockey player, but we invite him to hang with us, anyway."

Everyone was a comedian tonight. I nodded at Jackson, who elbowed his friend and then cocked his curly head.

"I was at the game today and saw you get hit," Jackson replied. "You okay?"

"I'm fine." I nodded. "I got the air knocked out of me. It happens."

Lying about how I was doing was second nature to me thanks to years of practice.

"That's why I'll stick to rowing," Jackson replied. "No danger of getting cross-checked."

"Just an accidental oar to the face," Dane teased.

Jackson smiled, then slid his hand behind Dane's back. That move seemed way friendlier than besties. Or maybe it had been so long since I had one that I'd forgotten.

"Beer?" Jace offered, and reached for the cooler by his feet.

"Yes, please. I need something to get rid of that nasty taste of tequila," Kayden replied. "Not my fave."

Dane smirked. "You did shots already? Without us?"

"I was at Mad's. He's got a stash."

Jace handed out beer bottles, and we all clinked glasses. I took a long sip and my nerves eased.

"So, liquor, cigs, what else you got, Maddox?" Dane quipped.

"Edibles," Kayden blurted out, and offered a wicked smile. "A whole big bag of 'em. And they're freaking strong too. I am totally freaking high. Like, relaxed, but not, and everything is freaking...why do I like saying *freaking* so much? Sorry, where was I?"

"As you can tell, Kayden mistakenly ate too many." I

shook my head. "Shit, I should've brought the bag with me. But I wasn't sure if I'd actually step foot in here tonight."

"I'm glad you did," Dane replied. "It's good to have an actual conversation with you. Now tell me more about these edibles, where'd you get them? You buy them here?"

"Nope, back home. I slid them into my equipment bag when I came through the border."

"Risky."

I shrugged. "I guess. Didn't think about it. It's legal where I come from."

"I know what we're doing later. Afterparty in Rocher's room!" Jace called out.

"Yes!" Dane high-fived him.

"No fucking way." I pointed at Kayden. "Bad enough I let this one in there earlier. He nearly broke my chair."

Jackson chuckled. "How'd that happen?"

"He sat in it."

Everyone laughed, and I took another gulp of my beer. I hated to admit it, would *never* admit it, but I was actually having, wait for it…a good time. I didn't like peopling, but these guys were tolerable. In small doses.

Until Kayden turned around and slapped his ass. "My big, bouncy, hockey butt cannot be sustained by your tiny furniture, Mad."

"Good thing it's not your chair then," I bit out and rolled my eyes. I really wanted to stare at his ass, but I didn't give in to temptation. "Or your room. And it's fine. Sturdy as hell."

"No, it's not. You gotta get a bigger chair just for me. For our study sessions."

"Don't be ridiculous."

"I'll come shopping with you," Kayden insisted. "We can do a sit test."

"I'm so going to walk out of here if you keep up with this," I grumbled.

"You don't do a sit test, you do a fuck test," Jace

announced and looked at me. "Then you know it's sturdy. Can you fuck in it?"

"No comment," I snapped and gulped down the rest of my beer.

"Oooh," Jace smirked. "Looks like you need a new chair."

"I'm going back to the dorm. I need more THC for this conversation," I muttered and ran a hand through my hair.

"Hey," Jace motioned to the crowd. "Check it out. See those two girls over there? They're in my psych class. Hot, eh?"

Jace waved them over. One was blonde and the other brunette. Both pretty, if you were into women with big smiles and big…

"Jace! Oh my God, where have you been hiding?" The blonde one yelled out and reached for him. "Sam and I have been searching for you in this crowd forever!"

"I've been making the rounds." He hugged both women and then turned to the group. "Hailey and Sam, this is Kayden, Maddox, Dane, and Jackson."

"Are you all on Jace's hockey team?" Hailey asked as she looked up at Kayden. "Well, you must be for sure."

Kayden blushed and took another sip of his beer.

"Are you guys gonna stand here in the corner all night?" Sam asked. "I want to dance. Who's with me?"

Jace volunteered, and so did Dane and Jackson.

"I'm out," I replied.

"Come on," Hailey encouraged. "Kayden?"

"Okay." He put the empty bottle aside and glanced at me. "You sure you don't want to join us?"

"Go already," I snapped and turned away, reaching for the cooler and another beer.

Anything to wash away the bitter taste of jealousy that was now burning a hole in my gut. Was Kayden going to hook up with her? I was gonna down another drink and get the hell out of here before I had a chance to find out.

"One dance, and I'll be back, Mad," Kayden said.

I refused to look at him, waving him off, gulping down half the beer in record time. I needed the buzz to kick in. Fast.

"You know what? I'm gonna sit this one out too," Jackson added. "I need another beer."

Dane looked puzzled, but nodded. The entourage of five pushed their way to the middle of the room and onto the makeshift dance floor.

Fuck it. I reached into my pocket for my cigs and lit up.

"So, you and Kayden are chummy," Jackson stated.

I shrugged, exhaled, and turned to look at him. "Completely against my better judgment."

"Nah. Kayden's a sweet guy. No one can resist him."

That was probably true as well. I glanced at the crowd and spotted Hailey talking to Kayden, and soon they were dancing together. Close. Really fucking close.

I pushed off the wall and turned around.

"I gotta go."

"Kayden wants you to stay," Jackson replied. "We all want you to stay. And you should. Stick around. Hang out with us."

"Look, you guys are cool, but I think Kayden's good for the night. And I've had all the socializing I can handle."

Jackson took a sip of beer and nodded. "Okay. Want me to walk back with you?"

"No," I bit out. "I mean, I'm good. Thanks for the offer."

I took one last drag and shoved the cigarette butt into my half empty beer bottle.

"Don't forget to drop by the third floor," Jackson added.

I nodded, even though I had no intention of ever doing so. Then I gave a reluctant wave and made my way around the perimeter of the room, careful to ensure that I didn't get anywhere near Kayden. I didn't want him to spot me leaving.

Once outside, I finally let go of the breath I didn't realize I'd been holding in.

There were a few people hanging around, but Ethan and Finn were gone, probably inside with the rest of the team. I was in such a rush to leave I hadn't noticed.

My stomach was in one giant knot. It had to be the beer and tequila, right? Drinking that mix was a mistake. Like coming to the party tonight. What the fuck was I thinking? I didn't fit in here. I didn't fit anywhere. Not like Kayden, who everyone, including Hailey, wanted to be around.

I was happy to be alone again, but walking through campus, the quiet was suffocating.

When I got back to my dorm, I kicked off my boots, threw off my jacket and shirt and flopped down on my bed. But sleep didn't come.

My phone buzzed. I didn't even bother to check. I knew who it was. And when there was a knock at my door ten minutes later, well, I ignored that too.

CHAPTER 21
KAYDEN

"Open up, Mad! Let me in!"

I knocked again, harder, louder. Why was he so goddamn stubborn like this?

"Mad! Why'd you take off like that?"

I was about to knock again when the door opened. Maddox stood in front of me in nothing but those ripped jeans and a scowl. Fuck, he was so damn sexy I couldn't think straight. Except to say, I wasn't straight. Nope. Definitely not.

Maddox crossed his arms and leaned against the door. "What the fuck are you doing here? Go back to the party."

He made to close the door, but I put my hand on it.

"You didn't even stay for fifteen minutes. And you shouldn't have walked home alone," I replied.

"I told you I'd stay for an hour. I stayed. I left," he scoffed. "And in case you can't tell Kay, I'm a big boy. I take care of myself."

"That's your line for everything; '*I don't need anyone*' or '*I don't like people*' or '*fuck off.*' Why? I need to know why."

Maddox shook his head and motioned to his room. "Get inside before you wake up the rest of this floor."

I stepped into his room, and it was dark, save for the glow from the lamp by his bedside.

"Why are you even here? Shouldn't you be sucking face with Hailey right now?" he snapped.

That sounded a lot like jealousy. And that wasn't my high talking. I was getting better at reading my angry bee. I bit back a laugh at that image. I'd been stung by Mad so many times, and I kept coming back for more.

"She's real nice," I murmured. "Pretty and fun. Sweet, too."

With every additional word that came out of my mouth, Maddox's blue eyes grew darker. His jaw clenched, his lips pursed in a pout. Oh yeah, I was on to something here. He wasn't happy that I might be interested in Hailey. Even though I wasn't. Not at all.

"But I don't want her," I confessed. "There's someone else I can't stop thinking about."

Shit, did I really admit that out loud?

"You mean Sam?" Maddox hissed, pacing back and forth.

I shook my head and sat down in his chair. There was no mistaking the ominous creak when I made contact.

"New chair, stat," I chuckled.

Maddox stopped pacing and stood in front of me, hands on his lean hips. My laughter dried up as I realized how close he was. So close, I could reach out and touch him. His chest was rising and falling, fast, like he was out of breath. He wasn't the only one. Pretty sure he could hear my heart pounding like a jackhammer.

When I realized he'd taken off from the party, I didn't hesitate to say goodbye to my friends and follow him home. I didn't care about anything else. Couldn't explain it. I just... wanted to be with him. Not that I knew what the hell I was doing. I'd never been with a guy. What if I made a move, and he pushed me away? For good?

There was only one way to find out.

"And no, I wasn't talking about Sam," I admitted. "I just met her, so I haven't had time to think about her. And I don't want to. There's only one person who's got all my attention lately. One person I always want to be with. Do you understand?"

I stared up at him, at those dark, bottomless blues. The flash of awareness that throbbed between us had my cock chubbing up in record time.

Maddox stepped up to me and leaned over, his hands gripping the armrests, so close that I could smell the tobacco and beer on his breath. I was so turned on that I was trembling, every muscle primed with anticipation. Strands of hair fell over his eyes, and I couldn't hold back any longer.

I reached up with one shaky hand and pushed his hair away, testing the softness of it, and watching for any sign that he wanted me to stop. His scowl eased, replaced with a heated expression that was just as fierce, his cheeks flushed, his breath choppy.

"Is this okay?" I asked, the words barely a whisper. "If not, I can stop. And apologize. Or go. You probably don't—"

Maddox was silent, and it scared me. He was preparing to unleash that sharp tongue of his. He was going to tell me to get out, get lost, and never come near him again.

But to my complete shock, Maddox slid over my lap and straddled my waist. And when he lowered himself over me, his hips meeting mine, his ass sitting snug against my dick, I couldn't help the filthy groan that rumbled out of my chest.

"Oh fuck," I whispered.

This was really happening. Maddox was touching me. I was touching him. My cock pulsed heavy and hard in my jeans, harder than I'd ever been. I was hot all over, flushed from head to toe.

"What the hell have you done to me, Kay?" Maddox growled.

He tilted his hips, rubbing against me. Holy shit, that

felt… it was… I was too turned on to form a complete sentence. Even in my head. My entire body throbbed with a heat and excitement that was pure lust. I wanted more. No, that wasn't right. I needed more.

"I could ask you the same thing."

When his lips hovered over mine, my balls drew up painfully tight, and my veins flooded with pleasure.

But Maddox didn't kiss me. At least, it wasn't like any other kiss I'd had. Instead, he unleashed that wicked tongue of his in the best way. He full-on attacked my mouth, devouring me. The intensity of the kiss, the shock of electricity when our mouths met; it was unreal. Kissing him was so much better than good. There was no hesitation, no tentative exploration. He went for it. When his tongue snaked around mine, teasing me, I nearly came in my pants. I gripped his hair tighter, angling his head for a deeper connection.

I swallowed his husky moan, and it snapped what was left of my control. We ate at each other's mouths with eager lips and aggressive tongues. I was desperate, and greedy for more. I couldn't get enough.

I moved one hand to slide down around his back, lower, until I reached his ass.

"More, Kay," Maddox demanded when we finally came up for air. "Keep touching me."

He pushed his ass back, and I slipped my hand under his jeans to grab one perfect, taut handful. I was right about him going commando.

"You've been teasing me all night in these jeans," I confessed. "Fuck, ever since that shower at the rink. It's all I can think about."

"I jerked off in that shower after you left. Couldn't stop myself," Maddox admitted, thrusting his hips against mine, harder, faster.

God, that was such a turn on.

"Do it now," I bit out. "I want to see."

I don't know where this demanding side of me came from, but here I was.

Maddox moaned as he scrambled to unzip his jeans. His dick jutted out, heavy and hard, the head red and leaking pre-come. I licked my lips at the sight. Never thought I'd be dying to taste a guy's cock, or his cum, but suddenly, I was thirsty for it. All of it.

As I glanced up his body, I still couldn't believe this was happening. I thought Maddox was hot before, but now? His lips swollen from *my* kisses? He was stunning and I couldn't look away.

Maddox spat in his hand and stroked himself off. Fuck, I loved that too. It was dirty, and so freaking sexy. Watching him jerk off had my climax racing to the finish line, and I tried frantically to think of a way to calm down so I wouldn't embarrass myself. No way was I ready to come yet.

"Kay," Maddox bit out, his forearm tensing with every pump of his hand.

I wanted to touch him so badly, but maybe that was too much, too soon? Desperate, I scrambled to undo my zipper, reaching inside my briefs, pulling out my cock, and giving myself a long, slow pump.

"Jesus Christ," Maddox whispered as he stared down at me.

What? Was there something wrong with my dick? Did he not like what he saw? All my usual insecurities flooded the forefront of my mind.

"I thought I'd been mistaken in the shower," he whispered. "But no, your cock is as gorgeous as the rest of you."

I jolted at his comment, surprised but elated. A compliment from Maddox turned me into a total praise slut and I wanted more. My dick was leaking like crazy. I added spit to create a smoother glide and gave myself a few pumps.

I thought jerking off solo was hot, but watching Maddox,

and him watching me? New kink unlocked. Until he took over, pushing my hand aside and wrapping those beautiful fingers around my dick. I wasn't prepared for the way his firm grip tormented my cock. His callused fingertips slid up and down my throbbing shaft, tugging faster, teasing me so good.

Then he took both of us in hand.

"Oh, God. Mad," I groaned out as he stroked us off.

It wasn't coordinated or smooth or anything like porn. Porn had nothing on the real thing. The scent of our pre-cum and the sweat from our bodies grew stronger. My thighs were rigid, my balls drawing up higher, tighter, pleasure crawling up my spine as his grip tightened.

"Come for me, Kay," Maddox growled.

That's all it took. Four words and I was a goner.

I came hard, my body jerking, ropes of cum covering Mad's hand, his cock, and mine. The visual of our stiff dicks rubbing against each other was burned into my retinas. There was no way I could ever unsee it.

Maddox's head fell back, the tendons in his neck rigid as he let out a feral groan. His forearm tensed as he unleashed all over me, over the two of us, more cum covering me. I reached for him again, gripping his neck, urging him closer. Our tongues tangled in wet, frenzied kisses. I didn't want to stop. I couldn't. Kissing him was addictive.

"Mad," I whispered his name against his lips.

I could hardly believe we'd had sex. It was nothing like I'd imagined and more than I'd dare to dream.

Until he suddenly tensed, pulling back, pushing my hand away, nearly toppling out of the chair.

"What the—" I asked, holding on to his arm so he wouldn't fall. "Mad, what's wrong?"

"Let go," he snapped. "Please."

I did as he asked and when he slid off my lap, I sat there, dick out, fucked out, covered in sticky cum and humiliation.

Not five seconds ago, I was on top of the world and now? Now I felt lower than dirt. And I was confused. What the hell happened?

"Are you okay? Did I do something you didn't like?"

"It's not you, Kay." Maddox shook his head. "It's me. It's all me. I…I can't deal with this. I…I need you to go."

He tucked himself away and zipped up, heading for the bathroom. When the door slammed shut, I didn't move. I sat there, in that cramped chair, stunned and feeling like a fool. With numb hands, I pulled my shirt off, and wiped myself down. After zipping up, I glanced around and spotted his button-down on the floor. Without thinking, I grabbed it and threw it on. Of course, it was too small. I couldn't button it, and the seams in the arms nearly burst, but it would do.

I waited a moment, hoping that Maddox would come back out and want to talk. That he'd want me to stay. But, as the minutes ticked by, I realized that was stupid. And I was acting the same.

There was no need to make a big deal, anyway. I came, he came. I satisfied my curiosity and my questions. It was casual sex. No biggie.

As I left his room, sweaty but chilled, a strange ache took hold of me.

Casual? My gut told me it was anything but.

CHAPTER 22
MADDOX

"Why the fuck did you kiss him?"

I could ask myself that question over and over, and I wasn't sure if I'd ever get an answer. What was wrong with me? Where did I even start? I stared at my reflection in the bathroom mirror and I had no idea who was looking back at me. My face was red and splotchy, and my lips were swollen. But what shocked me most was the softened expression in my eyes. I bent over the sink, my arms shaking, hell, my entire body was trembling. I thought I was going to pass out.

From the aftershock of that monster orgasm, or the reality that I'd kissed someone for the first time? Not someone. Kayden.

And not just kissed, had sex. I didn't even know what I was doing. I acted on instinct and I just…did it. Jerking us off together was hot as hell. Hotter than any fantasy I'd ever imagined.

Instead of splashing water on my face, I turned around and turned on the shower. I needed to scrub down and forget tonight ever happened. It was a mistake. A fucking powerful, world-imploding mistake. One I wasn't going to repeat.

You're an asshole.

No shit. Not just kissing Kayden, but after. Telling him to go, leaving him there. But it had to be done. I wasn't ready to process what had happened, never mind talk about it. I'd been so sure, so consistent in my efforts to keep people away, convinced that I'd never be like anyone else. I was damaged, a freak, unable to make any kind of connection.

Until now. Until him.

No.

I stood under the spray of the water and watched as the drying cum—mine and Kayden's—washed away. Why did that leave me with an ache in my chest? Was that regret? No. How could I be remorseful about something that felt so good?

It's just sex. Hormones. Totally normal. I guess I wasn't so different from everyone else as I'd imagined. But still, that's where it ended. We got off, and he was gone. End of.

Don't think about it.

Easier said than done. This must be why people hook up with strangers. Once it was over, it was over. Not for me. I had to see Kayden in class, on the ice, in the locker room, in the shower room. Don't even think about him naked in that shower again…ugh, too late.

And now, I'd never be able to sit in my fucking chair or work in my room without thinking about the way we went at each other. Like animals, unrestrained, uninhibited. The primal part of me wasn't dead, it was dormant. Not anymore. But, it was risky. Obliterating any remaining rules I had—and I didn't have many.

How was I gonna face Kayden? What would I say?

I'd act like nothing had happened. Be my usual self, and things would be fine. Besides, he was straight. Okay, more than likely bi. Whatever. It didn't matter. I didn't mean anything more to him than he meant to me. A quick orgasm and it was done. It was college. We were supposed to explore and experiment.

Odd thing was, I could only picture experimenting with him.

———

When I woke up the next day, my phone was silent. No text or call from Kayden. I was so fucking relieved. This was what I wanted. It was no big deal.

Two days later, same thing. I saw Kayden in economics class. He waved, but sat on the other side of the room. Cool. I got to listen to the lecture without interruption. Not that I was paying much attention, but still.

A week passed. Still nothing. Until I texted him about our economics study session. I didn't want to reach out, but if he needed help, I wasn't going to turn him away.

Kayden's response?

Kayden: Not this week. I'm good.

Good. Fine. His regular tutor probably had it covered. We had midterms. I wondered how his studying was going. Not that I was thinking about Kayden.

Just, you know, every day…

Two weeks later, Thanksgiving had come and gone, and still no word from Kayden.

I became more agitated with each passing day. I should've been happy. I'd had weeks to myself. It was peaceful, quiet. No one to bother me about friendship bracelets, or what kind of music I listened to, or teased me about my scowl. Who needed that shit, anyway? Not me. The only time I saw Kayden was in class, or at practice. He kept his distance and so did I. There was a word or two exchanged, but that was it. And this was Kayden? A word or two wasn't his usual. Whatever. It wasn't my problem anymore.

By the time early December hit, we'd gotten our

midterm results back. I aced all my exams, including economics. Then I wondered how Kayden did. Which wasn't like me. Why did I give a fuck? I shouldn't. I didn't. Still, I didn't want him to fail or anything. He was probably fine. Or was he?

Before I knew it, my hands were typing out a message.

Maddox: How'd midterms go?

I headed off to the gym for a workout. An hour later, sweaty but still wired, I checked my phone. No reply. I walked back to the dorm, but I couldn't concentrate on any of my projects.

Next thing I knew, I was stomping up to the third floor. I passed Jackson in the hallway, and he stopped short when he noticed me.

"Maddox, hey, how are you?" he asked. "It's been a while."

"Um, I'm okay. I'm looking for Kayden," I said quietly. "Is he around?"

"He's in his room," Jackson replied, raising one eyebrow. "But maybe hold off on the snark. I think he's had a bad day. In fact, he's been quiet the past couple of weeks."

Shit.

"I want to know how he did on the econ test."

"Aren't you in the same class?"

"Yeah," I muttered.

"Then why didn't you ask him when you saw him?"

"We didn't talk to each other. Not today. And not for the past few weeks."

My face heated, and I bit my lower lip in frustration.

Jackson paused and stared at me. "You guys were getting along the night of that party. What happened?"

"Nothing happened," I snapped. Nothing and everything. "And we weren't getting along."

Unless shoving my tongue down Kayden's throat and stroking him off, counted.

"Okay." Jackson held his hands up. "I'm just making an observation. You left the party, and Kayden followed you home. I thought that maybe—"

"Maybe what?" I bit out and stared at him.

Jackson paused, but his eyes told me he had more to say. Had Kayden told him about the kiss? The hand job?

"I thought you guys were friends," Jackson added.

"We're not. I mean, sort of," I paused, searching for words that took forever to say. "Look, I really need to talk to him."

Then I glanced around. I didn't know which room was his. Fuck, I was an idiot.

"Kayden's room is 333," Jackson smirked.

"Thanks."

Jackson nodded. "Well, I have to get to class. See you around."

I nodded and walked down the hallway, searching for Kayden's room. When I found it, I knocked once and waited. Sweat pooled in my pits, my lower back, the base of my neck. Fuck, even my hands were clammy. I swiped a hand through my hair and shifted from one foot to the other, waiting, my nerves riding high.

But when Kayden finally opened the door, nerves gave way to concern. His bright golden eyes were red-rimmed. Bloodshot. There were dark circles underneath, too. And his smile was nowhere to be seen. He looked how I felt.

"What's wrong?" I blurted out.

"I got sixty on my econ midterm. And I got sixty-five on my social policy one. That's what's wrong. I'm fucked. If I don't get at least eighty-five on these finals, I can say goodbye to my scholarship, and that means goodbye to hockey, and—"

Kayden started to hyperventilate, and I stepped into the room, closing the door quickly.

"Sit down. Head between your knees."

"Why don't you j-just l-leave," he gasped. "I don't want you here."

He went so pale, so fast, I thought he was going to pass out.

"Sit down, Kay. Now."

Kayden sat down on his bed, and I headed for the bathroom.

He needed water, and maybe a towel to breathe into? That would do since there wasn't a paper bag around. I grabbed the glass that was sitting on the edge of the sink, filled it up, and plucked a hand towel from the rack.

When I returned to his bedroom, I found him sitting in the same position, elbows on his thighs, head in his hands. I crouched down in front of him and offered the glass, but he shook his head. He was breathing in and out so fast and I was mirroring him, my chest tight as hell.

"Take a sip. Slowly," I encouraged. "And you're not going to lose your scholarship. Or hockey. I'm going to help you. Okay?"

"Why are you being nice?" he choked out. "And why are you still here? Shouldn't you be leaving? Isn't that what you want? To get away from me?"

"Stay calm, Kay. Take a long, deep breath. In through your nose, out through your—"

"I'm not that stupid, Mad! I know how to fucking breathe!" he snapped.

I jolted, lost my balance, and fell on my ass. Thankfully, I didn't have far to go. The glass of water, on the other hand, spilled everywhere. At least I had the towel to mop it up.

I sat there, drenched, and started wiping up. Kayden bit his lower lip, then laughter filled the room.

"I'm sorry," he chuckled as he stared at me. "I shouldn't laugh. But between falling on your ass like that, and your expression, it's too freaking funny."

I gave him my best finger and was tempted to throw the

wet towel at him. "I was going to suggest you put the towel over your mouth to calm your breathing, but since it's wet and you already know how to breathe, I'll shut up."

"Thanks," Kayden whispered, smiling at me.

I was so goddamn relieved. Thank fuck sweet Kay was back.

There was only room for one snarky asshole on our team, and I was not relinquishing my title.

CHAPTER 23

KAYDEN

wanted to stay mad. *At* Mad. He'd ghosted me for weeks. Well, I ghosted him too. Still, he was the one who didn't want to talk about what happened that night. He couldn't even look me in the eye, in class, or on the ice.

I left his room that night, and I'd been walking around in a fog ever since. Thank fuck for the routine of workouts and practice. But even that wasn't enough to get my concentration back. And barely passing those midterms pushed my self-doubt to the brink. Turns out, I sucked at everything that mattered at my age; school and sex.

Maddox sat on the floor of my room, his T-shirt wet and clinging to his abs. Instead of acting like a jerk, I offered my hand.

I waited. And waited.

Finally, he grabbed hold of it. His palm met mine and the shockwave that rocked my body brought me right back to the night of the party. That kiss we shared was not a fluke. Not the kiss, not the hand job, none of it.

I hauled him up off the floor. Only now he was standing, and with me sitting, his denim-covered dick was right in front of my face. *Fuck, don't think about his cock.* How could I not? It's all I'd been thinking about for weeks.

Then he threw off his wet T-shirt, and his abs were front and center. The ones I'd come all over. My cum, his. My dirty mind started racing, my earlier panic all but forgotten.

"Uh, what are you—"

"Care to share?" he asked.

"Huh?"

All the blood rushed south so fast I couldn't hardly think. Or hear.

"A shirt? Can you spare one? You know, since it's your fault I'm wet," he sniped.

"Yeah, uh, dresser. Second drawer."

Maddox stalked across the room, and I tracked every movement like I was watching my opponent on the ice, readying myself, planning my next move. Only, he wasn't my opponent. He was the guy I wanted to fuck.

I let out a loud groan and fell back on my bed, covering my eyes.

"Are you okay?" He asked. "Are you still having problems breathing?"

Fuck yes.

"Sort of." I looked over and he was still half naked. "Put a shirt on already."

"Hey, I'm the bitchy one," he reminded me. "Knock it off."

"I'll knock it off when you put some clothes on," I grumbled.

When Maddox turned away, I quickly adjusted myself. But I couldn't calm my dick down. I grabbed a fleece blanket and pulled it over my lap. Maddox glanced back over his shoulder and gave me a pointed look. Nothing new there.

"Show me your test results," he barked.

"No." I shook my head. "No way. It's humiliating enough that I barely passed. What did you get? A hundred?"

Maddox paused. "We're not talking about me."

"Is this a pity project for you?" I snapped.

"We've already been through this. Shut up already and listen to me."

Maddox pulled out my favorite T-shirt, one that I'd had forever. The original navy blue was now grey, and it sported a lobster holding a beer in its claws. The shirt fit me perfectly, but it was big on him. Still, I swallowed hard when he put it on. It looked good, better than on me. Like it was made for him. Then again, he could wear anything and make it look cool.

He sauntered over and sat down beside me.

"I got ninety-seven, alright," he admitted. "And you're not a fucking pity project. I...I want to help you. I might be a cranky pain in the ass, but I'm not a monster."

I stared into his eyes, intense as always. Dark, and full of secrets. He was wary. Of me? Of letting people see the kindness in him? Why?

"I never said you were," I muttered. "But I feel so dumb compared to you."

"Don't ever use that word to describe yourself," Maddox implored, leaning closer. "And remember Coach's latest speech? I'm not into the rah-rah, woo-woo shit, but he's right. If you go into a game with a defeatist mindset, it's already over. You might as well stay home."

"Hockey's different," I argued. "I'm good at that."

"You're going to get your eighty-five. We just need to sit down and focus on the methods that make it easier for you to interpret the material. That's all."

I nodded, his insistence sparking hope. Maybe Mad was right.

"You should consider changing your major from computer science to psychology," I offered.

Maddox snorted. "No thanks. I've had enough therapy to know I'm not the empathetic kind."

Therapy? For what? Then I remembered the tattoos on his

shoulders. Remembrance. Vigilance. Every time I learned something new about him, I wanted to learn more. One question always led to another.

Maddox leaned back on my bed, lying down, hands under his head. He looked damn good on my bed. What would it feel like if I was stretched out naked over him? Kissing him? Coming with him?

I began sweating. A lot. Was it my hormones or was I coming down with a bug?

"Are we going to talk about, you know, that night?" he mumbled.

He rolled over, facing me, and the bed shook. Then I imagined the bed shaking for a much filthier reason.

"What?"

"Kay."

I ran a hand through my hair, holding my head again.

"You said you couldn't. That's why I left you alone. I figured you wanted to forget. That you didn't like what we did."

"Are you fucking kidding? Forget that kiss?" he bit out. "It was my first. There's no forgetting that. And it was hot. More than hot. Jesus, we were going at each other like animals. We nearly broke my chair in the process."

I laughed at that. I'd never be able to look at an office chair the same way.

"Yeah, we did."

Maddox licked his lips, and I remembered exactly how he tasted, and how those lips felt on mine. Not the drinking, not the high... nothing could make me forget that kiss, either. It wasn't my first, but it was the hottest. And what was worse? I wanted another taste. More than one.

"Stop staring at me like that," he growled and suddenly sat up. Then he slid off the bed and paced in front of me. "And what happened that night... happened. But it's done. It can't happen again. We're teammates, for fuck's sake. If anyone else finds out—"

"I know," I sighed.

It would be a fucking mess. One I didn't need. Figured. The first person I really wanted, who wanted me, and I couldn't do anything about it.

Or, we could fool around in secret? Who would that hurt? No one.

"Or—" I started.

"Kay."

"What?" I looked up.

I fought the urge to reach for him. My roommate wasn't around. We were alone. We had this small but surprisingly sturdy bed. And I wanted to get naked. I wanted Mad. And I wanted to forget about school, and scholarships, and anything except feeling good.

"Don't even think about it," he bit out. "Let's get started on a plan for your finals."

I heard the words coming out of his mouth, but I wasn't paying attention. Instead, I threw off the heavy blanket and then my t-shirt.

"What the fuck are you doing?" Maddox hissed.

"Getting comfortable. It's warm in here."

"It's not that hot. And like you told me earlier, put the shirt back on."

"Why? Does my naked chest bother you?" I teased.

"Don't say naked."

I leaned back on my forearms, legs splayed wide. There was no hiding the bulge in my jeans. Another few seconds and my dick was going to rip right through this denim. And I didn't miss the way Maddox's eyes roamed over me, the way he licked his lips.

"Come here," I whispered and crooked one finger.

Since when did I tempt anyone into bed? Like, never.

Like, now.

"No." Maddox stood at the edge, in between my legs. "Get up. We're going to the library."

"But I feel lightheaded."

No shit. All the blood in my body was in my dick.

"Are you dizzy?" Maddox asked.

"No. But I might need a kiss."

Mad's reaction was just what I figured. He rolled his eyes and shook his head.

"Get up. Grab your shit."

He headed for the door.

"Aren't you gonna wait for me?" I asked.

"In the hallway. Put a shirt on and get *that*," he pointed to my crotch. "Under control."

"Give me five minutes."

"Five? More like one."

"Three!" I called out before he slammed the door.

I ran into the bathroom, unzipped, and took myself in hand. No way was this boner going away on its own. I fumbled for the bottle of moisturizer and squirted a glob in my hand, then jacked off with hard, frantic strokes. Imagining Maddox was kissing me again, jerking me off, sucking me off. Holy fuck, did I want him to suck me off. And then I pictured him kneeling behind me, eating my ass. Jesus, I wanted that too. Then I'd turn around and return the favor.

Fuck, fuck, that was hot.

I wondered how it would feel to have his fingers in my ass, his cock. My asshole clenched tight, my curiosity a runaway train. One filthy image after another pushed my climax to the edge, my balls drawing up high.

Replaying that kiss, it was like Mad was right here with me, taking control of my mouth, and giving me all the pleasure.

"Oh God. Yes!"

My orgasm unleashed, one intense wave after another, my

body jerking, ropes of cum shooting all over the sink. My aim was off and cum dripped down the counter to the floor.

"Shit," I moaned, trying to catch my breath.

Grabbing a towel, I wiped off the sink, turned the water on full blast, and washed the rest of the cum away. Then I splashed my face, cleaned up, and zipped up. My legs were shaky, and my hands too, but at least my anxiety was gone.

I sauntered out to my bedroom, threw on a fleece jacket and my puffer vest. Grabbing my backpack, I headed for the door.

Maddox was leaning up against the opposite wall, arms crossed, a knowing smirk on his face.

"You good now?" he asked.

"Oh, yeah."

"Oh, Jesus."

"What? You told me to get it under control. I did. Fastest hand job in history. But at least now I can concentrate."

Maddox pushed off the wall and started walking away.

"Try that before your next exam," he called out over his shoulder.

Man, he was smart.

CHAPTER 24

MADDOX

Don't think about what Kayden was doing in the bathroom.

Right.

He smelled like cum and sweat and everything I remembered about that night. Not to mention, the walls in this dorm were thin. Even standing in the hallway, I could hear him. No way I missed that loud moan and what it meant. It took all of my willpower to stay put, when all I really wanted was to push off the wall and push open that door. To give in to temptation.

This wasn't me. I wasn't ruled by my dick.

Until that fucking kiss. It was like a switch flipped inside me, and now that it was turned on, *I* was turned on, and I couldn't undo it. I didn't understand it and I didn't like it. But the scary thing was, I was starting to like *him*.

That was the biggest mystery of all.

How'd I let this happen? I was safe in my world. Alone. No one to bother me. No one to touch me. Hurt me. Not that I would get hurt. Fuck, now I was being dramatic. There was nothing to get worked up over. Sex was no big deal. Blow your mind and body kind of sex, but still.

We walked across campus to the library, and I tried *not* to look at him but it was impossible. I was so aware of Kayden now. Every breath, every smile, every burst of chatter, was magnified.

"We have another away game coming up. You excited?"

I nodded, grateful for small talk. "It's gonna be a good one. I can feel the momentum building."

"Yeah, things are clicking with the team. Axel and Jace are still at odds, but they're both killing it. And I think Silas could be great if he focused more. Half the time, his head's far away. Hit and miss."

"Maybe he's got personal shit to deal with. He did take a year off," I replied. "Anyone know why?"

Kayden shook his head. "Nope. And I don't want to be the one to ask. He's not real friendly."

"Neither am I, and that didn't stop you," I scoffed.

"True," Kayden shrugged. "Maybe I'll invite him out one night. We can grab a bite, shoot the shit. If it's just the two of us, he might start talking. It's worth a shot."

I wasn't happy with that idea. Just the two of them sounded like a date.

Listen to yourself. That's ridiculous.

Still, it didn't stop the possessive urge I had when it came to Kayden. First, the girls at the party and now this. I should've popped edibles earlier. I needed to relax and forget about that fucking kiss…

"And speaking of the away game, we've got a two-night stay instead of one," Kayden added.

That's right. We were off to Maryland. And Kayden would be sleeping with me. No, not *with* me. Next to me.

"What about it?"

"Nothing," Kayden muttered, as we headed up the library steps.

He ran ahead of me and opened the door, motioning for me to first.

"Stop doing that," I bit out.

"What?"

"Holding doors for me. Knock it off."

"Jesus, you're bitchy today."

"Today?" I snapped and walked ahead of him. "Every day. Stop doing it. I can open my own fucking door."

He kept holding the door, and I begrudgingly relented.

We headed inside and I went straight for the desk, requesting a private study room. Usually you had to book online way in advance. Thankfully, the third floor had a cancellation, so we grabbed it. The librarian handed over a keycard, and Kayden and I headed for the elevator.

The study room was at the end of the hall, and offered no windows, and no distractions. But when Kayden closed the door, suddenly this room was a bad idea. Because it was at the end of the hall, and offered no windows, and no distractions…

Just the two of us. And now it was way too fucking hot in here. I yanked at the collar of my shirt. Kayden's shirt. That didn't help matters at all.

"Let's go over the test results and see which parts you had trouble with," I croaked out.

Kayden snorted. "Like, all of them?"

"Kay," I warned.

He nodded, pulled his laptop out of his bag, and we sat down. I grabbed my tablet and my water bottle. I was fine. I could do this.

Until Kayden's massive thigh brushed against mine. I tried to move away, but there was no space. This room wasn't designed with massive hockey players in mind.

Kayden started talking, but I was too busy trying *not* to think about how good it felt to be this close to him. I wanted closer.

"—And that's the one that really confused me," Kayden stated and stared at me. "I think we should review that first."

"Uh, sorry, what?" I shook my head. "Repeat that."

Kayden smiled and licked his lips. My cock started filling and Christ, I didn't need a hard-on now. I shifted in my seat, but I kept rubbing up against Kayden.

"Can you move over?" I snapped.

"Sorry, there's no place to go," he replied. "And I said, my problems started with the third question on the test. Multiple choice always screws me up. I can't stand them. I get confused and I never get the right answer."

I cleared my throat. "Right. Uh, let's see."

I took his offered laptop and reviewed the entire test, highlighting the incorrect answers and the concepts they described. See, I could do this. I wasn't dickstracted. I mean, distracted.

"Let's start with the question about GDP—"

"Is that like DP, but greater?" Kayden chuckled at his inane quip. "Great double penetration?"

My body flushed hot as I thought about anything to do with penetration, double or otherwise. What would it feel like to fuck Kayden. Would he want that? Would he be into being fucked? The thought of taking his ass made my dick harden so fast *I* was now the one in danger of hyperventilating.

"Stop," I managed to whisper.

He put his arm around the back of my chair, and his body heat enveloped me. Why did that feel so damn good?

"What? I'm kidding."

"Stop with the sex jokes. Just… don't."

"Fine. No jokes," Kayden muttered.

I reached for my water bottle and took a long gulp. I was in desperate need of cooling off.

He leaned in closer. "I'm curious about getting fucked in the ass."

I choked on my water and shook my head. "Not funny, Kay."

"I'm not laughing," he replied as he stared at me.

He wasn't. His face was flushed, and he was looking at my mouth like I was a drug, and he needed his fix. And he wasn't the only one.

I popped up out of the chair, needing space. Before I did something we'd both regret. Kayden did the same, but I stepped back, leaning against the wall. I needed a moment. Time to think. If thinking wasn't overridden by my cock.

"Mad."

Kayden leaned into me. All I could see and smell was him.

Our mouths didn't so much meet as crash together. Kay tasted better than I remembered, so good that I moaned loudly when his tongue licked mine. I nipped his lower lip and sucked on it. The dirty groan he let out had me scrambling to get closer. He reached for me, sliding one big hand through my hair and tugging gently, the other cupping my ass. One spike of pleasure after another rolled through my body, white-hot lightning surging through my veins. Was I going to get burned? Probably. But I didn't care.

When Kayden suddenly let go, I protested.

"What the fuck?" I panted, licking my swollen lips, suddenly panicking. Had I done something wrong?

Apparently not.

Kayden dropped to his knees, and I started to shake.

"Kay?"

"I came so hard earlier. Thinking about this. About you and me. Now it's your turn."

No one outside this room could see what we were doing, but they could probably hear. I was so turned on that I didn't care. And when he reached for my zipper and delved his hand inside my jeans, my balls drew up tight, throbbing hard.

"I need to know what you taste like," he admitted as he pulled out my dick, spat on it, then started stroking me off.

"Oh fuck. Fuck, fuck," I moaned, my thighs rigid, anticipation racing up my spine.

Kayden's chuckle rumbled loudly as he jacked me off.

"That's better than fuck off," he teased. "And I haven't even licked the head yet."

"Don't say licked. Or head," I gasped, trying not to come already. "And if you want to do it, do it already."

I watched, mesmerized, as Kayden leaned forward, sticking out his tongue and swirling it around the head of my cock. The image was filthy and provocative, and I wasn't proud of the needy moan that ripped out of my throat. I couldn't help it. Then he stuck his tongue in my slit. One teasing lick and I was so excited I was counting hockey stats in my head to calm down. My thighs quaked; hell, I was trembling all over.

"Fuck, you taste better than I imagined," Kayden whispered as he slid the head of my cock into his mouth and sucked hard.

But I resisted the urge to punch my hips forward. After all, he was a virgin. We both were.

Wait, not anymore.

CHAPTER 25

KAYDEN

f someone asked me a month ago if I was curious about what a cock tastes like, I'd have said no. But now? How the fuck had I been missing out?

Maddox was freaking delicious. Musky, salty, bitter. Incredible. And getting on my knees for him wasn't something I'd imagine I'd get off on, but did. I had no idea what I was doing and relied on my instinct—and my memory of that porn site Jackson recommended—to guide me. Not that porn prepared me for taking an actual dick in the mouth. And licking Mad's cock was one thing. Giving him actual head? I wasn't sure I was ready to swallow his entire monster cock yet, but I really wanted to taste his cum.

Then I remembered where we were. Deep-throating was the least of my worries. Getting caught having sex in the library might get us kicked out. Of the building. Out of school?

Too late. I didn't want to stop. Couldn't.

My dick was throbbing hard, despite my earlier orgasm. I ignored it. I wanted to please Maddox. I licked his cockhead again and used my spit to jack him off. Maddox's filthy groan was loud, and I wondered if anyone walking past our room could hear. The very idea made my heart beat out of control, my adrenaline pumping wild and hot.

I swallowed and tried to take more of him, but I gagged. Fuck, this was harder than it looked. Pun definitely intended.

"Fuck, Kay, don't stop," Maddox moaned and gripped my hair tighter. "Don't stop. So good."

I nearly came in my pants hearing his praise.

When I looked up, his dark eyes met mine, and I shivered, every hair on my body standing on end, goosebumps littering my skin.

Maybe I wasn't good at this, but I'd damn well give it my best try.

"Wanna come in your mouth, on your face," Maddox confessed.

My responding groan was muffled by his dick as I sucked harder, my hand frantically working in tandem. No way was I going to be satisfied with anything less than watching Maddox come apart. I needed to see the look of pleasure on his face and know that I was the one who brought him there. Me.

I pumped my hand, stroking the base of his dick while I continued to suck on the head. Then I reached up with my other hand, and cupped his balls, testing the heavy weight of them. Maddox punched his hips forward, and I gagged again, but managed to keep going.

"I'm gonna… shit, fuck, I'm coming," Maddox groaned as he stared down at me, never looking away.

His body tensed, and suddenly, my mouth was flooded with hot, salty cum. Too much. I swallowed some of it, but most of it dripped out of my mouth, and down my face. I was a filthy mess, and I had no idea how I was going to walk out of here without everyone knowing exactly what I'd done.

Maddox shuddered, panting hard, and fuck, he was gorgeous when he let go. And now that I'd seen it, I couldn't ever imagine him any other way.

"Kay," he whispered my name.

His softened cock slipped out of my lips and his hips fell back as he slumped against the wall.

"I… you…that was…you are—" he paused, running a hand over his face. "Oh my God, I can't speak."

I bit back a laugh. I was so fucking pleased with myself. I hadn't come, but I didn't care. Getting him off made me feel like I was flying—like I did when I was barreling down the ice.

Then I noticed that his hands were shaking. Mine too. In fact, my entire body was trembling, and my knees ached. My knees…The last thing I needed was an injury right now. I stood up, lightheaded, and wiped my face with my hand. Too late, I realized I'd need something else to get rid of all the cum.

Maddox tucked his dick back in his jeans and zipped up, then bent over, hands on his thighs, still breathing hard.

"My bag," Maddox whispered. "Wipes."

"You carry wipes with you?"

"Of course. What if you're stuck someplace without soap to wash up?" he bit out.

I shrugged.

"Ew, Kay."

"What? I had your dick in my mouth. I think I can handle a few bathroom germs."

"Hey!"

"No complaints," I laughed. "In fact, for a newbie giving head, I think I did pretty good."

I reached for his bag, rifling through it until I found the package of hand wipes. I pulled it out, wiped off my face and hands, and threw it in the garbage. I took another one and wiped down the stains on my shirt and the floor. It wasn't perfect, but it would do for now.

"I'm giving you a perfect score," Maddox replied as he leaned back. "Because I've never come that hard in my life.

But shouldn't we be freaking out by now? What the fuck are we doing?"

I stepped closer, hands on his hips, leaning into him. And the amazing thing was, he let me.

"It feels too good to stop," I confessed.

He nodded and then surprised me again. Without pause, he leaned up and kissed me.

"Thought you didn't want my germs," I teased.

"They're mine, but I don't mind sharing. But only with you," he quipped.

This time, when he reached for me, the kiss was deep and dirty, his tongue tormenting mine. Every kiss was hotter than the last. Like the first time. Like every time we touched.

"Are you ready?" he asked me when we finally broke for air.

"For anal?" I blurted out.

Clearly, I was still horny as fuck, and Maddox found that hilarious. He laughed and it was genuine. And seeing him smile like that, at me, was almost as satisfying as his orgasm face.

"Studying, Kay. Remember? That's why we're here."

"Couldn't anal be considered studying? Like the blow job, you know, I'm in training."

"Enough with the jokes. Sit your ass down and let's get studying."

He pushed at my shoulders, and I reluctantly backed away and sat down.

"Fine. But I want to revisit the anal talk," I added.

"Will you stop saying anal?" he hissed.

"I'm ordering a dildo."

"Holy shit, what have I unleashed?" Maddox grumbled as he sat down beside me. "Come on. Time to focus."

"If coding doesn't work out for you, there's always teaching."

Maddox snorted. "Hard no."

I slid my hand over his thigh and squeezed. "Hard yes."

Maddox leaned over and kissed me again. When he sat back, the smirk on his face was as irresistible as his scowl.

"At least I know a surefire way to get you to stop talking," he replied. "Two, in fact."

"Shut up and tutor me."

Maddox

Two hours later, Kayden and I snuck out of the library as quietly and quickly as we could. No doubt the room smelled like sex, but I'm sure we weren't the first ones to get down and dirty in there. Horny college students probably favored it. There were no windows, and the door locked. Plus, there were no cameras. At least, I didn't think so.

Oh well. Too late to worry about it now.

And getting caught was the least of it. I was more concerned that I was fucking around with Kayden to begin with. The fact I couldn't resist him made me want to jump on a plane and head home. Or head anywhere and not look back. But that wasn't rational. I needed to get my goddamn degree, get noticed by the scouts, and get my life going. Then I could go wherever I wanted. Or wherever I was traded. I had to get drafted first.

And I had to remind myself that what we were doing was hooking up. It didn't mean anything more than that. And it gave me pleasure. Pleasure I never thought I'd experience. Why deny myself?

Since we were both starving (for food), but not keen on the cafeteria offerings, we headed into town. Kayden's phone buzzed as we were walking.

"Jackson and Dane are already at Boots and Burgers. Wanna join them?"

I didn't want to people, but we were headed there anyway.

"Sure."

Okay, maybe it wouldn't kill me to get to know Dane better. He was a great player and a good captain. So far. And he was a friend of Kayden's so… Not that I cared what Dane thought about me. He knew I was a snarky ass, but that's all he knew. And he was protective of Kayden. So, I figured, it wouldn't do any harm to play nice for once. Besides, too much assholery could create tension that I didn't need.

Yeah, and fucking around with your teammate isn't going to create tension?

I suddenly realized that Kayden and I were risking a lot by fucking around. Like skating on an unfamiliar lake, one break in the ice, and we were done for. If our teammates found out, well, there would be blowback, right? And what if the scouts found out? It was difficult enough getting drafted, never mind being a queer player. And yeah, I realized I was that. Never thought I'd have an epiphany about my sexuality like this, but then again, wasn't that part of what college was about? Finding out who you are?

Then I thought about how many hockey pros were openly queer. I could only think of one. One. Out of a thousand. Those odds weren't looking good.

"What are you thinking about?" Kayden asked me as we strolled past the many shops that lined main street.

"Nothing."

"Do you really want me to keep asking? Because I will."

"No one can ever find out about us," I blurted out.

Kayden stopped short and turned to me. His lips were red, swollen, a dead giveaway as to what he'd been up to. Mine were the same. How were we going to explain this away? Only a short while ago, he had my dick in his mouth, and now we were going to meet up with his friends, our teammates, and pretend nothing happened.

"I'm serious. Hockey is the only reason I'm here."

Kayden nodded, then looked away. "I know. I'm the same."

"And?"

"And what? I agree with you. This is fun, but that's all it is."

Then he started walking again. And me? I stood there, lost for words. I should've been relieved that he was in agreement. We could fuck around, but no one would know. That was perfect, right? No hassle, no stress.

Then I thought about the party. The way Hailey had been all over Kayden.

With every kiss between us, Kayden became more confident. Hell, he'd blown me in the library, for fuck's sake. Did that mean he wanted to hook up with other guys? And women too? And why did I care? It was none of my business who he wanted to fuck around with. None.

I stomped off after him, not sure why his laid-back attitude grated on my nerves. So much for my good mood. Bitchy Mad was back. With a vengeance.

CHAPTER 26
KAYDEN

The cold was bitter. Not the weather. I meant Maddox.

Ever since that blowjob in the library, he was walking around in a piss-poor mood. Not sure why. After all, he was the one who came. He should've been smiling for weeks, right? I know I was. I'd never thought giving head would be such a rush, but it was.

Until Maddox's bad attitude soured mine.

He barely spoke to me the rest of that evening, and Dane and Jackson watched us with concern. I waved it off, and when Dane asked me about it the next day, I said that Maddox and I had another disagreement. We didn't. The total opposite. Maddox wanted to keep our fucking around on the down low, and that was fine by me. So why was he so cranky? Or maybe I was thinking way too much about his reaction. He was, after all, a self-proclaimed grump. Maybe after the orgasm, he reverted to his usual mode.

Still, I assumed things between us were different. That he wasn't just my new fuck buddy, but my friend. Now, I wasn't so sure we were anything. I thought we'd finally reached a point of understanding between us, and then Maddox withdrew into himself. Not that I should be obsessed about him. I had more important things to focus on than my sex life. Days went by with no communication from Maddox. I found it unsettling, but what could I do?

So, instead of sitting beside Maddox on the drive down to Maryland, I sat beside Dane. At least he'd talk to me. Willingly.

"Where's your bestie?" Dane quipped.

"He's so far from that." I shook my head. "And he's at the back of the bus, as usual. Ignoring me. He's hot and cold, and either way, I always get burned."

"What are you talking about, Kay?" Dane whispered.

I couldn't help the fiery blush that heated my cheeks. "Not here."

"No shit. Your face gives everything away."

I playfully smacked his shoulder in retaliation.

Instead of sleeping the whole trip, I got out my notes and studied. My regular tutor had fired off a list of items for me to follow up on. He was alright, but I learned more in one session with Maddox than in several sessions with my school-assigned tutor.

After working for two hours, I grabbed a protein bar from my backpack, gulped down an energy drink, and went back at it. I didn't need the extra caffeine or stimulation, but I was nervous as fuck about this trip and this game. And about the rest of the semester, the courses that I was struggling with. Not to mention sharing a room with Maddox again.

I should have talked to Coach and told him that my personal feelings for Maddox required me to switch rooms. But I wasn't ready for the interrogation that would follow. And I'd have to actually define my feelings first, and that was scary as fuck. I'd never been so confused, consumed, or downright amused by anyone as I was with Maddox. I wanted to hug him really tight and not let go. Which was funny as fuck because he was so *not* the huggable type. I wanted him, for sure. Our chemistry was hot as fuck. But it was everything else that left me wondering what the hell I was doing. Still, I didn't notice or want anyone else. Only him.

Finally, after two hours of studying, my eyes grew heavy. I fell asleep and woke up to Dane nudging me with his elbow.

"We're here."

Here meaning the hotel. Which meant a shared room with Maddox. I went from sleepy to anxiety code red in less than ten seconds.

We lumbered off the bus, and entered the hotel. Maddox was on his phone, ignoring everyone. I turned to Dane and I didn't hold back my eye roll.

Once I had my hotel key card in hand, I headed for my room. I didn't look back for Maddox or wonder when—or if —he was following me. I just wanted to hit my mattress and sleep. But since I got to the room first, I was confronted by a problem. A big one.

Only one fucking bed. Was this a joke?

Picking up the hotel phone, I called the front desk.

"Hi, I'm in room 435, but there's been a mistake. We have a double room booked, not a king."

"Hold, please."

I paced in place while cheesy music played in my ear.

"Thank you for waiting. This is Jenna speaking. How can I assist you?"

"This is Kayden Melnyk in room 435. Sutton University room block. There's only one king bed in this room. Our requests are always two doubles."

"One moment," she replied. "Oh yes, I see that. But I'm sorry, we have a convention going on and we had to re-work the room scheduling. Some of your teammates are in the same situation."

"So, that's it? There's nothing you can do?"

"I'm sorry, but we're all booked up."

"Fuck!" I yelled out just as Maddox entered the room. When he spotted the bed, he dropped his bag. "I mean, sorry, uh, thanks for the info."

I hung up and shook my head. "Before you go ballistic, I just called the front desk, and there's nothing they can do. The entire hotel is fully booked."

Maddox shrugged and slipped off his leather jacket.

"Whatever. I'm too fucking tired to care. I'll take the right side."

Then he headed for the bathroom. Huh. As soon as the door closed, I called Dane.

"Hey, did you get stuck in a room with only one bed?" I asked.

"Uh, no. But Axel and Ethan did. So did Jace and Finn. And you?"

"Yes."

"Shit, bud, I'm sorry."

"It's a problem, Dane. But not for the reason you're thinking," I whispered. "Maddox and I have...you know...we kissed the night of that party. More than that. We got off, together, and it was the hottest fucking thing I've experienced in my life, and then in the library the other week I sucked him off and—"

"Whoa, bud, slow down. One piece of shocking information at a time. Back up, I need details. About the kiss and everything else. I guess that porn site inspired you, eh?" Dane chuckled.

I slapped a hand over my head. "This isn't funny, D."

"And this happened weeks ago, but you're just telling me now? How long were you gonna keep this a secret?"

Dane sounded hurt. Which I didn't intend. I wanted to tell him, fuck did I want to tell him, but I also wanted to respect Maddox's privacy. And, I was still in shock that I'd had sex. Not just because it was with a guy. Just, sex in general.

"I almost didn't believe it happened. And it was good. No, not that. It was incredible. Better than I'd imagined and… well, we agreed not to tell anyone. It's just a casual thing anyway. It doesn't mean anything."

Yeah, right.

"I get you. You know I do, given what me and Jackson are going through," Dane replied. "But Jackson and I aren't on the same team. So, you better know what you're doing, Kay."

"I don't. That's the fucking problem."

"And now you're sharing the same bed—"

"Exactly," I sighed.

"Well, as long as no one finds out, do what you want. But you gotta separate work from play or hockey from fucking. Nothing can interfere with our game, right?"

I dropped onto the bed. "Ugh."

"Can you?" Dane asked.

"Yes," I replied. "Of course. That's all it is."

I sounded confident. It was no problem.

"Or you could approach Coach for a room change," Dane offered.

"He'd insist on a reason why. And I'm not ready to go there. I'm fine. It's fine."

"I wish I could offer you advice. The only thing I can say is—" Dane paused. "Try to keep your voices down. The walls in hotels aren't soundproof."

"Not funny."

"Not joking."

"Dane," I started. "How did you, you know, know that what you felt for Jackson was more than sex?"

There was a pause on the other end of the line.

"Back in high school, when Jackson and I were fooling around in secret, I kept telling myself it was just hormones. But whenever I'd see him talking to another guy, it drove me crazy. I wondered if he was interested in them. I thought about him all the time. Wanted to be with him and only him. And he was the one I confided in. About everything."

I thought about the need I had to know all about Maddox. Was that just curiosity or did it mean more? I'd told him about my learning disorder and my ADHD. And it felt good to be open like that. To have someone finally see me. All of me.

"Thanks, Dane."

"Hey, you wouldn't be the first guy to fall for a teammate. Of that, I'm sure. But I'm not gonna lie, it does make me worry. About you, and the game."

"I know. And I can't afford to fuck up. I need this team."

"We sure as shit need you. Remember that."

The bathroom door opened, and Maddox stepped out.

"I gotta go," I muttered.

"See you in the morning."

I tapped end and threw my phone on the bed.

"You sure you're okay?" I asked Maddox. "Three months ago, you didn't even want to share a room with me, never mind a bed."

He threw his shirt off and started to undo his jeans. Uh, that was not the response I was anticipating. And him getting naked didn't help my poor, confused dick at all. Maddox didn't reply. He just pushed his jeans off and threw them on the bed. Clad in nothing but tight black briefs, he stared at me for a moment, then slid under the sheets.

I guess I got my answer.

Searching my backpack with sweaty hands, I grabbed my meds and a bottle of water, and downed my pills. Then I headed for the bathroom to wash up.

By the time I got back out, Maddox was already snoring.

Huh. So much for my worries. I wondered if this meant he was done. With me, and with sex. While I was still rocking a semi and trying to get my mind off being alone in bed with him, he was obviously not concerned. Or interested. My earlier fears turned to frustration. I stomped over to the left side of the bed and got in. But with Maddox close, almost naked, and smelling so fucking good, there was no way I was going to be able to sleep. And knowing that I didn't affect him the way he did me, I let out a sigh. A loud one.

I tossed and turned for God knows how long. Until Maddox's snoring ceased.

"Knock it off," he grumbled.

"I can't help it," I bit out. "I can't sleep."

"I thought I was on a ship with all the fucking movement going on."

"Excuse me for being wired," I replied. "I can't just tune everything off and fall asleep like you."

Maddox sighed and rolled over to face me. "I didn't sleep on the bus. I'm fucking exhausted."

Oh.

"Sorry," I muttered.

I rolled away, facing the window, and willed myself to relax. Right. I could hear Mad's every breath and I so wanted to turn over, pin him to the bed, and kiss the ever-loving shit out of him.

Then, I didn't have to. Maddox threw one leg and one arm over me.

What the fuck?

"Think of me as your weighted blanket. Now shut up and go to sleep. We both need it."

I could sacrifice sleep for sex, but he was right. We had a game tomorrow, and I wasn't going to turn down his offer. Or fuck up the game.

Closing my eyes, I listened to the sound of Maddox's slow, even breaths and soaked up the heavy weight of his body hugging mine. Soon, my eyes grew heavy.

And my dreams? He was right there, too.

CHAPTER 27

MADDOX

woke up at seven, plastered to Kayden's back. My arm and leg were still wrapped around him, holding him close, and I didn't want to move. Not from this position or this bed. Huh. For a guy who couldn't stand to be touched, I was becoming addicted to Kayden's.

My therapist would call this a breakthrough. I called it a freaking miracle.

And my cock, now rested after a full night's sleep, was also very happy to be sleeping next to the big guy. Then I remembered where we were.

Roll away from Kayden and hit the shower.

I didn't budge. Until I felt Kayden suddenly shift in my arms. Then I quickly let go. But I continued to stare at him, wondering how the hell I'd ended up here. He rolled over and faced me, his sandy hair a wavy mess around his face, his golden eyes sleepy.

"Hey," he murmured and reached out to cup my face.

"Hey."

His touch was gentle, and that startled me more than anything.

I swallowed past the huge lump in my throat. And when

he leaned over and kissed me, I let him. More than that, I took control of the kiss, teasing him with my tongue, all the while pushing at his shoulders, urging him to his back.

Straddling his waist, I rocked my hips, my morning wood rubbing against his. The loud groan that rumbled out of his chest made me shiver, lust sparking like wildfire in my veins.

"Get these briefs off," I demanded. "Now."

"Fuck," Kayden whimpered and slid his hands down my back and over my ass. We both struggled to get out of our underwear as fast as possible, and when our naked cocks brushed against each other, hard, hot, and leaking, I rubbed myself all over him. I needed to come so fucking bad.

"Next time," I moaned against his mouth. "I want to eat your ass."

"Fuck yes," he moaned. "I want that too."

Kayden gripped my ass cheeks tightly as he thrust his hips in tandem with mine. We humped frantically, and all the while I devoured his mouth, needing his taste, so fucking greedy for it.

"Kay," I groaned as my body took over, my hips pumping hard and fast.

"Come with me," Kayden urged.

I pumped my hips one more time, and then I unleashed, my body jerking hard with the force of my orgasm. Kayden called out my name, lashing my skin with his cum, both of us a sweaty, sticky mess.

I collapsed on top of him, panting, too blissed out to move.

"This is a much better way to get your hips flexors ready for the game," Kayden teased.

"Mmm," I whispered against his shoulder, then gently nipped the skin and licked it. "I think you're on to something there."

One of his hands slid up my back, then up higher to my shoulder, my neck. I tensed, so unused to being touched like that. Kayden's hands were gentle now, slow, and easy. I trembled a few times, then I figured it was just aftershocks. But when he traced one of the tattoos on my right arm, the trembling intensified.

Suddenly, he stopped.

"Shit, I'm sorry."

"It's okay," I replied, my head still tucked under his chin. "I'm still not used to being touched like that."

"Does this skull and snake represent someone?"

I moved my head, looking into his eyes.

"I...I don't want to talk about it. Not today. But, someday, alright?"

He nodded and then slid his hand back around to grip my neck, bringing me in for a long, deep kiss. It didn't matter if it was fast and dirty, or slow and sweet, kissing Kayden was so freaking incredible. Fuck, I could lie here all day and make out with him.

"See," I finally said when we came up for air. "You freaked out for nothing."

"What?"

"Your call with Dane."

"You heard?"

"You're not exactly quiet, Kay."

His face turned pink, his freckles darkening, and I did the unthinkable. I kissed him. No, not his mouth. His cheek.

I leaned back and Kay stared at me, mouth open, eyes wide.

"What?" I bit out.

"Nothing." Kayden shook his head and hugged me tighter. So tight I was surprised I could draw breath.

But our cum was drying, and it was starting to get itchy.

"Shower, breakfast, rink," I declared as I reluctantly pulled away.

Kayden stared up at me, his hands wandering up my stomach, higher, until he reached my nipples. When he ran the pads of his fingers over them, I jolted. Who knew that would turn me on?

"Good?" he whispered as he licked his lips.

"Very. But we don't have time to explore that now."

"Later?"

I nodded.

Then I took hold of his hands and pulled them away from my chest. He interlocked our fingers tightly, and suddenly, my mouth was dry, my heart knocking hard against my ribs. Holding his hands make me nervous as hell. Kayden tugged, and I leaned forward, taking his lips again. Harder this time, kissing him soundly, my tongue snaking around his. We didn't let go of each other. Not until our phones started chiming.

"Reality calls," I reminded him.

"Reality bites," he whispered and smiled against my lips.

"Sounds like me," I quipped.

"That's what I thought at first, but no," Kayden looked at me, his expression serious. "You're all bark and no bite."

"A pretty fierce bark."

"Eh, I'm getting used to it."

Kayden

By the time Mad and I showered, changed, and ate breakfast, it was time to head for the bus.

And when we arrived at the rink, I was pumped up. Feeling better than I had in a long time.

See? I could handle whatever this was with me and Mad. Sex. Really hot, intense sex that led to amazing orgasms that cleared my head and gave me that much-needed oomph. I chatted up all the guys, high-fiving them, offering words of encouragement, getting them amped up for the game. Maddox kept himself to himself. Which was fine. I knew there was no interfering with his pre-game ritual.

Dane skated up to me as we finished our warm-up.

"You're in an extra good mood," he whispered. "Don't tell me you and Mad—"

I tried to hold back my smile, but I couldn't.

"Your face, Kay. Everyone will know or suspect you got laid and the questions will start."

Shit, I didn't think about that.

"I can't help it. Why didn't anyone ever tell me that having an orgasm before a game was the best thing ever? I feel like I could play hockey in the freaking Olympics right now and win gold."

"Oh my God. Is Maddox aware of what he's unleashed?" Dane teased.

I glanced at the net and Maddox glared back at me, shaking his head.

"I think so."

"Oh no," Dane muttered.

"What?"

"That look on your face. I fucking know that look, Kay. You like him. More than like?"

"Well, I did ask you how you knew about Jackson. It shouldn't be that much of a shock."

"Yeah, but Maddox? I mean, he's hot, but volatile as fuck. Are you sure you know what you're doing?"

"He may be all that, but he has his reasons. He's so much more than that. And yes, despite my shitty grades, I'm not totally stupid. I can handle this."

"I never said you were that. Never." Dane looked at me, hurt in his eyes.

"I'm sorry. I know you didn't mean it that way," I replied quickly. "It's gonna be fine. I'm sure this feeling is just tempo-rary. It'll burn itself out and then we'll move on. That's what happens, right? It's fun for a while and then it's done. Nothing lasts forever."

Well, maybe for some people. Like Dane and Jackson.

They were in love. Okay, maybe I liked Maddox more than a hook up. And yes, whenever I was with him, I was free-falling into something I knew nothing about but wanted anyway. And I was a committed player. Once the game got going, I was all in. It was the same way with Maddox.

"Remember what I said. It can't interfere with the game," Dane added.

I nodded, positive in my decision.

Coach called us back to the bench for a final talk before the game started.

"Melnyk, Moss, Rowland, Lund, St. Pierre, you're up. Show them how it's done!"

The ref skated onto the ice and blew his whistle, getting everyone's attention. And when I stepped out, I was ready.

First period, and we're on fire. Dane scored, then Axel. I also got my first assist of the season. I was so revved up that when I skated past Maddox, he offered his blocker to me, and I tapped it. It wasn't a pat on the ass, but I'd take it. And thank God, Playing Rockland College wasn't the mayhem that was us against Boston.

For the rest of the game, it seemed like nothing could stop us.

We were up 3-0 by the second period. Rockland still hadn't scored, and it didn't look like it was about to happen anytime soon. All our guys were glued to the fucking puck in every play, with none of us letting up. Their goalie started looking tired; after so many shots on goal, we wore him down.

By the time the third period rolled around, though, we'd hit a bit of a bump. Silas, up until this point, was killing it. Until he let one of Rockland's forwards slip past him. The guy fired a wicked slapshot, and we held our collective breath as the puck took flight.

It was a beautiful corner shot. But it was no match for Mad's reflexes. No goal. And while Rockland's crowd sat silent, everyone on our team celebrated. We jumped off the bench and yelled as loud as we could, then I got the team chanting Maddox's name.

And by the time the final buzzer sounded, it was 3-0 Cougars. Shut the fuck up, it was a shutout! The bench was lit. Even Coach was smiling.

We rushed from our box to center ice to celebrate. Everyone except Maddox.

He was skating in front of his net, tapping the bar, and watching us. I could sense that he wanted to join in, but also that he needed to hold back. He didn't like crowds or being crowded. I gave him that space, but once we calmed down, which, let's face it, for a group of college players, takes a while, I ambled over to give him a hug.

He needed one, whether he liked it or not. And what was more surprising? He let me. For about five seconds. Then he pushed me away and told me to fuck off.

That was the moment I knew I was falling hard for Maddox Rocher.

Three hours later, I was still riding the high of that win. And the fact I got to share it with Maddox. And we'd sure as fuck share another celebration tonight. In private.

Since we played an evening game, we were out at a late team supper, and then one more night in our hotel before leaving first thing in the morning. I glanced down the table. Maddox had taken the seat on the end again. Trying to keep our distance, even though I didn't want any.

When I thought about this morning, how intense it was to come together like that, I realized how badly I wanted him. I wanted more. But I hadn't brought lube or condoms or anything like that with me. Then again, we kept going back and forth, and it's not like I was expecting anything to happen on this trip. I wasn't sure what we were doing, except everything that felt good.

I hadn't lied. I wanted him to fuck me. But I also knew that I had to prepare for anal. And that meant, I had online purchases to make. And more experimenting to do. Then I'd be ready. Until then, hand jobs and blow jobs would have to do. Just thinking about having sex with Maddox had my body flushing hot and my brain short-circuiting. Between that and the adrenaline rush of a win, my hormones were out of control. And I wasn't sure how I was gonna make normal conversation with my teammates.

Until Dane nudged me.

"You okay there? Why so quiet?"

"What?" I croaked, then cleared my throat. "I mean, yes, I'm good. Amazing. You?"

"On top of the fucking world." He smiled and held his glass up. "Hey guys, let's have a toast. To a shutout! We shut down Rockland and we're just getting started!"

Everyone raised their glasses and cheered.

Thankfully, that got me out of my headspace and forced me to think of topics other than sex.

As we finished up our dinner, I opened my backpack, pulled out the bag of bracelets I'd made, and passed them around. Yup, I'd made good use of that kit. All in team colors, of course, green and gold. Well, almost all of them…

"Hey, Kayden!" Jace called out. "Why does Rocher get black and yellow?"

"That's simple," I replied with a smile. "Cause he's my angry bee."

Maddox shook his head and gave me two of his best fingers while all the guys clapped and hollered. I don't think he minded the joke, though. He still wore the damn bracelet. And seeing it on him filled me with a pride I hadn't expected.

"What does it say?" Jace asked Maddox.

"Salty."

That got laughs and more claps.

"And, of course, Kayden is sweet," Jace teased.

I shrugged and tried not to blush. Hah.

"Please don't tell me I actually have to wear this thing," Axel grumbled.

"Come on," Jace taunted from across the table. "Are you really that uptight?"

"I don't like jewelry."

"No one's asking you to wear it every day. Just tonight. Be a team player," Jace replied. "And lighten up."

It was just for fun. Coach was wearing his too. Hell, all the guys were. Even Silas, who'd been all but silent during dinner. He'd played a great game today. We were finally synching up on the ice.

Afterward, as everyone was filing out of the restaurant, Silas came up to me and pulled me aside.

"Do you think you could make a few extra bracelets?" he asked quietly, his face serious.

I thought he was being sarcastic at first, but he looked sincere. I nodded.

"Sure." I smiled at him. "You want any particular words or sayings for them?"

"My jersey number? And one with the name Josiah on it? My younger brother loves stuff like this. It would mean a lot."

"Of course. Is he going to be at one of our home games?" I asked. "I'd love to meet him."

Silas bit his lower lip.

"Maybe in a month or two."

He didn't offer a reason why, and I didn't press.

"Can't wait."

"Thanks."

I watched as he walked away.

"Hey!" I called out, and Silas turned around. "Me and Dane usually hang out after practice. You wanna join us?"

"No," Silas replied. "I mean, I can't. But thanks for offering."

"Sure. If you're ever at the west end dorm, I'm in 333. Drop by and say hi."

Silas nodded and headed back down the hallway.

"Wow, he talks."

I turned around to find Dane with a shocked expression on his face.

"Yeah, he does," I replied.

"What did he want?"

"A couple of bracelets. For his brother."

"That's...surprisingly sweet."

"See? You can't always judge by first impressions. Maddox is the same."

Dane's expression told me he wasn't buying it.

"Only to you Kay. You and your *bee*," he teased. "You are shit at trying to hide, my friend."

I looked around, but everyone had left. Including Maddox. He was probably on his way upstairs. To our bedroom. Our bed.

I waved him off. "Please. No one suspects anything."

"I don't know. I think Jace is on to you. And, as much as Maddox likes to put on that resting bitch face, he does stare at you an awful lot."

"Really?" That was surprising. It made my heart take off running. "Like how?"

"Like he's very aware of you. Like, his eyes are super-glued to your ass."

"He does that?" I squeaked, completely surprised. "Shit, that's hot."

"Oh boy, what's he unleashed with you?"

I chuckled. "A horny beast, Dane. A horny fucking beast."

"Jesus, Kay, TMI."

"Hey, you said I could come to you or Jackson if I had questions. And I have them. A lot of them. Like, do you enjoy anal? And if so, any tips on how I prep for that?"

Dane's eyes bugged out, and he pulled me into the nearest alcove.

"Christ, Kayden, give me a bit more warning next time."

"What? We were talking about me being horny. Asking about fucking shouldn't be shocking."

Dane sighed and ran a hand over his hair. "I...holy shit, Jackson's going to kill me, but yes. We do that. Along with other things. But you don't have to. Only if you want it, and you're comfortable with it. For me, I prefer to top, but—"

"Ooh, this is getting good." I rubbed my hands together. "Teach me, oh wise one."

He rolled his eyes.

"The only thing I can say is, take it slow. Use lots of lube. I mean *lots* of it. And if you don't enjoy it, don't do it. And yeah, you might want to prep with a dildo. See if you like penetration before you go for the real thing," Dane whispered. "Then, there's douching."

"Wait, I need to record this so I don't forget."

"Trust me, you won't," Dane replied and glanced around. A couple of people got off the elevator and headed our way. "This isn't the best time or place for this conversation. Let me text you some info, alright? A couple of sites you can check out. And if you have more questions, ask away. Just, not in public."

"Awesome, thanks D."

He gripped my shoulder and stared at me. "Just do what feels right to you. Don't be pressured into something you're not into."

"Maddox wouldn't ever do that."

Dane shrugged. "You know him better than I do. Or, at all."

"I'm starting to. And I want to know more."

"Holy shit."

"Exactly."

Dane and I headed for the elevators, and he got off on the second floor while I continued to the fourth.

When I got to my room, the lights were already on, and I could hear the water in the bathroom running. I stripped off my clothes and got into bed, my body thrumming with anticipation. Sure, I was sore and exhausted from the game, but I was vibrating with adrenaline. Lust. I'd never felt so aware of my body.

When Maddox finally stalked out of the bathroom, wearing nothing but my bracelet, I couldn't hide how much I wanted him.

Living up to our Cougar namesake, he stalked around the bed, and pounced on me. The game was over but our fun was just beginning.

CHAPTER 29

MADDOX

A WEEK BEFORE CHRISTMAS BREAK

"Come home with me."

"What?"

Kayden and I were in the library again, in a private room, studying. Or trying to. For the past two hours, he kept squeezing my thigh and dropping heated kisses on my neck, and it was driving me crazy. He drove me crazy. We'd been fooling around any chance we could get, and it was only getting better, hotter, and more addictive.

I didn't just want his touch—I needed it. Craved it. We hadn't gone any further than hand jobs and blow jobs, though, because we were always rushed. We didn't want to get caught, either by his roommate or the students on my floor. We both wanted more, but there was never any time. Or maybe we were both too scared to take that next step. It was sex, and yet, I knew it was way more.

I was in over my head. I liked being with him. And it sparked a panic inside me. A panic that was getting bigger. The voice in my head told me I was no good for someone like him.

And now this?

"Come home with me for Christmas," Kayden repeated.

No way. Me and family didn't mix. I didn't have one anymore, and I wasn't about to face a pity party from his.

I shook my head.

"I'm staying here. I've got to finish up a coding job, and I'm going to enjoy the peace while the hordes of students are gone."

"You shouldn't spend the holiday alone," Kayden replied.

"I spent Thanksgiving alone, so what's the difference?"

"You mean you didn't go home to Toronto?"

"Nope," I muttered. "And for what? I don't have a home there anymore."

I wasn't saying that to get his sympathy. It was the blunt truth.

"What about Daniel? You said his family fostered you."

I'd told Kayden a bit about my life back home in Toronto. Not a lot of detail. Just that I had no family left, and that I had to be fostered for a few years. Part of me wanted to spill my guts about the rest of it. The why. The other part of me wanted to stay silent. Move on. Not let it tarnish everything I was working toward. And I was still getting used to the fact that I had someone, other than my therapist, to tell.

"I did, but that was before I turned eighteen. I don't have to go back there now. And he's got his own family. I'm not a part of that anymore. Besides, he invited me, but I already said no."

That wasn't Daniel talking; it was all me. I appreciated everything he'd done for me, helping me navigate life when I had to leave my father's place. But being around Daniel, his wife, and his kid made me wish for things I wanted but would never have. My mom, the only family I had, was gone. Now it was just me.

"I still want you to come home with me," Kayden implored.

I stared at him. At the honeyed eyes, golden freckles, and wide smile that had a chokehold on me. One that was getting way too tight. I couldn't breathe, and I needed to be let loose.

Meeting his family sounded like dating. And I didn't want Kayden to think we were in any kind of relationship at this point. Nothing beyond sex. And hockey. And school. Okay, maybe we were friends who fucked. Fuck buddies. No, I wasn't anyone's 'buddy.' In fact, trying to put any kind of label on what was happening made me itchy as hell. Relationships had rules, and the only ones I followed were my own.

"No," I repeated, and shoved his hand off my leg. "Fucking around has been fun, but it's time we call it quits."

"Just like that?"

I recognized the hurt in Kayden's voice, and I saw in it his eyes. But it couldn't be helped. I wasn't cut out to be… whatever this was we were doing. Or I was playing at. The only game I was good at was hockey. Anything else felt totally out of my league.

"Yeah, just like that," I bit out, grabbed my shit, and got up. "I gotta go."

I expected Kayden to stop me, but he just sat there, staring.

"And finals?"

"We can squeeze in one more study session. Just no more touching."

"Got it," he snapped and looked away.

"Kay, look. I was honest with you. I'm just coming to terms with the fact that I'm gay, never mind, anything else. And I told you I'm not cut out for this shit."

"This shit?"

"You know what I mean."

"No, I really don't. Cause I thought you were into me, I thought you liked me, hell, maybe even—" he paused and shook his head. "Whatever. It's just me being stupid again."

"What did I say about you calling yourself that?" I bit out.

"You're right." He glared at me. I'd never seen him this angry. "This time, you're the one who's acting dumb. Just go already."

I headed for the door, and I didn't look back. This was better for both of us. Kayden was under enough pressure with his classes. What if we got caught? The last thing he needed was to be outed. And me? With every passing week, I realized that one day I'd be okay with telling people I was queer. But telling people I was into Kayden? That was a whole other thing. A truth that could threaten everything we were working for.

I walked back to the dorm, but unfortunately, Dane spotted me when I was halfway across campus.

"Maddox!" he called out and ran up to me.

"What?"

"I just wanted to say hi," Dane replied. "Wait. I thought Kayden had a study session with you today?"

"He did," I snapped. "It's done."

Dane looked at me, his expression confused. "Okay, sorry I mentioned it. Everything all right?"

"I'm helping him with his course. That's all. There's nothing else going on."

Dane raised one eyebrow. Shit. He knew. He fucking knew. Duh, he's Kayden's closest friend. Why was I surprised?

"You know?" I bit out.

He nodded. "He needed advice, someone to talk to. To figure things out."

"And he told you everything?"

"Not everything, but enough. And he came to me because —" Dane looked around and then whispered. "Fuck it. He came to me because I'm queer. Jackson and I are together. And when Kayden came to us with questions about possibly being into a guy, of course he told me. He thought he was straight until—"

"Until me."

Fuck, fuck.

Dane nodded. "But I haven't said anything to anyone. I wouldn't. I'm only out to a few close friends, and I'd never do that to anyone."

I nodded.

"But I have to tell you, the two of you being involved and on the same team is risky."

"Not anymore."

Dane stared at me. "What do you mean? What did you do?"

"What I should've done weeks ago. Put a stop to it," I hissed. "Like you said, it's risky. And neither of us needs that right now."

Dane's expression went from concerned to angry. "Where is he?"

"Still at the library."

"If you've hurt him, I—"

"No one's hurt, Dane. There are no feelings involved, okay? It was sex. And it's done. Now we're back to being… nothing."

Those words tasted vile, but it was necessary. I should've cut this thing off before it started. Letting my dick rule my brain was the biggest mistake.

Then I glanced down at my wrist. At that damn bracelet Kayden made. The one I'd yet to take off. *Salty. Angry bee…* The ridiculous words reverberated in my head, and they wouldn't leave. I wanted to rip the bracelet off and throw it in the garbage. Never look at it again. But when I touched it, I couldn't.

What the fuck was wrong with me?

"You've been a grumpy prick since you got here, but that was fine," Dane snapped. "I didn't care. As long as you played hard and gave your all on the ice, that's all that mattered to me. But I know Kayden. He doesn't take friendship lightly. And you know what? You're all he's talked about for months, so don't tell me there are no feelings involved. Kayden sees something in you. What, I have no fucking idea."

Dane stormed off in the direction of the library, and I stood there with nothing left to say.

What did Kayden see in me? I didn't have a clue either.

CHAPTER 30
KAYDEN

CHRISTMAS

"Kaybear, is everything okay? You've been so quiet ever since Dane and Jackson left."

I'd invited my friends back home, and it had been a welcome distraction. After finals, Dane and Jackson spent two days with my family, then headed back to Arkansas to see theirs. And being alone again had me thinking about Maddox. Where was he? What was he doing? Was he really okay?

I stared at my plate, full of delicious food that I had no desire to eat, and ignored my mother's question. I'm surprised she noticed at all, given that our family table was chaos and noisy as fuck. Yup, I wasn't the only chatterbox in the family.

And I didn't even know where to begin. Should I say anything? If I told her I was hung up on someone at school, more questions would follow. Like, who was the girl? That would be the assumption. Then they'd need *all* the details. Was I really ready to come out and tell my family that I'm bi? Part of me said, *Fuck yes*. Because I wanted Maddox. More than wanted. And his gender was the least of it. But given that he'd walked out of the library and I hadn't seen or texted him since, maybe it was pointless. Why bother upsetting my family over a fling that was done before it even began?

"I'm tired. Between hockey and studies, I'm worn out. I worked so hard to get through finals."

I was worried sick I was going to fail and get kicked out of school.

"Did your tutor help?"

"They did."

"You had more than one?"

Oops. "Yeah. Another student in my elective helped me out."

"That's good. But I hope you've also made time to have fun. Any cute girls catch your eye?"

I rolled mine. Oh man, if only she knew.

"There was someone. But they're not interested in dating me."

Maddox was okay fucking around, but as soon as I invited him here, boom. Everything imploded. I'd asked him to come home with me again the day we were leaving campus. We argued in the dorm, and he stormed off. Dane told me that maybe I was better off leaving Maddox alone. I was starting to wonder if he was right.

And yet, it was too late. I already knew I wanted more than a quick make-out session with Maddox here and there. I wanted to be with him all the time. And yeah, I still wanted him to fuck me. I'd even ordered that dildo and started experimenting. I was more than ready for it. For him. For all of it. There was an idea in my head, a ridiculous one, that me and Maddox were like Dane and Jackson. We could be boyfriends. Fuck, just saying the word gave me chills. I'd had a crush or two on girls in high school, but nothing, nothing like this. I was in over my head but I didn't know what to do.

"I can't believe that. And if so, it's their loss," Mom replied, and patted my hand.

"It's complicated."

"It shouldn't be. Either she likes you, or she doesn't."

"He doesn't!" I blurted out and slammed my fork down.

Suddenly, the entire table quieted. Fuck. *Way to go Kay.* Can't do anything the normal way.

"Did you say *he*?" Mom asked.

"Uh, well, I mean—" I paused, my face burning hot. "Yes."

Dad leaned forward. "What's going on?"

I stared at him across the table. My dad's a giant bear of a man and I get my size, and my hazel eyes, from him. Mom's only five-six and petite. But of the two of them, Mom's the one who's fiercely protective, the one who enforced the rules in the house. Dad had a more laid-back approach to parenting. I had a feeling that was about to change. And given the way he was staring at me, it was happening right this fucking minute.

"I fell for someone," I confessed. "A guy on my hockey team. I'm bi. Merry Christmas!"

Oh, my god. I actually said all that out loud.

Everyone at the table stared at me.

"What?"

"You've got it bad for one of your teammates?" my sister Janina yelled out. "That's so hot."

"Nina!" Mom called out.

"What? Tell us his name! Show us his picture!" Nina insisted.

I bit back a laugh and then I realized there was nothing funny about this situation. I had it bad for Maddox, but the reverse wasn't true.

"I don't have a picture. Maddox—" I paused, remembering that neither of us was planning to come out. Shit. Not that anyone in my family would say a word. And I knew

Nina would hound me until she got the truth. "Sorry. I shouldn't have said anything. Don't repeat his name."

My younger sisters, Reena and Jenna, pulled out their phones.

"I'm googling him," Reena announced as she and Jenna giggled.

Oh Jesus. Me and my big fucking mouth.

My dad tapped the table. "A teammate?"

"It just happened."

"Are you out of your mind?" My dad barked. "You're under the radar of professional league scouts. If it comes out that you've been…involved with your teammate, forget your chances of ever playing at that level!"

"Vic," Mom whispered to my dad and reached for his hand. "Calm down."

"Calm down? Do you want our son to screw up his entire future for some guy?"

"He's not some guy. His name is Maddox," I countered. "Look, there's nothing to worry about. He's not interested in me, so there's no problem. Okay? Can we forget I said anything and go back to our usual Christmas food coma?"

"Why didn't you tell us you were gay?" my brother Alec asked.

"I'm bi. And do I have to tell you guys everything? I just started to realize it myself, I haven't even come to terms with it yet—" I shook my head. "Please, can we change the subject?"

I poked at my mashed potatoes and forced myself to take a bite. It was great, but my appetite was off. Suddenly, I was in the sin bin and everyone around me was staring like I'd let them down.

"You know we love you no matter what. And if you're bi, well, then, that's who you are," Mom announced. "It's the teammate situation your dad is concerned about. Plus, the professional hockey world isn't exactly a hallmark of queer acceptance."

"Like I said, there's nothing to talk about," I repeated. "It's over."

Rory, who was the youngest—and quietest—brother, spoke up. "Maybe we can set you up while you're here for the weekend? My friend Geoff is gay and single."

Maddox was right to turn down my offer to come home with me.

"No one's setting me up, and no one's asking me any more questions," I stated. "Now please, pass the gravy."

"I found him!" Reena announced loudly. "It's Maddox Rocher, right?"

"What? Where?" I asked.

"School socials. They posted pics from the last game. Let's see…he's a goalie from Canada," Reena announced as she tapped her phone. "Ooh, there's one photo here with his mask off. He's gorgeous."

Fuck, did I know it.

"Let's see," Nina asked, and Reena passed over her phone.

Then it was on to the next family member and the phone did the whole tour of the table. Holy shit, my family was wild.

"He's got quite the scowl on him," Nina commented. "Is he always like that?"

I nodded, stuffing in a forkful of turkey so I wouldn't start gushing like the fool I was. Scowl or not—or maybe because of it—Maddox always had my attention. And when one of his rare smiles appeared, any hint of one, I ached with a sweet kind of intensity that I'd never experienced for anyone. His grin totally wrecked me. It made me feel like I'd won the damn lottery. Who was I kidding? His pout did the same thing. Because I knew that there was so much more to him than angry glares and sharp words. He'd researched the best reading apps for my dyslexia and helped me break down the concepts I struggled with. He bought me that journal. And he was surprisingly protective. Like that time on the bus when he told Axel off.

Then there was the way he kissed me, touched me. Like he couldn't get enough. I guess now he had. Christ, I was gone for him. And I was dreading my return to school. I had to act like we were strangers again. How was I going to do that?

I put my fork down and my gaze locked on the bracelet on my wrist. I wondered if Maddox had thrown his away. He'd been wearing it ever since I gave it to him, but probably not anymore. And why did that make me feel even worse? My stomach clenched tight. No way was I going to be able to finish my meal.

"So, what happened, Kay? Why'd you break up?" Nina demanded.

"We weren't really together, so there's no breakup," I muttered.

Sure as hell felt like it, though. They might as well hear the whole pathetic thing.

"I invited him here for Christmas," I confessed. "He freaked out. And that was that."

"He doesn't have any family of his own?" Mom asked.

"Nope. His mom passed away when he was thirteen. And his dad's gone too. There's something really bad there that he won't talk about."

That comment was met with awkward silence. Man, I sure knew how to get a party going.

"I think we've had enough of this conversation," Dad announced and pointed at my sisters. "No more questions. Leave Kayden alone."

I was grateful. But also, annoyed? My dad glanced at me and gave me '*the look*.' The one that said after dinner, he and my mom were going to sit down with me for a long talk. I already knew what was coming.

Don't fuck up your hockey dreams. Maddox sounds like trouble. Stay away.

Everyone began eating again. I sipped on my Diet Coke and ignored the food and the talk around me. Then my thoughts wandered back to my obsession. Was Maddox alone? Probably. That made the ache in my chest worse. My hand itched to pick up my phone and text him, but I held back.

Being silent had never felt so wrong.

CHAPTER 31
MADDOX

t was a new semester, but it felt like September.

I saw Kayden at practice, but it was awkward. There were polite nods and *'hey, how's it going'* so no one on the team questioned us. I guessed he'd done okay with his finals. I didn't ask, even though I wanted to. He must've done well because he was still here, right? And me? My sleep was shit, my concentration and appetite too. It wasn't difficult for me to figure out why.

I missed him. And I didn't miss anyone, except my mom.

But how could I want for a guy who annoyed me half the time and confounded me the rest? Okay, so Kayden didn't annoy me anymore. Maybe I liked him. A lot. So much that it was physically painful for me to walk into my room. That goddamn chair was like staring at a neon sign, reminding me about our first kiss. And everything that followed. Every touch was branded in my brain, burned into my memory. I'd never forget.

And Christmas, by myself? It was more like Halloween, with only the ghosts of students past roaming the halls. And it really fucking bothered me. I never minded being alone before. But I did now. The quiet was too much. Lonely. Depressing. And I hated it.

So, I did something monumentally dumb. I searched for Kayden's socials and followed him.

He'd posted a few pics of his family holiday. But he wasn't smiling in any of the photos. In fact, Kayden's expression looked a lot like mine. Every day I berated myself for what I'd said to him. Had I hurt him? I kept telling myself what we had was just sex, but there was no way I was buying that shit now. I was feeling stuff I never imagined I was capable of.

Then I thought about our next practice, next game, our season's stats. Would me and Kayden being together really fuck things up? Did other teammates fuck around? Who knew? If they were, what did it matter as long as it didn't interfere with the game?

For the first time in years, I wanted something more than hockey. I wanted Kayden. A relationship with him? Boyfriends? I could hardly believe it, but there it was. Acknowledging the truth had my brain freaked out, but my gut finally stopped hurting. I had to talk to him. Even though I didn't know if confronting him was going to make my life a total mess or be the strangest, best thing ever.

I'd hardly left my room since everyone returned to campus. I was still figuring out what I wanted to say to Kayden and how, but I'd decided today was the day. We had practice, but afterward, we needed to talk. If he'd talk to me. He would, right? This was Kayden. No way would he ghost me if I tried to approach him. Would I have to apologize? Ugh, I hated saying sorry. That right there was a testament as to how much I was in over my head for this guy. I didn't apologize to anyone.

Still, as confident as I was that he would talk to me, my nerves were riding high when I entered the rink. As usual, me and Silas were the first guys here, and slowly, the rest of our teammates trickled in. There was the usual talk—about Christmas break, raunchy jokes, and comments about our upcoming game against the number one college hockey team, Langston.

I didn't hear Kayden's voice, but I knew exactly when he arrived. Call it a premonition, but it was weird. I'd never been in tune with anyone like that before. It was frightening how badly I wanted to see him, so much that my body began to tremble the moment he stepped into the room.

I rushed to put on my gear, trying to hide the fact that my hands were shaking.

When I looked up and saw Kayden staring right back at me, I nearly blurted out my relief that he was here. And that he was finally looking at me. Really looking at me. Then I realized *he* had on *my* resting bitch face. This wasn't going to be as easy as I'd imagined.

"Hey Maddox, what's going on?" Ethan asked out loud, our teammates turning to stare. "Why's Kayden scowling, and you look like you're lost? You guys switch personalities?"

The guys laughed at that, but I didn't find it funny at all. Accurate, but not amusing.

"At least we have personalities, Ethan. That's more than I can say for you," I spat out.

"Ooh, the snark is back! Thank fuck," Jace quipped and gave me a nod.

I nodded in return. Damn fucking right. I might be starting to like the guys around here, but that didn't mean I was gonna start smiling or acting nice or anything.

"Don't tell me you're still wearing that stupid bracelet," Axel sneered as he stepped closer to me. He glanced from me to Kayden again. "What are you guys, like BFFs now?"

Axel turned to me with sharp eyes. Did he know? Could everyone tell how I felt about Kayden?

"We've won the last two games, so it stays," I bit out, recalling the superstitions hockey players are known for. "Are you okay with that? You wanna see what brand of underwear I have on too?"

Axel gave me his middle finger and stalked away. Asshole. I turned to Kayden and the look he gave me said he was scared as fuck they were on to us.

So much for my confidence.

———

Practice was brutal. It felt like I hadn't stepped foot in the gym for a year. Coach was in a demanding mood too, pushing drill after drill, until hours later, we were all sweaty and sore and begging for practice to end.

Kayden loosened up and started talking to everyone. Except me. I was counting down the seconds until this practice was over so I could finally talk to him alone.

Coach blew his whistle and motioned for everyone to gather close. I skated up to the group and glanced at Kayden. He was looking anywhere but at me. The knot in my stomach tightened.

"You guys are slow today and I get it," Banning bellowed. "We've come back from the holiday break. Too much food and not enough activity. But now's not the time to slack off."

Banning paused and looked directly at Silas. The defenseman was leaning on his stick, sweat soaking his beard, and he didn't look happy. And I didn't miss the way Coach bit his lip and shook his head.

"I don't need to remind you who we're facing on Saturday. But Langston College is not infallible. They've had a lot of lineup changes this season. And they've lost another star player, this time, to Wheaton U. Rest up tonight, do a light workout tomorrow, and be back here in two days, ready to win that game," Banning crossed his arms. "Good practice. Get out of here."

I skated back to my net, grabbed my stick and my blocker,

and followed the rest of my teammates off the ice. I needed to grab Kayden's attention, but I had to find the right moment. Thankfully, he was busy chatting up Dane, and while the rest of the team showered, changed, and left, Kayden was one of the last ones standing. With his friend. Who was now giving me the stink eye. No surprise there.

Once I had my jersey off and then my chest protector, I ambled over to Kayden, my hands sweaty, my heart beating like a wild thing.

"I need to talk to you."

Dane turned silent.

Kayden finally turned around and looked at me. I stared up at him, and I forgot everything that I was going to say. Not that I was going to say it here, with Dane listening. But still, my mouth was dry, and a horrible lump sat in my throat. He could deny it all he wanted, but he was hurt. Angry yes, but hurt more than anything. I could see it in his eyes. He was shit at hiding how he felt.

"If it's about the econ class, don't worry. I got eighty-seven on the final and I got my C on the course. And I don't need any further help—"

"It's not that."

"Then no, I don't want to talk to you."

"I didn't ask if you wanted to. I said I need to."

Kayden shook his head. "Not now."

"Kayden, is everything okay?" Dane asked as he stepped up to us.

"Everything's fine," I snapped.

"Is it?" Dane bit out and glared at me. "And I wasn't asking you."

Dane was dressed, ready to leave. He pointed to the door. "Hurry up, Kay. I'll be waiting outside."

Kayden nodded, and I watched as Dane stalked off. When the door slammed shut, and we were alone, I didn't waste a second.

"Kay, I—"

"I'm not mad," he replied as he leaned against his stall. "I mean, I was. Maybe still am, but I'll get over it. You were right. We were playing at something we shouldn't have. It's not worth it. Hockey comes first."

All I heard was 'it's not worth it.' *I* wasn't worth it.

"I'm such an idiot," I bit out.

"No, you're the smart one, remember?" he scoffed. "I was reminded of that over the holidays."

"What are you talking about?"

Kayden licked his lips, and it took every ounce of strength I had left to not reach up and kiss the fuck out of him. Every day without him was excruciatingly long. I was going out of my damn mind.

"I told my parents about you," he whispered. "Not details, just the basics."

Holy fuck. I was not expecting that.

"They're more concerned about us being teammates than the fact that I'm bi. The last thing they want is for me to screw up my hockey future. But I told them it's no problem because it's done."

I shook my head. "Do you really want that? To be done?"

My body was shaking, and I was sure I was going to pass out. I placed one hand on the stall beside him and leaned in closer. Jesus, there was something about us now, hot and sweaty from practice, that turned me on like nothing else. I wanted out of the rest of my equipment. More than that, I needed to get naked and rub myself all over Kayden. I wanted to kiss him, listen to his moans, watch him come, and yes, taste his cum.

"Does this feel like a mistake?" I asked him, reaching up and cupping his jaw.

He hadn't shaved in days and the reddish-blonde stubble was rough against my fingers. I could only imagine how it would feel against my lips, my thighs, and fuck, even my ass.

His sharp inhale was all the motivation I needed to finally say what I'd been holding on to.

"I can't think about anything else. I can't study, I can't sleep." I paused and licked my lips. "I freaked out when you invited me home. I knew what was happening between us was way more than fucking, and it scares me. What I feel for you... I can't even begin to describe it, Kay. And I don't know what the fuck I'm doing except what feels right. And that's you. Only you."

I wasn't the only one shaking.

"Mad," Kayden whispered my name, his eyes never leaving mine, and I shivered. "You can't keep doing this. Not with me. I need to know you're not going to turn around tomorrow and tell me to fuck off again."

I grinned at that, the knot in my stomach finally easing. "Well, it *is* my favorite saying."

"I'm serious."

"So am I." I stepped closer, until our bodies touched, not wanting to be anywhere else. "And I can't guarantee I won't push you away. I told you, I don't know what the fuck I'm doing. Plus, you know I'm a moody ass."

Kayden reached down and cupped said ass. My cock was aching in my jock, so hard I nearly lost my train of thought.

"I want to be with you," I confessed, my words barely a whisper. "I'm asking for one more chance."

Kayden bit his lower lip. "What about the team? What about hockey?"

"Off the ice, it's you and me. We keep this private. On the ice, we do what we always do. We can separate the two. We can do this."

"Our relationship? Our rules?" Kayden asked.

"Fucking right."

He stared at me, and I held my breath, waiting for his answer. The only thing I heard was the frenzied pounding of my heartbeat.

"Even though we're keeping this secret, I want to be exclusive," Kayden added. "No one else."

"Yes."

I barely got the word out and we lunged for each other, the kiss mauling and greedy. His scruff teased my lips, the burn so good. Christ, I was frantic for his taste.

To me, days without touching Kayden felt like a whole fucking year.

CHAPTER 32
KAYDEN

Was this real? Was Maddox my boyfriend? Holy shit. I almost couldn't believe it. Not his admission, not my reaction, and not the fact that he was dropping to his knees in front of me right now, and tearing at my pants.

"What are you doing? Anyone could come in here," I hissed. "What about hiding, for fuck's sake?"

"They're all long gone," he replied as he made quick work of my jockstrap. "Now shut up and let me apologize the way I need to."

I wanted to laugh at his comment, but I was too turned on. My cock was already throbbing, leaking, but then I remembered where we were. And where we'd been.

"But I need to shower first, I—"

Maddox teased the head of my dick with his wicked tongue. Suddenly, I didn't care where we were or how sweaty I was; all I needed was more of his hot, wet, incredible mouth. And his filthy eagerness sparked mine.

"You really are a dirty fucking boy," I whispered.

He moaned and looked up at me, his dark eyes watering, his lips stretched wide around my cock. He jacked me off with his hand while he bobbed his head up and down, taking me halfway down his throat before gagging.

Maddox pulled off and shook his head. "I'm gonna try my best to suck you all the way down, Kay, but you've got a big fucking dick."

I bit back a laugh at his honesty.

"You don't have to take it all," I reassured him. "Or any of it. Breathe heavy on my cock and I'll come."

Maddox's responding grin made my knees weak. I was never getting used to the sight of that smile. Then he leaned forward and took me in his mouth again, and I forgot about everything except how damn good it was.

Both of us beginners, but quick learners when it came to each other.

His hot tongue swirled around my cockhead and when he sucked long and hard, my knees locked up tight. I grabbed hold of his hair, mesmerized by the sight of my cock moving in and out of his mouth. The pleasure was unreal, so good that I was gonna come embarrassingly fast. He didn't take me all the way, but it didn't matter. *Maddox was giving me head in our locker room...* Between his deep groans and skillful tongue, getting sucked off was sexier than anything I could have imagined. And I was pretty sure my awestruck whimpers said it all.

I slapped one sweaty hand on the stall behind me, trying to keep myself upright as he completely wrecked me, ripping away my control and any remaining inhibitions. I pumped my hips and when he swallowed me again, deeper this time, my climax hit the breaking point.

"Oh God, Mad, I'm gonna come," I panted. "Pull off if you don't want my load."

Maddox didn't let up, his hand stroking faster, his mouth sucking harder. My balls drew up painfully tight, ripples of pleasure turning to shockwaves. I shoved my other hand in my mouth, biting down hard on my knuckles to keep from screaming out loud as I came in a heated rush.

We weren't new to sex anymore, but I still couldn't believe it could be this good. That Maddox wanted me this way. So intense, like nothing else mattered. I closed my eyes for a second, overcome. When I opened them again, oh yeah, it was real all right. Maddox leaned back, breathing hard, my cum dripping down his lips, his chin. I thought the thrill of winning a game or getting high was tough to beat, but nothing, nothing compared to the way he and I came together.

Then he grabbed my jersey from the bench, took a long inhale, and swiped it across his face. That move was just as hot as everything else we shared.

"Dirty is right," he whispered, his voice hoarse. "I came, hands-free, in my jock. And you, Kay, are the reason why."

More cum leaked out of my dick. I slid down until my ass hit the floor, too fucked out to move.

"Mad," I whispered as I stared at him. "I—"

My phone buzzed.

"Shit. That's Dane. Fuck, he's been waiting for me in the hallway all this time."

"Sounds like he's getting impatient. You better get going."

"I wonder if he heard us?"

"Doubtful," Maddox shrugged. "But still, that's kinda hot."

"Mad," I warned.

"At least you don't have swollen lips and beard burn." Maddox let out a dirty chuckle. "Well, not as much as me."

"Fuck."

"What? Dane already knows."

"Yeah, but he's not exactly rooting for us at this point."

"Not yet," Maddox smirked.

I leaned over and gave him a kiss. "I gotta hit the showers."

"I'd join you, but then we'll never leave," he replied.

"Come to my room tonight. We'll study, order pizza, then wreck my bed."

I wanted to be there right now.

"Can I stay?"

"Overnight?"

"You don't have a roommate. And yeah, I wanna stay. All night."

I was gonna run right back to my dorm and find that dildo I'd ordered. We'd waited long enough, and I was ready for *all* the fucking.

Maddox rubbed his jaw. "But what if *your* roommate notices and starts asking where you've been all night?"

I waved that off.

"Pfft. Please. He doesn't care. He's a total pothead and in his own world."

"A pothead, eh? I might need to meet this guy," Maddox teased. "You can stay. But don't hog the blankets."

"I'd never," I quipped and kissed him again.

"Stop flirting and get your ass moving. Before Dane walks in here."

"Be prepared," I added, standing up, suddenly light-headed. Between the blow job and that gruelling practice, my body was shot. "He's probably going to want to talk to you. I can't hide for shit."

"I'm ready for it."

I smiled at that, then reached into my stall for my phone and texted Dane a quick '*I'll be right out.*' Then I headed off to take the fastest scrub down in history. By the time I was leaving the showers, wrapped only in a towel, Maddox was on his way in. He passed me and yanked on the towel, exposing my ass.

"Get out of here before I change my mind," Maddox warned, eyeing me up with a heated intensity that had my semi turning hard again. "My room. Three hours."

I nodded and started walking away, calling out over my shoulder. "You order the pizza. I'll bring the dildo."

"Now that's the kind of studying I'm down for."

I quickly got dressed and headed out to find Dane standing in the hallway, arms crossed, expression flat.

"Uh, sorry about the delay," I announced, my face heating.

"Too busy sucking face with Maddox?"

There was no point in denying it. "We talked first."

"As long as you know what you're doing."

I nodded and kept walking. The rink was a ghost town. We passed Coach Banning's office and even that was empty.

Dane and I headed out of the sports facility and into the cold December air.

"Kay—" Dane started.

"It's all right, D. Trust me."

Did I trust myself?

Like Maddox, I didn't know anything about being a boyfriend. We were both going to stumble around in this relationship until we found out where the hell it was going.

"You better. If this gets out—"

"It won't."

Then I thought about what just happened. My first reaction was, *Jesus, I want more.* My second was, *if anyone caught us, we'd be done.*

"We talked it out. We're not gonna stop seeing each other, and only each other," I admitted. "He freaked out about the Christmas invite, but that's normal, right? This is all new to us."

Dane stopped walking. I turned to face him.

"What?" I asked.

"So, you guys are like, exclusive or something?"

"Yeah."

Dane shook his head. "That's, uh, wow. Fuck, I need a moment."

I chuckled. "No one's more shocked than me. Well, Maddox is."

"No shit." Dane smiled at me. "I thought he had ice water in his veins. But then I figure, if anyone's going to melt him, it'd be you."

"He's—" I paused, trying to find the words to explain what was happening. It took me a while. "I've never felt this way about anyone. Call it a crush, or obsession, or maybe even l—"

No way was I going to use the 'L-word.' I'd fallen for Maddox, but was it infatuation or so much more? I knew the answer. It looked like Dane knew it too, given the way he was staring at me. But saying it out loud was frightening as fuck.

My friend gave me a reassuring pat on the shoulder. "I know what you mean. First time for everything. It's pretty crazy, right?"

"Fuck yeah. It would be awesome if we could be open about it. Not hide."

"Are you really prepared for that? Me and Jackson have been talking about it for months. I'm ready, I know I am, but I freeze up when we're actually in public. I hate that I'm still scared, and I feel like shit for letting him down."

Then I thought about what it would be like to hold Maddox's hand while we walked around campus. To kiss him whenever and wherever. There'd be stares and comments for sure. Not everyone was accepting.

"You're not letting him down, you're coming out when you feel it's right," I reassured my friend. "And maybe I'm naïve. Telling my family I'm bi is one thing, but everyone else? That's a whole different thing."

"I've gotta say it," Dane added. "The one person you should tell is Coach."

"What? No. He'll kick me and Mad off the team for sure."

Dane shook his head. "I don't think so. He was cool when I told him I was gay."

"That's different. Jackson's not on our team."

"Even more reason why you should speak up. Think about it," Dane replied. "Better that Coach finds out from you than hearing a rumor or catching you in the act."

The high I was riding came crashing back down to earth. Dane had a point.

"I'll think about it," I muttered.

"And don't fuck around in the locker room," Dane quipped. "While it's hot as hell, you're more than likely going to be found out."

I couldn't help but smile. "Totally worth it."

CHAPTER 33

MADDOX

our hours had passed, and Kayden hadn't arrived. I picked up my phone and texted him.

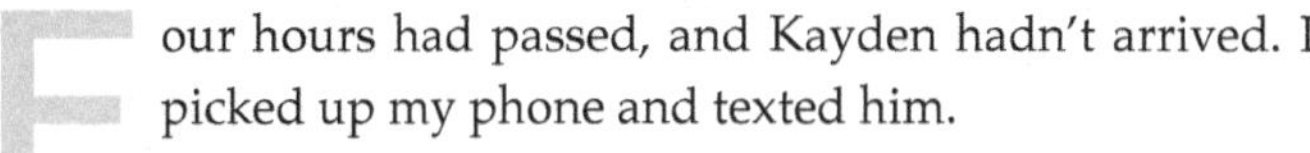

He'd be here. He said he would. He was all in.

Unless Dane said something to him? Convinced Kay that I wasn't worth the hassle, after all?

I'd ordered pizza, but it was now cold. I couldn't eat it, anyway. It wasn't like me to doubt myself. Not to this degree. And I hated feeling needy, like if I didn't see or hear from Kay in the next half hour, I was going to start pacing the floor. Too late…

My phone finally buzzed, and the relief was palpable. Until I glanced down and saw it was a message from Daniel.

Daniel: Your father's lawyer stopped by the house today. He said he tried to call you several times and since I'm your emergency contact…

I'd been ignoring any calls I didn't recognize. Four in the last two weeks alone.

Maddox: Shit, not this again. What does he want?

Daniel: They've finalized the paperwork

Maddox: I don't want anything of his. Nothing.

Daniel: You're the sole beneficiary

Maddox: It makes me sick to even think about it

Daniel: You can donate most of it, but you have to deal with it

Maddox: Most of it? All of it.

Daniel: You can do whatever you want with it. But you need to deal with the lawyer. Email him back if you don't want to talk on the phone... On a lighter note, how's school? hockey? I read about your latest win. You guys are on fire.

Maddox: It's really good. Things are better.

Daniel: And the teammate you were rooming with on the road, Kayden? How's that going?

If only Daniel knew.

Maddox: He and I are good

I paused, unsure if I should tell Daniel all of it. Fuck it.

Maddox: More than good

Daniel: You mean…

Maddox: I've learned a lot in the past few months. And I'm not talking about school. Turns out, I'm gay.

Daniel: So, you and Kayden are dating?

Maddox: Yeah. But we're keeping it a secret. And don't even start. Nothing you say is gonna change my mind.

Daniel: I know that. But be careful.

Maddox: Careful is for middle age

Daniel: Ouch. Well, you know where to find me if the shit hits the fan. Or the ice.

Maddox: Thanks

Daniel: Are you coming home for your next break? We always have a place for you.

Maddox: I'm not sure yet. But I'll let you know.

Daniel: Okay, take care. TTYL

I threw my phone aside, stretched out on my bed, and stared up at the ceiling.

Go upstairs and see if he's in his room.

I hated waiting around, so I got up and reached for my black hoodie when there was a knock at my door. When I wrenched it open, there was Kayden, backpack clutched tightly to his chest, looking fidgety as hell.

"You okay?" I asked, concerned.

"Yeah. Fine. Sure," he rambled. "Sorry, I'm late. Dane and I got to talking and then when I got back to my room, I was… busy."

I knew what that meant. Sexy images of Kayden playing with himself, pushing that dildo in his ass, made my cock fill.

"Are you going to stand out in the hallway all night or come in?" I teased.

Kayden swallowed hard and nodded, but he didn't move. The big guy was nervous. I shouldn't find it cute (God, I can't even believe I said that word…), but he was. I stepped aside, and he wandered into my room, setting his bag down and shoving his hands in his back pockets. I shut and locked the door.

"You really ordered pizza," he blurted out.

I chuckled at his surprised expression. "Yeah, of course. Because you're always hungry. You want a slice?"

He shook his head. "No. I'm too fucking nervous to eat."

I stalked up to him and slid my arms around his waist, pulling him in tight. Kayden was hard all over, but it wasn't just his muscle tone. He was rigid, tense. And that wouldn't do.

"Relax," I whispered as I reached up and gave him a reassuring kiss. "We don't have to have sex."

"But I—" Kayden paused and licked his lips. "I prepped for it."

"That's hot as fuck," I admitted. "But we're only going to do it if we're both ready."

"I am. I want it. No, that's not right. I fucking *need* it. But, also, yeah, anal is…a lot. And I'm pretty sure that dildo is no match for your cock."

More filthy images bombarded me, but I summoned my control. Soon enough.

"Don't feed my ego," I quipped and drew back. "Now sit, eat pizza, pop an edible—one—and chill."

"Uh, okay."

Kayden looked around my room like he was afraid to sit down.

"We'll save the fucking for another night," I reassured him. "Or day. I'm too tired."

I wasn't, but I didn't want my boyfriend to be any more freaked out than he was. Or I was. Not about the fucking, but the fact I used the word 'boyfriend.'

"You mean, not at all?"

Kayden nearly shouted the words, like I'd shocked him. I bit back a laugh. At least my comment got him out of his head.

Wandering over to my desk, I grabbed the pizza box and placed it on my bed. Then I pulled out my baggie of edibles, grabbed two, and wandered over to offer Kayden one. He popped it in his mouth, and I did the same.

"Coke or water?" I offered. "That's all I've got. Well, tequila, but I know it's not your favorite."

"Coke."

He sat on the bed, worrying his bottom lip.

"Baby, you need to stop thinking about it, okay?"

We stared at each other in shock.

"Wait, what did you call me?" he asked.

"Uh." Shit, now I was the one who was nervous. "Just eat the damn pizza already."

Kayden slid his hand around my waist.

"Nope." I tried to pull back. "Not happening."

"My angry bee is back," he quipped. "So sexy. Come here."

Who was I kidding? I slid over his lap and attacked his mouth, kissing away his teasing words and any remaining tension. When I slid my tongue over his, there was only one thing I was hungry for.

And Kayden was it.

Kayden

Maddox didn't do anything by half measure. That

included kissing. Deep, drugging kisses that had me falling back on his bed, greedy for more. And with every brush of his lips and tongue, his hands, fuck, his whole body rubbing against mine, my nerves melted away. It was the same on the ice. Once the game was in motion, I was all in.

I'd spent two hours in the bathroom getting ready for tonight. Shaving took me ten minutes. Getting my ass prepped, though, took an hour and fifty. Most of it was spent lubing up, and staring at the massive fake cock I'd purchased. Watching porn on my phone while playing with my ass did the trick. I stood with one foot on the toilet, dick in hand, dildo in the other. And when I finally pushed the rubber cock into my hole, I cried out so loudly I'm sure everyone in the dorm heard me.

It was painful at first, then painfully addictive. The fullness in my ass sparked nerves I never knew existed. I could only imagine what it would be like when Maddox pushed his hot, hard cock in there. Would we use a condom? Neither of us had been with anyone, and I really wanted to feel his bare dick in my ass. And his cum.

Which brought me back to what we were doing now…

Maddox moaned loudly, and I swallowed the sound, groaning in response. I ate at his mouth, nipping his lower lip and soothing it with my tongue.

He moaned loudly and leaned back, shoving the pizza box off the bed to make room, then tugged on my shirt.

"Take it off, Kay," he demanded.

I followed him, sitting up, reaching for my shirt, and yanking it off as fast as I could. Then my jeans and my briefs, until I was naked, thrumming with so much anticipation I was shaking hard. Maddox did the same, stripping off his jeans and taking his cock in hand, giving it firm, fast strokes. I swallowed hard at the sight of him.

"You're so fucking gorgeous," I whispered as I lay down

on the bed. I stroked my cock frantically, my hand moving in tandem with his. "Want you so bad."

"Kay," Maddox moaned and slid back over me.

I cupped his face and brought him in for another breath-stealing kiss, unable to get enough. His hard dick rubbed against mine, and I could come, just like this. Maddox, however, had a different plan. He turned his head and kissed a path down my jaw, my neck, and then lower, over my collarbone, and my nipples.

"Fuck yes," I growled, so turned on I was shivering. "Don't stop."

He licked and sucked on my skin, then gently bit down on the hardened nub of my nipple. The pleasure was so intense that I grasped his hair and held him tightly to my chest. But not for long. Maddox continued to torment me with those wicked lips of his as he made his way down my abs, lower. When his hot breath brushed my throbbing cock, I jerked hard, trying to keep from coming too soon.

"Hold on to your knees, baby."

I shuddered when he called me that. Fuck, I was trembling all over. Pulling my knees back, I watched as he lowered his head. Instead of taking my cock in his mouth, he moved lower, until his tongue teased my crease.

"Oh fuck, yes, do it. Please. Please."

I wanted his tongue in my ass so badly.

"Love to hear you beg for it," Maddox groaned.

He glanced up at me, his blue eyes dark, feverish.

"Now I want to hear you scream for it."

Maddox lowered his head and teased the rim of my hole with his wicked tongue, and fuck yes, I gave in to his demand.

He slid his tongue over my taint and balls, then tormented my hole again. Shoving his face in my ass, his scruff rubbed against my skin, the pleasure intensifying. When he finally pushed the tip of his tongue inside me, my hips came off the bed, and I struggled to hold on to my legs. Maddox didn't let up, licking and eating my ass so good I couldn't breathe, let alone think.

"Mad…Oh God, don't stop."

But after one last, teasing lick, Maddox did just that, leaning back and sitting up. He was panting hard, licking his lips, and fuck, he was tasting me. It was dirty and so sexy to watch. More pre-cum leaked out of my dick, and I finally gave it attention. I let go of one of my knees, spat in my hand, and jacked off.

"Get the lube," I moaned as I stroked off. "Now."

Maddox leaned over and reached under the pillow beside me, pulling out a tube of lube.

He poured a generous amount into his palm, warmed up his hands, and pushed mine away. Taking over, he stroked me off as I writhed and pleaded for more.

And when his other slick hand teased the rim of my asshole, I was more than ready for it.

"Yes," I whispered. "Do it."

"Kay."

Maddox paused and when I glanced up, a dark pink flush stained his cheekbones.

"Baby, are you sure?" he asked me.

This time, it was my turn to snark. "Hurry up already, before I do it myself. Or maybe you'd like that? You wanna watch me?"

Maddox let out a dirty chuckle. "Later. First, I want inside your ass."

"That makes two of us."

He pushed one lubed finger in my hole, and thank fuck I'd prepped. There was pain mixed with pleasure, and I wanted more of it. All of it.

"It's good," I panted. "More."

Maddox slid another finger in and shit, that was a lot. My hard-on flagged to a semi. Until Maddox drilled deeper.

There was no mistaking the exact moment when he hit my prostate. The pleasure was so intense, I could only cry out and beg for more.

"Add another finger," I encouraged. "Almost there."

When he pushed a third finger inside me, I couldn't speak at all. Until he started to fuck me like that, and I pumped my hips, reaching for more.

"Good. I'm good," I panted. "Need you. Get your cock inside me."

"Condom?" Maddox asked.

I shook my head. "There's been no one else. And I don't want that. Do you?"

Maddox didn't reply. Instead, he poured more lube on his hands and slicked up his dick. Oh shit, this was really happening. My boyfriend was going to fuck me, bare, and come in my ass. His hands shook as he kneeled between my legs, and strands of his hair fell into his eyes. When he notched the head of his cock to my hole, I tried not to tense up. Tried to remember every piece of advice I'd googled about bottoming and then some.

But when Maddox pushed inside of me, slow but steady, all the questions and worries I had were silenced. The burn in my ass intensified, and I let out a desperate moan.

I was right. That dildo had nothing on the real thing.

CHAPTER 34

MADDOX

Ask me to describe myself and I'd give you five words. More like three.

Ask me to describe the reality of my dick in Kayden's ass and I could write a whole fucking essay about it. Both of us were slick with sweat, lube, and pre-cum. My twin bed barely fit the both of us, but it didn't matter. Nothing was better than being naked with Kayden. And watching us come together, me inside him, nothing between us, it completely blew my mind.

And I was about to blow my load in no short order.

When I was finally all the way inside him, his ass strangling my dick, I paused for a second, trying to calm down so I wouldn't come too soon. He stared up at me, trusting, and it made the shiver that ran through my body turn to shakes. Logically, I was prepared for the mechanics of sex. It was everything else that happened when I touched Kayden that was scary as fuck. The tightness in my chest, the drop of my stomach. And the knowledge that I was more concerned about his pleasure than mine. I wanted to give it all to him.

Me, the loner brat, putting someone else first? Total mindfuck.

I pushed my dick all the way in, and hell, he was so slick and tight; it was unreal. My eyes nearly rolled back in my head. I panted hard, rocking my hips gently at first. I set my forearms on the bed and leaned down until we were eye to eye. His chest hair teased my slick skin.

"You good?" I whispered.

Kayden quickly nodded. I couldn't resist his lips, mauling him in a possessive way that said everything I couldn't. Given my tongue was just in his ass, I thought maybe he'd pull away. But I should've known better. Kayden was as hungry for me as I was for him, kissing me back, sucking on my tongue. I thrust again, harder this time, and his fingers dug into my ass cheeks, pulling me in tighter.

"Fuck me," he moaned against my lips. "I'm ready."

I didn't need to be told twice.

I gave him one more kiss, then reluctantly pulled away from his tempting lips. Leaning back, I spread my knees, gripped his meaty thighs, ready to pound that beautiful hockey ass of his.

When I punched my hips forward, Kayden cried out my name. I did it again, my hips finding a steady rhythm, fucking into him with short, tight strokes. My brain shut down and my body took over. I thrust harder, faster, rutting in and out of him, as the bed creaked, and our grunts and moans grew louder.

"Harder," Kayden whimpered. "So close."

"Fuck, Kay."

Kayden tugged on his cock, his tense forearm working furiously. I held on tighter, fucking him faster, my climax building with every thrust. I needed more. I needed Kay to come.

"So good," I moaned. "Being inside you is… fuck Kay, I can't even…I can't hold on."

"Don't. Let go. I wanna feel it," he keened. "Need your cum."

My balls drew up tight, my climax tipping over the edge.

"Yes!" I growled as my orgasm unleashed, ripples of pleasure coursing through my body, flooding every part of me. It was so intense that my legs went numb, and breathing was impossible.

My body jerked hard as I unloaded my cum in his ass. And Kayden was right there with me, shouting my name, his hole squeezing my cock. Our eyes locked as he came, and I couldn't look away.

Until I felt his hot cum on my abs. Seeing and smelling his cum gave me a visceral satisfaction. Kayden was mine. I made him come.

"Wow," Kayden panted as we stared at each other, hot, sweaty, and completely fucked out. "I mean…wow…that's all I can say."

"Fucking right," I nodded, breathless. "I…I think I'm gonna pass out now. Wake me up in twelve hours."

I collapsed on his chest. Kayden slid his hands around my waist and squeezed me tightly. And, yeah, I didn't mind that at all. His hugs, or the fact that I was covered in his cum.

"We're really good at that," Kayden declared.

I buried my face in his throat and tried to bury my sudden laughter. But I couldn't. I hardly recognized the sound coming out of my chest, but damn, it felt good.

"You know what Coach says—practice hard, play harder," I teased, kissing Kayden's neck.

"I'm ready for that if you are. All the practice. All the playtime."

"No argument here."

I really didn't want to move, but I had to. Before we fell asleep glued to each other. Reluctantly, I peeled myself away from his body. He winced when I pulled out, and I startled, watching my cum drip out of his hole. I didn't know that anything could be that hot, but seeing the proof that I'd been inside Kayden turned me on like nothing else. Without thinking, I reached for him, rubbing his hole.

"You okay?"

"Oh yeah. Don't stop." Kayden closed his eyes and another husky moan rumbled out of his chest.

"Shhh," I whispered, suddenly aware that there were other people in this dorm.

Kayden opened his eyes, and the cheeky smile on his face had my heart beating double time. "*Now* you're telling me to be quiet?"

I rolled my eyes. "Yes."

"Do you know how many times I've been kept awake by other students and their loud fucking? Too many times," Kayden scoffed. "No one pays attention to the moans."

"Maybe you're right."

"Of course I am."

"And if they see you leaving here tomorrow?" I asked.

"We'll tell them we had a hot threesome."

My smile faded. "No fucking way."

"No sharing?" Kayden quipped.

"Nope. You're mine," I replied and punctuated my statement with a hard kiss. "Only mine. And that's it."

"Same goes," Kayden smirked and kissed me back. "But if anyone asks, that can be our story. Plenty of straight guys do it."

I shrugged. "I guess. But I'm not worried. I don't talk to anyone on this floor."

"Shocking."

I reached down and pinched his ass. "I talk to the guys on the team. And Jackson."

"I know. What's up with that?"

"You. It's all your fault."

I kissed him again, longer this time. Each kiss more addictive than the last.

"Shower, pizza, and sleep?" I suggested.

Kayden grinned. "Yes to all of that."

I rolled off him but I moved too fast, and nearly toppled when I made to stand up.

"You alright?" he asked, reaching out to steady me.

"I'm the one who should be asking you. Are you sore?"

"Not that bad, but ask me again tomorrow," Kayden replied as he stood up, pulling me into his larger body. "Thank fuck I used that dildo."

Another smile let loose. At this rate, I wouldn't recognize my face.

"Stop it," I replied, squeezing his waist.

"What?"

"You know what," I leaned up and nipped his jaw. "Teasing me. Now go get your incredible ass in my shower."

"Only if you're coming with me."

"It's a tight fit," I replied, and glanced up at him. The glint in his golden eyes had me shaking my head. "Don't even."

"But there are so many jokes, Mad."

"Come on. We need to eat and go to sleep so we can save some of our energy for the next game."

Kayden nodded, taking my hand and tugging me into the bathroom. I wasn't lying. It was a really tight fit, especially given Kayden's size, but we made it work. Another make-out session led to mutual hand jobs. And another orgasm later, we crashed.

Totally depleted, we flopped down on my bed, ate the entire cold pizza, and passed out.

It was the best sleep I'd had in seven years.

Kayden

Taking a dick up the ass is a lot harder than it looks on screen. And if you're not careful, porn can set you up for unrealistic sexpectations. Even with the prep of that dildo, I woke up the next morning with a sore freaking ass. Thank

God we weren't playing today because I'd be limping on *and* off the ice. But the prep was worth it. And the actual fucking? It was more than I could've imagined. Intense, sexy, incredible. And I knew it had everything to do with Maddox.

I couldn't have given myself like that to just any guy. Not my first time. Maybe not any time. Did that mean I was demi too? Probably. No shade to anyone, do what feels right for you. For me, it took trust. Trust, and a shitload of lube. I was so gone for Maddox and I knew that my emotions played into it. Even though I was scared of the potential pain, and worried I might not enjoy anal at all, I knew Maddox would never hurt me.

I suspected Maddox was the same. Given how prickly he usually was and how he didn't warm to anyone easily. Or allow anyone to touch him at all, never mind like this.

Speaking of touching, I ran my hand over his right shoulder, over the detailed tattoos that I was fascinated with. The skull eating a nasty-looking snake. It was very different from the tattoos on his left arm; a large fish, surrounded by a variety of sea creatures. Both tattoos were beautiful in their own way, but I favoured the fish. Then I remembered he didn't want to be touched there. I pulled my hand back, but it was too late.

"Vigilance."

I stopped moving at Maddox's sleep-roughened voice.

"The snake. It's the very definition of my father. He was a narcissist and an abuser. And the skull represents me. Because I'm not afraid of him anymore, but I still need a reminder to protect myself. Always."

I notched my face to his neck and kissed him gently. Maddox's body tensed and then he relaxed into me.

"Jesus, Mad, I'm so sorry," I whispered.

"He died two years ago in a car accident. He was doing 140 on a highway and lost control of the car. Kind of fitting since he was always losing control," Maddox sighed. "My father, Corey Grange, was from Toronto; that's where my parents met. He was a professional hockey player in Europe at the time and would come home for the summers. They divorced when I was four. Anyway, after that, Mom and I moved to New Brunswick. I only saw my father once or twice a year. He was a stranger to me. If I was lucky, I got a card on my birthday and a visit at Christmas. That was the extent of our relationship. But it didn't really bother me. I had my mom and we had each other. She was…everything."

Maddox paused and reached over his shoulder, placing his hand on mine.

"Genevieve Rocher was a force to be reckoned with. Strong. Bold. Full of life. The kind of person who walks into a room and everyone gravitates towards, you know? That's why she didn't get along with my dad. He couldn't control her," Maddox murmured. "She was an environmental scientist, and that's where my love for all things ocean comes from. The tattoos on my left arm are all in memory of her."

They were beautiful. *Strong. Bold. Full of life.*

"When I was eight, she started getting sick. She lost her appetite, she had trouble sleeping, and her blood pressure skyrocketed. She went to the doctor and after many rounds of tests, she was diagnosed with kidney disease. There were medications and dialysis, but things got progressively worse. She was waiting for a transplant for years," Maddox paused, his fingers gripping mine harder. "When I was just shy of my thirteenth birthday, she developed an infection. Which led to sepsis. And then, just like that, she was gone."

I hugged Maddox as tight as I could, wishing I could take away his heartbreak.

"I thought losing her was hell, but things got worse. By this time, my father was retired from playing and he'd moved back to Toronto to start up a contracting business. The week my mom died, he came to get me. He threw out her stuff, packed up all of mine, and moved me in with him. I was livid that he'd wiped out every trace of her, and that he'd taken me away from the only home I'd ever known. And I was still in shock, angry, hurt. Most of all, I was scared. I had no other family, and the only one I had left was a father I didn't even know."

It was the most he'd ever talked to me. The words poured out of him, the pain in his voice unmistakable.

"Mom always taught me to stand up for myself. I was a quiet kid, but when I made my mind up about something, that was it. My father, on the other hand, hated that I'd talk back to him. That I dared to question his authority. His way was the only way. I found that out not long after I moved in. He had all these rules about everything; what I should be studying, and eating, and listening to. Whenever I'd fuck up, he'd punish me. The first time I pushed back, he slapped me so fast, so hard, I almost didn't believe it happened. Then, the slaps became backhands, and punches. Pretty soon, it was happening more often than I want to remember."

Maddox paused, his body quaking in my arms.

"He said he was doing it to prepare me for the real world. To toughen me up."

"Fuck, Mad."

"I didn't have anywhere else to go, so, I kept my secret for years. Until one night, just after I turned sixteen. After he… beat me, he made a disgusting joke about my mom's death. It tipped me right over the fucking edge. The next day, I told Daniel what was happening. He suspected for a while that something was wrong. A few of the players on my team had noticed the bruises. But whenever he asked me, I played it off with an excuse; I hurt myself skateboarding or stuff like that."

Maddox stopped talking. When he glanced over his shoulder, the pain in his eyes hit me right in the gut.

"And then my life imploded again when I came forward against my father. I had to talk to social workers, the police, therapists. My dad was charged with assault but never tried.

Court backlog resulted in so many delays that the charges were eventually stayed. The only thing I had was a restraining order. And Daniel." Maddox shuddered and then rolled over, facing me. "I got out, I got help, and I got better. Or, as good as I'm gonna get. But I'll never be the person I was before him. My defense is up and it's there to stay. I'm telling you this because, I never thought you and I would end up here. And I want you to know why I am the way I am. And while this is great now, I can't promise things. Or, that I won't push you away again. I wasn't lying when I said I don't know how to do this."

I reached for him, and he nestled between my legs, staring down at me.

"You don't need to *do* anything."

"What?"

I looked up at him and pushed a lock of stray hair behind his ear. "Be yourself. We're figuring this out, so there's no pressure. And I like you exactly the way you are. In fact, I'd say that given where we are now, and how we ended up here, I like your scowl as much as your smile."

Maddox shook his head. "I don't smile."

"Now you do."

He rolled his eyes. "Feeling cocky this morning, eh?"

"Oh yeah."

"I didn't—" Maddox paused. "I didn't hurt you, did I?"

"No. I mean, my ass is kinda sore, but it's the good kind. And it was worth it, because you and me? It's freaking amazing."

Maddox leaned down and kissed me. But it was barely a brush of his lips, and then he was pulling back. I cupped his face, urging him to stay close.

"Kiss me like you mean it," I whispered. "Boyfriend."

Maddox did just that.

CHAPTER 35

KAYDEN

Maddox and I made out slowly, kissing for ages. Not caring about morning breath, our lips swollen, our lungs in desperate need of air. There was no class to get to, no game to prepare for, no student event to sit in on. And hey, Coach wanted everyone on the team to get in a light workout. We figured this would count.

I thought maybe Maddox would want to be alone after all that talk about his piece of shit father. But he held on to me tightly, and didn't let go.

My phone chimed, and Maddox and I reluctantly separated. I reached down and grabbed my bag, searching for my phone. When I saw the reminders piling up, I sighed.

"Shit. I forgot my meds last night."

I yanked out my pill case.

"I'll get you a glass of water," Maddox offered and slid out of bed.

I watched him strut to the bathroom and yes, he was strutting, whether or not he was aware of it. Between his taut body, his tats, and that high, sweet ass of his, I was all but drooling.

By the time I plucked my pills out, Maddox had returned holding two glasses of water.

Screwing around in the dark was one thing. But seeing his body now had my heart hammering against my ribcage.

He passed me a glass, and I popped my meds, then gratefully gulped down the water. I watched as Maddox did the same, mesmerized by the way his Adam's apple bobbed up and down. It brought me back to the locker room and that wicked blow job. Then I noticed he'd put his silver earring back in. Just when I thought he couldn't get any hotter.

"You're staring," he snarked.

"You're gorgeous."

He looked down, pieces of his dark hair sliding over his eyes.

"Stop."

"It's the truth."

"Kay," he growled.

"Yes, baby?"

Maddox's head shot up, and I noticed the goosebumps all over his skin.

"Wanna go workout?" he asked.

That was… not what I was expecting him to say.

"Food first."

"Naturally. But not the caf." Maddox got up. "Their eggs are crap."

"The All-Day Breakfast Diner. Best omelets around," I paused. "Do you want me to text Dane and Jackson and see if they want to join us? Maybe Jace too?"

Maddox nodded, finished his water, then took my empty glass. I quickly group texted the guys, then headed for the bathroom. After washing up, we got dressed and headed into town. It was snowing hard, and the air had a bite to it. I pulled my beanie down to cover my ears and glanced at Maddox, who didn't seem as bothered by the cold as me. He didn't wear a hat, but he'd layered a puffer coat over his leather jacket. Only Maddox could make wearing two jackets look cool.

"Aren't you freezing?" I asked him. "I'm so fucking cold."

"Are you forgetting where I come from?" he chuckled. "And you've got a parka, gloves, and a hat on. What else do you need?"

"Shared body warmth." I waggled my eyebrows.

"You're such a horndog, Kay."

"You say that like it's a bad thing."

"Not while we're out in public. If anyone overhears—"

"They won't," I assured him. "And remember our story. You, me, and a hot girl named Summer."

"Summer? Where did that come from?"

"Don't know," I replied. "Oh, wait. It's a girl from back home. I kind of had a thing for her my last year of high school. Summer Smith. Big blue eyes, long dark hair. She's so cute. And she works part time at the ice cream café in town. Her mom owns the shop. I used to stop in every weekend. I probably gained ten pounds alone that year."

Maddox stopped walking, and I stopped rambling.

"I don't want to hear any more, Kay."

Jealous Mad was so fucking hot.

"I said she's cute. That's all," I replied, chuckling. "Are you sure you're gonna be able to control this possessive side in public? What if a hot girl—or guy—starts flirting with me?"

"Don't even."

I laughed harder.

"Summer," Maddox grumbled and started walking again. "I don't like it."

"Hey, Maddox isn't exactly a common name either," I snarked back.

I was getting better at it, thanks to my favorite tutor.

"I wasn't talking about her name," he replied with a sigh. "Did you see her when you went back home for Christmas?"

"Um, I mean, I stopped in at the café on Saturday with my brothers and sister. And she was working. But I barely noticed her."

"But she's the one you thought of for this fake threesome we've supposedly had?" Maddox bit out.

"Okay, pick another name."

"Why? When you've already set your sights on *Summer*," Maddox snapped.

"Aw, is this our first fight?" I quipped.

Maddox bit his lower lip and stared up at me.

"Did you take any edibles this morning?" he asked.

"Nope, just my regular meds."

"Just checking."

I grinned at him, and he rolled his eyes. He was so adorably jealous that I wanted to pull him into my arms and kiss him, but yeah, now was not the time.

When we finally strolled up to the All-Day Breakfast, Jace, Dane, and Jackson were already there, sitting at a booth at the back. Jace sat across from Dane and Jackson, but when he spotted us, he slipped out of the bench and moved beside them. I slid into Jace's empty spot, Maddox following. It was snug fit, but I had no complaints.

"What did you guys get up to last night? Any good parties?" I asked.

"Nope," Jace replied. "I was wiped after practice. Ate dinner and fell asleep watching a movie on my laptop."

"Me and Jackson were the same," Dane replied. "What about you two?"

Thank fuck my cheeks were already reddened from the cold.

"Same."

"Except Kay here ate most of my dinner," Maddox added.

"You should've ordered a bigger pizza."

"Is there a bigger one than extra-large?" he quipped.

"Party size, duh." I smiled at him.

When I turned to face my friends, the guys were staring, first at me, then at Maddox. "Yes?"

"Nothing," Dane replied quickly. "You both seem like you're in really good moods. And for Maddox, that's saying a lot."

Maddox offered his favorite finger in response and Dane laughed it off.

"Carbs, sleep, and a day off," I replied. "It's the trifecta of a perfect day."

Sex was in there too. Holy shit, was it ever. I replayed the night in my head, one dirty image after another, and I started to sweat. Dane smirked at me and this time it was my turn to roll my eyes. Until I turned to Maddox. The way he was looking at me, like I was on the menu instead of breakfast, made my heart take off like a hungry player after the puck.

"It's freezing outside, but it's hot as hell in here," Jackson announced.

"I second that," Jace quipped.

"Where's Maddie?" I asked, changing the subject, searching for our usual waitress. "Have you guys ordered yet?"

"Nope," Dane replied. "But I think we've all worked up an appetite."

I snorted at that. Me and Maddox sure as hell did. There was silence around the table. I coughed into my fist, trying to clear my throat.

"Um, so, what are you guys up to after this?" I asked.

Before my friends could reply, Maddie appeared to take our orders. OJ all around, four-egg omelets, and hash browns for everyone but Jace, who chose scrambled egg whites and toast. Thankfully, I didn't have to get my phone out to read the menu here. I knew everything by heart.

"Gym, then studying. You?" Jace asked.

"Same."

"So, you gonna tell us what's really going on here?" Jace

pointed between me and Maddox. "Not that you need to say anything, but what the fuck?"

"Nothing's going on," Maddox whispered. "Nothing that concerns anyone but me and Kay."

"Look," Jace leaned forward. "I don't care who you fuck around with, okay? I'm bi, so I'm cool. But what about the team finding out?"

"Why should they care?" I asked.

"What if you two have a fight and the tension bleeds into the game? What then?" he asked.

"It's not gonna happen," I argued.

"Everyone says that, and then—*bam*—it happens," Jace countered. "Trust me. You think you know someone because you're fucking them and then they turn around and stab you in the back."

What? I wanted to ask Jace about his comment, since it sounded like he'd had a really bad personal experience. Unfortunately, Maddie arrived at that exact moment to deliver our breakfast. She quickly dropped off the plates and left us alone again.

"That's not going to happen. And worrying that maybe, sometime down the line, there might be a problem?" I scoffed. "Come on."

"At least tell Coach. Better you do it than he finds out from someone else," Jace replied.

"I've already suggested that," Dane added.

I was getting anxious, a knot forming where my stomach usually was. Maddox reached underneath the table and squeezed my thigh. Turning to him, I was about to ask the question when I already recognized his answer.

"We should tell him," Maddox announced. "Let's do it."

"Are you serious?"

"Absolutely."

"What if he suspends us? Or worse?" I asked.

"For fucking? There's nothing in the rule book that says

what we're doing is wrong. We're not violating any code of conduct," Maddox turned to Dane. "That I know of."

Dane shrugged.

"And even if there *is* a rule, it's too late. We've already broken it," Maddox added. "And you know how I feel about other people's rules."

"Just Coach?" I asked.

Maddox nodded.

I paused, thinking about it. Could I be as fearless as Mad? I hesitated. Not because I was afraid of Coach's backlash, but because I wanted to protect Maddox. Thinking about everything he'd told me this morning, everything he'd been through with his dad, it made me want to shield him from all the bad stuff. Would Coach go ballistic? I had no way of knowing. Then again, maybe this was the best plan. Coach hadn't freaked out on Dane.

I glanced at Maddox again, and I knew what I wanted to do.

"Okay, I'm in. We'll do it tomorrow," I replied. "After we crush Langston."

Maddox nodded. "Now that that's sorted, can we eat our freaking breakfast? After all, we've got a game to prepare for."

Damn right, we did.

CHAPTER 36

MADDOX

After scarfing down breakfast and then taking a walk around town, the five of us headed off to the gym to burn off our calories. And our tension. There was a shitload of that. Most of it went unsaid. What else was there to talk about?

I honestly had no idea how Coach Banning was gonna react to the news that me and Kayden were fucking. Okay, dating. I reminded myself not to swear in front of Coach, but it wouldn't be easy. And if Banning so much as suggested he'd pull Kayden off the team, or punish him in any way for what was going on between us, I would protest, and protest hard.

We couldn't have been the first teammates to fuck around. No way.

Still, it's not like we were both out. Or that we were gonna shove our relationship in anyone's face. It was all under control. Nothing was going to change. We'd still play our asses off, we'd still win games, we'd still be ourselves.

I sounded confident, but who the fuck knew?

Dane and Jackson left the gym first, then Jace. Me and Kayden stayed behind and worked on the weight machines.

The only problem was, I was getting turned on watching him. And I wasn't the only one who was staring. I saw plenty of students, girls and guys, checking Kayden out. No wonder. He was built like a Viking—tall, ripped, hot as fuck. And who could miss that bouncy ass? Odd thing was, Kayden didn't even notice the attention, or if he did, he didn't care. But I did. I wanted to tell all of them to get lost. Stop staring at what's mine.

Kayden was on his back, doing bench presses, while I stood behind him, spotting. And taking in the view, of course. He made lifting over a hundred pounds look easy. When he finally put the weighted bar down, he stared up at me and licked his lips. If I wasn't already sweating through my tank top, I would be now. Then I imagined straddling his face while he ate my ass and suddenly it was time to leave.

"Shower, dorm," I grunted and stalked off to the locker room.

I needed a cold fucking shower.

Stripping down, I did just that. I never thought twice about getting naked in a change room and showering with other guys, but now? If Kayden so much as stepped near me, I wouldn't have to come out. My hard dick would do it for me.

I washed up as fast as I could and dried off in record time. Kayden sauntered into the change room when I was coming out of the showers. I did my best *not* to eye him up. Okay, I stared at his ass while he walked away, but I made sure to do it while no one was looking.

I got dressed, reached for my phone, and texted him.

> Maddox: Take a right when you leave the gym. I'll be waiting around the corner.

Then I grabbed my bag and headed for the door. The

windchill was biting today, so I walked around to the side of the building.

Leaning against the brick wall, the air was so cold my breath looked like plumes of smoke. Speaking of which... despite the carbs and the workout, my nerves were sparking. I pulled out my cigs and lit one up, inhaling deep, letting the warmth seep into my lungs.

I hadn't had the urge to smoke lately, but this morning was a lot for me to handle. Not just waking up in bed with Kayden, but all that stuff about my father and my mom. Stuff that I always buried deep. I didn't like to think about it, talk about it, or, worst of all, feel it. Then there was the fact that Kayden and I had to tell Coach about our relationship.

Not that we'd done anything wrong. But given our team-mates' reactions at breakfast, it was starting to feel that way.

I thought about where I wanted to be in a few years. Playing for a professional hockey team, traveling North America, maybe the world. Hockey had been my only goal, the one glimmer of hope that I clung to when I was at my lowest. Me and Kayden wouldn't change that, would it? I shook my head. I was getting way ahead of myself.

Who knows what next week would bring, never mind next year? And yet, when I pictured the future, I saw him there. I couldn't explain it. It wasn't logical, but he was there.

"Not this again. I thought you were done with the smoking."

Kayden sauntered up to me, his beanie pushing his hair into his eyes, a teasing grin on his face. The coldness that lived inside of me thawed. Just a little.

"I didn't promise anything," I replied with a smirk.

"But you could."

"Come here," I motioned to him, then dropped the butt on the ground.

Kayden stepped up to me, leaning in, blanketing me with

his body. His size alone could have triggered me, but it didn't. Just like I knew that something was off the minute my father took over my life, I knew that Kayden would never hurt me. My instincts were never wrong.

"Thanks for teasing me back there," I whispered. "I was trying *not* to get a boner in the gym."

"Me teasing? You were the one walking around in those tight shorts and tank top. Everyone was staring."

I shook my head. "You've got that the wrong way around."

"No way," he countered. So humble, my Kay. "Is that why you took off so quickly? Did I make you hard?"

I glanced around. No one was walking by on the street. Or if they were, they had their hoods up and were walking fast, given the weather.

Reaching up, I kissed him, but I made it quick.

"I was picturing you on that bench, naked," I confessed, watching his eyes darken. "Me straddling your face while you ate my ass."

"Fuck, Mad."

We lunged for each other, slamming our mouths together, the kiss so fierce and hot that I didn't feel the bite of winter air around me anymore. But I sure as hell loved the sting when Kayden gently bit my lower lip, then sucked on it. Anytime Kayden touched me, my inhibitions melted away. I couldn't think. The only thing that mattered was getting closer, kissing him deeper. More, more, more.

"Kayden? Maddox?"

We both froze at the sound of our names. When I turned around, I spotted Axel standing at the far end of the alley, duffel bag in hand, staring at us.

"Holy shit," he whispered.

Goddamn it.

Kayden stumbled back from me so fast he nearly fell on

the icy ground. I steadied him as best I could, but my stomach clenched tight when I saw the panic on his face.

"What the hell are you doing here?" I snapped.

He held up his bag. "Going to the gym like Coach asked, where else? What the fuck's going on here? Are you guys together?"

"Get lost, Lund," I bit out.

"Now it all makes sense. Sharing a room on the road, and all the fuss about those stupid bracelets," Axel sneered. "Does Coach know?"

I moved to stand in front of Kayden. My boyfriend was eerily silent.

"I said, get lost. And mind your own damn business."

"I'm making it mine. Banning doesn't know, does he?" Axel scoffed as he walked closer. "You don't have to answer. I can tell by Kayden's face. He's shit at playing it cool. Well, that's about to change."

"Don't." I stalked up to him. "We're going to tell him. Until then, keep your mouth shut."

Axel shook his head. "This isn't good for the team. You know it, and I know it. It's intense enough playing at this level. We don't need personal shit fucking things up."

"Nothing is getting fucked up," I insisted.

Axel stepped closer and pointed at me. "You can't guarantee that. And what happens when the rest of the team finds out about you two? And the teams we play against? You think about the scrutiny you're going to face when they find out you're queer? It's going to be a shitshow. Guaranteed. How's that going to affect our game?"

I wasn't in total denial. Axel wasn't totally wrong.

"It won't be a problem," Kayden finally replied. "It happened and now it's done. Over."

I was frozen again and no, I wasn't talking about the temperature.

"Kay."

"Go, Axel. Alright? Leave. Please," Kayden whispered.

Axel glanced at Kayden and then back at me again. "Come clean to Coach before I do it for you."

With that final warning, he turned and stalked off. Leaving me and Kay standing there, staring at each other, snowflakes kissing our faces.

"It's done?" I spat out.

"I had to tell him something to get him to back off," Kayden bit out. "I don't trust him. He's going to tell everyone."

I ran a frozen hand through my hair and bit back a scream. Nothing was ever fucking simple.

"What do you want to do?" Kayden asked me.

"We tell Coach. We tell the rest of the team. Then we deal with the consequences."

"And if the team doesn't accept it?"

I held my breath. "I don't know."

"That's a shit answer, Mad."

"What do you want me to say? I'm not psychic, Kay."

Maybe this was crazy. What was I thinking? I'd finally eked out a bit of happiness, then bam, it was ripped away from me. Serves me right for letting my guard down, for thinking with my dick, and not my head. Not just my dick. My heart was involved in this madness, too. Even worse.

"Let's go," Kayden muttered, and motioned to the street.

We walked in silence, the crunch of the snow under our boots. The closer we got to the rink, the more I felt like puking. When we finally arrived, and knocked on Coach Banning's door, I thought I was going to faint.

"Enter!"

Kayden opened the door, and we stepped inside.

"What's up?" Coach asked as we closed the door and sat down.

"We have something important to tell you," I muttered and clenched my hands together so tight I was cutting off my circulation.

"If it's about tomorrow's game—"

"No," Kaden interrupted. "It's personal."

Coach leaned back in his chair and stared at Kayden and then me. Banning could read a play and the players. I was sure we didn't need to say anything else. He knew. He fucking knew. Then it dawned on me that our coach wasn't much older than us. Maybe by a decade? Thirty, thirty-one? But I'm sure he was a hell of a lot wiser.

"Kayden and I are—" I stared at Banning. Would it be rude to say, *'we're fucking?'* Definitely. "You know, involved."

Coach ran both hands through his hair and cupped the back of his head. He smashed his lips together and dropped his head back, staring at the ceiling.

I glanced over at Kayden. He looked as terrified as I felt.

"Are you freaking kidding me?" Banning muttered and then placed both hands on his desk.

"This is not the kind of thing we'd joke about," I replied.

"Technically, there's nothing I can say. You're not breaking any rules. There's no policy at Sutton U about intra-team relationships—" Coach paused.

"But?" Kayden added.

"Does anyone else on the team know?"

I nodded.

"Dane and Jace. Axel—" I paused. "Axel just found out. He caught us kissing. He's pretty concerned about how this will affect our on-ice performance. All of them are, but Axel's more…insistent."

"I'd have to agree with the concerns. When personal feelings get involved, things can get heated, and we lose our perspective. Truthfully, I've never been faced with this situation before," Coach admitted. "Players coming out to me, yes.

But two teammates that are dating, no. Or is that the right word? Did this happen, past tense, or is it still going on?"

I looked over at Kayden again. Without thinking, I reached for his hand.

"We're in a relationship," I croaked.

Banning was shocked. Kayden was shocked.

But no one more than me.

CHAPTER 37

KAYDEN

"And nothing that happens between us is going to affect our play," Maddox insisted. "We're committed to this team and to winning. All in."

Coach Banning said nothing in response. I gripped Maddox's hand tighter.

"We aren't planning on coming out, though. Or, at least, not yet," I stated. "But we're worried that Axel might start talking about us. And that if he does, and rumors start, it might force our hand. He's pissed."

Banning raised one eyebrow. "Axel can raise his concerns with me privately. But he doesn't have a right to out anyone. Might be a good idea to speak to an LGBTQ rep here on campus."

"It's not only our team; it's the hockey world in general that's not accepting," Maddox looked at me and then back at Coach. "Even if Kayden and I weren't together, I don't know for sure that I'd want to come out."

Banning sighed and leaned forward. "I played in the league for five years, and I knew a couple of guys who were queer but kept it hidden. They waited until they retired to come out. It's not right, it's not fair, but unfortunately, change in the hockey community is slow," he paused. "Back to the here and now, moving forward, we go on as is. But if there are any issues, you need to tell me. We can't have your relationship affecting our season. Not when we're so close to our goal. I need all your efforts focused on the ice. Got it?"

"Yes, Coach," Maddox and I said at the same time.

"Good, now get out of my office."

A sudden knock at the door had Maddox and I letting go of each other's hand.

"Come in!" Coach yelled out.

The door opened and Axel looked surprised to see us. Like he didn't think we were going to take his threat seriously? Asshole.

"I can come back later—" Axel started.

"No, I don't have time later," Coach barked. "Get in here and close the door. Let's get this over with."

There were no empty seats in the office, so once Axel shut the door, he moved to stand beside me.

Banning steepled his hands.

"Maddox and Kayden told me about what happened. For everyone's reference, the team is status quo. That means whenever any of you—" he paused and glared at Axel. "And I mean any of you, step onto the rink, any rink, wearing the Sutton Cougars uniform, you're all teammates and focused on playing the best game you can. Off the ice, what you do is your business. And *only* your business. Are we clear?"

Maddox and I quickly nodded, and Axel too.

"We all have too much at stake at this point in the season. Keep in mind that scouts will be attending games and taking notes. Play hard, stick to your job, and do what you do best out there. Save your personal shit for personal time. That's all."

Axel headed for the door first, with Maddox and I following.

"And one more thing," Banning added. We turned to face

him. "You guys are some of the most talented players I've ever had the privilege of coaching at this level. I don't say that lightly. And I don't want to see any of you achieve anything less than greatness."

I felt calmer, but I wasn't sure how Maddox was doing. Or what Axel was going to say. Not until we left Banning's office.

"Look, maybe I overreacted a bit—" Axel started.

"You think?" Maddox snapped and took off down the hallway.

I turned to Axel.

"We were planning on telling Coach. We're not stupid," I whispered.

"I didn't say that you—" Axel raised up his hands. "Look, I don't want anything to fuck up this season. You don't know the kind of pressure I'm under."

"We're all under it. All of us. I'm on scholarship, and I struggle with my classes because I have dyslexia," I blurted out. "What do you think I'm going through every day?"

Axel stared at me and slumped back against the wall.

"Sorry," he muttered and shook his head. "I had no idea."

"That's what happens when you make a judgment about something you know nothing about," I replied. "Maddox and I take hockey as seriously as you do. Nothing gets in the way of it. You've seen us play. Trust in that."

I didn't have anything left to say to Axel. I stalked off in search of Maddox, who was now out of sight.

Probably halfway to the dorm by now…

I made my way down the long hallway and through the front doors, and when I stepped outside, I found him standing on the steps, staring at his phone.

"I've had enough drama for one day," I sighed. "Let's go back to the dorm and study. I've got an essay coming up, and I'm nervous as fuck."

Maddox looked up at me.

"I got a message from Daniel. He's driving down here tonight. He'll be at the game tomorrow."

"That's great!" I exclaimed. "We need all the support we can get."

I went to hug him and then realized where we were standing. Putting my hands back in my pockets, I stared at him.

Maddox didn't say anything. He stood there, head down.

"Are you okay? Aren't you stoked he'll be here to watch you play?"

"I am." Maddox looked up at me. "But, also, surprised. That he'd do that. For me."

"Well, he *is* your foster family."

"Was. But that doesn't mean he has to come see me now."

We started down the stairs and walked along the pathway.

"Obviously, you mean a lot to him."

Maddox's cheeks flushed as he nodded.

"I wasn't exactly the easiest kid to deal with," Maddox admitted. "But he's been more like a dad to me than my own. And I…I don't want to let him down, you know? There's only a handful of people whose opinions I care about. And Daniel's one of them."

"I can't wait to meet him."

Maddox didn't respond at first. Shit, did he not want me to meet Daniel?

"I told him," Maddox finally replied. "About you. About us."

He didn't say anything else and he didn't have to. I realized what it meant. And how much I meant to Maddox.

When we arrived at the dorm, we headed straight to his room. Once inside, we dropped our bags and tossed our jackets off. I sat in his chair, beckoning him to sit on my lap.

Maddox put his arms around my neck, sliding in nice and tight. Nothing between us. I cupped his face, running my thumb along his lips, across his cheekbone.

"So, you told Daniel we're together. Does this mean you *more* than like me?" I asked, pulling him in close, teasing his mouth with a soft kiss.

A loud moan rumbled out of his chest. It had me pulling him in even tighter.

"Like isn't the right word, Kay," he confessed, taking my lips in a claiming kiss. "I'm sure you've already figured me out. My feelings are never in the middle. All or nothing. Even though I might not say it or show it, you've gotta know that you're all of it. Do you understand what I'm saying?"

Maddox didn't need to say the words. I doubted he might ever say them. But looking up at his steely blues, I didn't see lust. I saw the truth staring right back at me.

"Yes," I whispered. "I've fallen so hard for you, Mad. It's like the first time I stepped foot on the ice. My legs are wobbly, my knees are weak, and I'm scared I'm going to get hurt. But it's still the most incredible thing that's ever happened to me."

Maddox gave me a smile I'd never seen before. One that literally took my breath away.

We didn't just fuck that night. There was love there, too.

Maddox – later that night

Kayden was out cold beside me, intermittently snoring and talking in his sleep. I'd say he was adorable, but thinking the word, never mind saying it, had me shaking my head at myself.

Despite—or maybe because of—the most intense sex we'd ever had, I was too amped up to join him in dreamland. Overloaded with emotions I wasn't prepared for. I thought after what I went through with my dad that I'd be able to face anything.

Turns out, I wasn't prepared to fall in love with Kayden.

I'd gotten so used to holding everyone at arm's length,

and holding everything inside, that speaking sometimes was near painful. And unleashing my deepest feelings? Forget about it. But as I stared at Kayden, I knew that somehow, little by little, the words were going to come. I didn't know when. I didn't know how. But one day, I'd be ready. I could only hope Kayden would be patient enough to wait for me.

"What's wrong?"

Kayden's sleep-roughened voice distracted me from my thoughts.

"Nothing," I replied. "Go back to sleep."

"No. Something's bothering you. I can tell."

"What are you, a mind reader?"

"No. I'm attuned to the many, many moods of my Maddox," he chuckled.

I slid back down beside him and tucked my face into his neck, taking a deep inhale, my unsettled heart still beating erratically.

"Don't give up on me, alright?" I whispered.

He hugged me tightly. I kissed his neck, then made my way up to his jaw, until he turned his head and our lips met.

"I didn't. And, I won't."

CHAPTER 38
KAYDEN

GAME DAY

was sweating a shit ton and the game had just started. I wasn't called up first, and that didn't help my nerves at all. Never content to sit still in the box, my knees were popping up and down, about to take flight. I was ready to launch myself over the boards the second Coach called a line change.

Dane, Ethan, and Colin were in position, along with Silas and Finn. And, of course, Maddox in goal. He looked calm. No, that wasn't right. He was calm. When I woke up this morning, I'd been my usual game day self, too much energy, too many nerves. My adrenaline went from zero to a hundred miles an hour in the blink of an eye. Maddox, on the other hand, kissed me good morning and quietly went about getting himself ready. No words spoken after that. Not that I let that stop me from talking. But he didn't mind my chatter. And I didn't mind the fact he didn't want to talk. I knew for sure that he was listening, his eyes following me no matter where I moved.

Until we got to the rink, where we parted ways. Maddox

put his headphones on and headed for his stall, and I did the same, walking up to Dane and Jace for my usual pre-game convo. I'd texted them ahead of my arrival to let them know what happened with Axel and Coach. They were concerned about Axel causing issues, but I wasn't. Between Coach's support, my friends, and of course, my boyfriend's, I was confident that nothing changed for us here on the ice.

And I needed that confidence today…

Coach tapped on my shoulder, and I focused on the now. "Remember what we talked about in practice. Keep a close eye on Joliet and Kourinko. They're so fast you're not going to see them coming until it's too late."

Langston College's star forwards. And they were that. Fast as fuck, from the first puck drop, which we lost, to the moment the ref called the first time out. But Langston's weakest link was their defense. Especially Delacourt and Whitman. Both guys were slow to react, and if we took advantage, it might tip the scales.

When I finally got my turn on the ice, the tension was so thick I was chewing on it—even with my mouthguard. We were closing in on the end of the first period and with no goals on either side, it was still anyone's game to take.

The face-off was ours, with Dane taking control of the puck before passing to Jace. Jace launched into the fray with impressive speed, and with a quick flick of his wrist, he shot the puck to Axel, who, in turn, took off with it like he was powered by jet fuel. It didn't matter how much I disliked Axel Lund as a person. As a hockey player, when he gets going, the guy's a goddamn force to be reckoned with. And after our confrontation outside Coach's office, I was starting to understand him. He didn't want to win, he needed it. And, given that Axel played for Langston College last year, it appeared he also had something to prove.

Axel skillfully deke'd around Delacourt, doing what he does best—making it possible for the play to happen. He passed back to Jace, and Jace doesn't hesitate to make his move, taking the shot. The puck zoomed past the goalie's blocker, and when the buzzer sounded, me and everyone else in the crowd erupted. Jace raised his stick in the air, shock and awe on his face.

Suddenly, we're up by one and anything's possible. But not for long. There's less than a minute on the clock and we've gotta make the most of it.

Coach was right about Langston's forwards. Soon, they're all over us. All over me. I get hit hard by Kourinko, slamming into the boards. Every bone in my body rattled while he skated away like nothing happened.

"Motherfucker," I muttered to myself, trying to catch my breath.

Silas skated up to me, concern on his face. "You alright, Kay?"

I nodded. "Fine. I'm fine. Thanks."

I'm tempted to make a fuss to the ref, but I know that's asking for a penalty we don't need. I shook off the hit—and my frustration—and got back into the fray.

We hold on to our lead. For that period. For the second.

By the time intermission is done, and the third period starts, we're rehydrated and ready to lock this thing down.

Maddox and I were true to our word. Out here, we're teammates. That's it. He's his usual grumpy self, scowling at everyone during the break, and I'm joking around to ease the tension. The only time I go near him is right before we're set to play. I skated around his net, tapped the bar twice, and headed back to my position.

Langston's also benefited from a break, and they came at us hard during the third period. But Maddox blocked several attempts on goal, holding steady. He looked like he was ready to play for hours.

The minutes counted down, and the atmosphere in the rink's completely electric.

I was sitting in the box when the final minute hit and I knew, I fucking knew, that we had this locked down. I was so proud of Maddox, and our team, that my emotions swelled up like a rising tide. It was the first time all game that I let myself go there.

We didn't score again. But Langston didn't score at all.

The buzzer sounded off and with it, the reality that we beat the top college team in the country. The game was over, but for the Sutton Cougars, the party was just beginning.

Maddox

My teammates flooded the ice, jumping around like they were part of a massive mosh pit, yelling, waving, celebrating. But I didn't hear any of it. I was still soaking up the reality that we'd won.

When I looked up at the crowd, I spotted Daniel and waved at him. It meant more to me than I'd ever admit seeing him standing there, cheering me on. He was on his feet, clapping and smiling at me, like any proud parent would. I looked around the venue, finally taking a moment to appreciate the scene, the fans, the moment...

Then, my heart nearly stopped when I saw a man in the crowd who looked eerily similar to my father. What the fuck? I dropped my stick, my legs numb, my pulse racing. I reached for my net to stay upright. I blinked and no, it was a stranger. Of course, it was.

He's dead. He's gone.

Normally, I coveted my mask. My protection. Now I wrenched it off so I could fucking breathe. I took a huge gulp of cold air, in and then out, slowly, until my nerves calmed. Shaking off that weird reaction, I skated toward center ice.

We'd won. We'd fucking done it.

I didn't want to get crammed in with my teammates, but I

still wanted to congratulate everyone. Upsetting Langston College was a huge win for us.

Kayden spotted me, skated over, and took hold of my arm, pulling me in for a hug. I was shaking hard. We clutched tightly for a moment, and then I let go and waved at the rest of the team. It was as close to a smile and a handshake as they were gonna get...

After basking in the thrill of our win, we cooled down, showered and changed. A team dinner was happening, and for once, I didn't crab about it. Not out loud, at any rate.

I slipped on my jacket when I heard a telltale buzz. When I reached for my phone, I saw the text from Daniel.

"Daniel's waiting outside," I said to Kayden, who was still getting dressed. "Join me when you're ready?

"Sounds good."

I headed for the hallway, and spotted Daniel standing at the far end. He wore a massive puffer coat and a beanie—or, as we Canadians call it, a tuque—looking like your typical hockey dad. When I finally reached him, he didn't move to touch me. He knew me.

Pushing aside my fear, I reached over and hugged him. After all, I wouldn't be here today if it weren't for his help. He patted my back gently, and when I stood back, his expression was as shocked as mine.

What the fuck did I do? Who am I right now?

"I'm so damn proud of you," he stated. "You were awesome out there. All of you."

"Thanks," I whispered, not comfortable with praise but not wanting to be a dick to one of my only friends. Courage on the ice was easy for me, but outside of it? I'd be working on it for a long while. "Join me and the rest of the team for dinner? I'm sure Coach Banning would love to talk shop with you."

"That'd be great. By the way—"

Daniel's question was interrupted by Kayden's sudden appearance.

"Hey, I'm Kayden Melnyk. And you must be Daniel Toth. It's an honor to meet you, sir."

Kayden held out his massive hand and Daniel's got swallowed up by it. My former coach and foster dad looked at me and then back up at Kayden. Way up.

"It's nice to meet you too, Kayden. I was impressed by your defensive skills out there. I'm going to be joining you guys for dinner, if that's okay?"

"Cool. Then you can give me the lowdown on this guy," Kayden pointed towards me.

"Hey!"

"What?" Kayden shrugged.

"Don't be taken in by his innocent expression," I warned Daniel.

My former coach was staring at us like he couldn't quite believe what was happening. *You and me both, Daniel.*

Daniel pointed to my wrist and then Kayden's. "What's that you're wearing? Team bracelets?"

"I made them," Kayden announced proudly. "You want one?"

"Absolutely," Daniel replied. "With Maddox's number and a grumpy face emoji."

Kayden chuckled. "I'm on it."

"You two are hilarious," I snarked, biting back a smile. "Let's get with the leaving already."

Kayden gripped my shoulder. "Come on, bee. We upset Langston College. Show your happy."

"Bee?" Daniel stared at me.

"Shit," Kayden whispered, his cheeks flushed.

"He nicknamed you *bee*?" Daniel asked me.

My face was overheating. Where was my mask when I needed it?

"Angry bee," Kayden corrected.

Daniel laughed out loud. "I love it! It's perfect."

He offered Kayden a high five. Jesus. These two were never going to let me hear the end of it. I threw up my hands in mock frustration, but really, it was all good. Who wouldn't like Kayden? Or that silly nickname? If he could melt my salt, he could do anything.

It wasn't until we stepped outside and I took a deep inhale of fresh air that I remembered what had happened after the game.

"I thought I saw him in the crowd," I blurted out.

"Saw who?" Kayden asked, stopping short.

"My father," I admitted. "That's weird, right? It was a panic attack. Probably from the stress of the game."

Daniel turned to me. "Not to mention the calls from the lawyers."

My father's estate. I couldn't put that off forever. I nodded.

"Have you been keeping up with your therapy?" Daniel asked.

I shrugged.

"Yeah, virtual sessions. But we talk mostly about school, and how I'm dealing with the environment here, " I paused. "Talking about my father takes a lot out of me, and most days, I don't have the energy to deal. And I hate talking about *him*, churning it all up again. I've been in therapy for four years now. When's it going to be enough?"

Never. Bruises faded with time, but the pain of his abuse stayed with me. It dug in deep, and I don't think it was ever leaving.

Kayden slid a hand to my back. Knowing that he had mine calmed me. I never thought I'd trust in anyone else like this, but I did.

"I don't know. But you're strong, and you're here. And look at you now. Can't you see the change?" Daniel asked me. "I can see it."

I stared at him, then glanced at Kayden.

"He's right," Kayden replied. "The first thing you ever said to me was *'fuck off.'* Now look at us."

I couldn't argue with that. But it got me wondering.

"What made you keep coming back?" I asked.

Kayden paused and bit his lower lip.

"Remember our first away game? When I told you about my dyslexia? Your reaction. It told me that you were so much more than an angry attitude. And I knew. I knew that I had to keep trying."

"Just like that, eh?"

"Just like that."

CHAPTER 39

KAYDEN

The night we beat Langston College was the night we came out to the team.

Not only me and Maddox, but Dane and Jace, too. In fact, Dane was the first one. At the after party at Ethan's house, of all places.

"I'm gay."

The announcement was made in the kitchen as we gathered around for celebratory shots. Dane's admission was followed by sudden silence. Except for the guys who choked on their drinks and coughed. The rest of them stood around gaping, mouths open, eyes wide.

"Not that it's anyone's business but my own," Dane continued with a sigh, reaching for another shot. "But I've come out to my closest friends and family and this is my next step. Y'all know Jackson. He's not just my best friend and roommate, he's my boyfriend. This is who I am. And that's all I have to say."

There were nods and murmurs from most of the guys. Was that a good sign or a bad one?

I glanced at Maddox, then at Jace. Everyone reached for another shot.

"Dane isn't the only queer player on our team," Jace declared as he stood beside Dane. "I'm bi. Like our captain said, this is who I am. And I'm not going to justify myself to anyone. Nothing changes on the ice. Nothing."

"We're cool," Ethan replied.

I was surprised—and pleased—that he was the first one to speak up. Finn nodded, then Julian, and even Silas murmured his agreement. Hell, I was shocked that Silas was even here. He'd never partied with us.

Sean and a few of the others shrugged but said nothing. I couldn't tell about Axel; he had his head down, staring at the glass in his hand.

I glanced at Maddox and he nodded. Better now than never.

"I'm bi too," I admitted. "But my situation is different—"

"Cause he's with me," Maddox added, joining me. "Kay and I are together."

More guys reached for the bottles of vodka and tequila that littered the kitchen island.

"Whoa," Ethan held a hand up. "One big news announcement at a time. I mean, I don't have any issue with anyone who's queer, but, teammates that are dating? Not gonna lie, that sounds pretty fucking intense."

"Jace said it best," Maddox replied. "Nothing changes. Kayden and I love hockey. It's all we want to do—"

"Besides each other," Finn snorted.

Maddox gave him his favorite finger. "We're both committed to the team and to winning."

Axel finally looked up and nodded at me. There was a hint of a smile on his face. It wasn't a total show of support, but I'd take it.

We hung around with the guys for a while, downing more shots and shooting the shit. Everyone seemed okay, but only time would tell.

Maddox and I headed back to the dorm. When we got to

his room, there was a question in my mind that had been waiting for too long.

"I want to ask you something—but don't say no right away," I started.

Maddox leaned against the door, sliding one hand around my waist, and the other over my ass, pulling me in tight.

"I'm listening."

"I want you to come—"

"Yes, please."

I laughed and kissed him quiet.

"Not that." I paused and looked into his eyes. "I want you to come with me when I volunteer next week."

Maddox's grip tightened. "You mean help out with the sports charity?"

I nodded.

"I haven't been back in a while, but it's time. And I know peopling isn't your thing, but if you saw these kids, Mad." I paused and leaned in closer. "They've been through so much already in their lives. If anyone can relate, it's you."

Maddox opened his mouth, but not a word or a sound came out.

"Mad?"

"Um, yeah. I'll go with you," he muttered. "But you're going to have to help me. I have no idea what to say or do."

"Just be yourself." I smiled at him. "Minus the swearing."

Maddox bit his lower lip. "Are you sure this is a good idea?"

It was the best idea.

The following week, Maddox made good on his promise and came with me to All For Play. We set up an adapted lacrosse game for the kids and having something structured to do helped ease Mad's anxiety. Two of the quietest kids in the group gravitated toward my boyfriend. I wasn't the least bit surprised as I watched both Maddox and the kids slowly warm to each other. They asked him tons of questions about being a goalie, and he patiently answered each one. In fact, it was the most relaxed I'd seen him in any social situation outside of hockey. He even cracked a smile. Several times.

If Maddox hadn't already stolen my heart, this would have clinched it.

Afterward, I told him I'd never been prouder. His response was typical; he rolled his eyes and played off like it was no big deal. But I knew it was. For him, *and* for us.

Maddox

Coming out to the team was *not* the shitshow I'd anticipated. And I was more than relieved that Kayden and I didn't have to hide. There were a few guys that looked uncomfortable with the news, but that was their problem, not ours.

It was dealing with the other stuff in my personal life that was daunting. Going back to my therapist, for one thing. Telling them about the panic attack I'd had after the game with Langston and dredging up the past again. I'd be in therapy for a long time. And you know what? That was okay. I was going to do what I had to in order to live my life on my terms.

A couple of weeks later, I finally got around to emailing my father's lawyer. It was time to get that over and done with. I had a plan for what I was going to do with my inheritance. And when the lawyer sent me the paperwork and everything was signed, I contacted an accountant and got my financial stuff in order. My mom had left me enough for college and savings, and I didn't need anything else. So, after discussing with Kayden and Daniel, I donated what my father left me to several charities, including All For Play. Anonymously, of course.

It didn't erase what my father had done, but it left me feeling lighter than I had in years. Tackling my painful past and doing something positive with it was its own kind of freedom. Slowly, the grip he'd had on me, even after death, was easing.

And when February rolled around, we were back on the ice. Only, this time, I wasn't the one in net. I was helping Kayden as a volunteer with All For Play's sledge hockey series.

After the volunteers—which included me, Jace, and Dane—helped get the kids into their sleds, Kayden pulled me aside.

"What do you think?" Kayden asked.

Proud parents were filling up the stands, waving, and taking pictures of the kids.

I glanced at him. "I think this is the most fun I've had on the ice since I started playing hockey."

"I told you," Kayden teased me.

"Yeah, yeah." I rubbed my nose with my middle finger.

Then I remembered who might be looking. Shit.

Kayden chuckled and squeezed my waist. "Can't take you anywhere."

"And yet, you do," I responded tartly.

"How about taking you home?" he asked me.

I swallowed hard. "You mean, like, meet the parents, home?"

"Yep."

"That's a big step."

Kayden nodded. "It is. But it doesn't have to be next week or next month. When you're ready."

Could I really do this? What if they didn't like me? And since when did I care about what other people thought of me? Since Kayden.

"And they'll love you," he added. "Because I do."

I'd never get used to Kayden saying those words.

"Your parents weren't happy about the whole 'dating a teammate' thing back at Christmas, right?" I replied. "What's changed?"

"What's our standing?" he asked.

I rolled my eyes. "We're the top-ranked team."

Kayden smirked. "Exactly. This is the best we've ever played. Our stats speak for themselves. And it's not just hockey. I'm doing better in school than I have in years, thanks to your support. I'm happy. Really fucking happy. And my parents know it because I talk about you constantly."

I bit my lower lip. "And what about the future? Going pro?"

"When we get drafted, we'll deal with it."

"You're confident," I replied, unable to contain a grin. "It's fucking hot, Kay."

"Don't give me that look, bee. Not now."

"What look?" I teased, licking my lips.

"You know exactly what look." Kayden shook his head and started skating backward. "Go teach the next generation how to be a goaltender."

"Never thought I'd be doing that," I quipped as I skated towards him.

"And yet, here you are."

"It's all because of you," I insisted.

Kayden cocked his head, a lock of his wavy hair falling into his hazel eyes. "It's us. Together. We make a great team, right?"

I caught up to him and took hold of Kayden's hand. There was no denying the truth.

"Best one ever."

EPILOGUE
KAYDEN

t didn't take much convincing to get Maddox to come home with me. This time. And for the entire summer, no less.

He was a bit overwhelmed about meeting my big family, but slowly, he came around. Rory was the first one he warmed to, as my brother was into everything tech, and my boyfriend was the same.

We got weekday jobs; me at a local tennis club and Maddox at a restaurant. The restaurant job was his therapist's idea. It was important for Mad to get out and meet people, and not isolate like he wanted to.

So, while I cleaned the clubhouse and took care of the courts, Maddox was busy managing delivery app orders. Maddox was fast, and he worked with a small team, so it worked out. And he was still taking freelance web gigs, so with all that, we had enough money for anything we wanted. Most of it went into our savings. We were planning a back-packing trip next summer to Italy and France. Maddox got interested in researching his mom's family history and discovered that his great-grandparents were from Normandy. Not only that, but he had distant relatives still living in northern France.

Most of the summer, we biked around southern Maine, exploring beaches, rivers, and parks. I had my dad's pickup truck for our beach days. On Fridays after work, we wandered into town for a lobster roll and, often, an ice cream. We ran into Summer a few times. Jealous brat that Maddox was, he always took hold of my hand. The weekends we spent at the beach, learning to surf, playing volleyball, and lazing about.

Like we were now. Spread out on towels, on our backs, getting burnt, watching the sun slowly dip into the horizon.

I glanced at my wrist, smiling.

"I know it was you," I blurted out.

"It was me what?" he muttered.

I turned to look at him and, for a moment, I forgot what I was going to say. Can you blame me? Maddox wore nothing but a black speedo, his earring, and my bracelet. Hot as hell. Oh, and he was rocking a new tattoo on his chest, over his left pec. He'd had it done in June. It was the number two made up of ten tiny bees.

Two and ten. Him and me. My angry bee. Or, just bee now. Not so angry anymore.

When he revealed the tattoo to me (on my twentieth birthday no less), I teared up. He still hadn't said he loved me, but he sure as fuck showed me.

"The bracelet kit," I replied. "You bought it for me. I thought at first that it was Dane, but it was you."

Maddox grunted, rolled over to his belly, and buried his face in his arms.

"You don't need to say anything," I quipped. "I know it was you."

He finally lifted his head, his eyes squinting.

"And?"

"You had it bad for me," I teased. "I knew it."

"Not had. Have," he replied with a smirk, leaned over, and kissed me.

"Right back at you, baby."

Maddox

A stolen kiss on a public beach was quick. Too quick.

"Time to go home?" I suggested.

Kayden got up so fast that he nearly tripped on his towel.

"I take it that's a 'yes'?" I chuckled, taking in the sight of my beautiful boyfriend, tanned, and looking fine as fuck in tight board shorts.

"It's a hell yes," he replied.

I couldn't help but smile in return. I was doing a lot of that this year and all because of Kayden.

We gathered up our towels, bodyboards, and backpacks. Once we got the truck loaded with our gear, he slipped into the driver's seat, and I got in beside him. We headed off down the road, taking the route that followed the coastline.

I reached for his free hand, interlocking our fingers tightly. I was doing a lot of that lately, too. And sometimes, in public. Coming out wasn't all easy, though. But once our teammates saw that who we were on the ice didn't change, they settled. Or they kept their opinions to themselves. Axel had no more issue, or if he did, he kept it to himself. Silas and most of the other guys told us straight up they had no problem. We moved on. And that number one college hockey spot that our team was vying for? We'd clinched it, one game at a time. Our successful hockey season was proof enough that Kayden and I were committed to the team and to winning.

"You okay?" Kayden asked me.

"Yeah, you know, thinking about this year. Everything that's happened. So many changes."

I squeezed his hand tighter.

"A lot of them," he replied. "The best kind."

It was true. I thought about my mom and what she'd say about all this. About me. About me and Kayden. The sun hit my shoulders, warm and comforting, like one of her hugs.

Be brave, honey.

"I love you."

The words were barely audible, but I'd said them.

Suddenly, Kayden let go of my hand, steered the car to the side of the road, and parked. We turned to each other, and he reached for me, cupping my neck.

I was shaking. So was he.

"Did you just say you loved me?"

I nodded, too choked up for a moment to do anything else.

"I broke my own rule."

Kayden smiled and pulled me in for a resounding kiss. I held on just as tight.

"I love you, too," he whispered against my lips. "And you didn't break anything. Remember? Our relationship, our rules."

"Right. And everyone else can fu…"

Kayden interrupted my favorite expression with another kiss.

And you know what? I didn't mind one bit.

Thank you for reading Rule Breaker! Rivals Axel and Jace get their story in Play Maker, Book 2, and Silas and Damien in Heart Taker, Book 3.

Want more of my MM romances? Check out my Wayward Lane rockstar romance series: Punk-In, B-Mine, and 4-Ever, and my Voyagers series: Oh Buoy, Starboard, The Cockpit, Endeavor, and Nauti or Nice.

BONUS SCENE

LIFE CHANGER

Kayden

"Are you sure you're ready to do this?"

I stared at my boyfriend Maddox as we sat in the truck I'd rented to drive home and waited patiently for his answer. Not that I expected him to say much. The closer the countdown to us leaving school, the quieter he got. Which only meant that when he did finally say something, I knew it was going to be…explosive.

"Yes," he snapped, his tone contradicting his word. "Now stop asking me."

He was sitting in the passenger seat, staring out of the window, with one hand tapping away on his thigh, and the other white knuckling the door. My beautiful bee was buzzing with nervous energy, and I knew it was all about meeting my family for the first time. Not just that, we'd be living with them for the summer. I came from a large family, most of whom were loud, and often incredibly nosy. But most of all, loving. Maddox, on the other hand, had gone through so much loss in his life already and he didn't trust easily. There was a protective wall around him, and he didn't take to people like I did.

Still, I knew that once Mad got to know my family, he would love them, and they, in turn, would love him. The fact that he was coming home with me said everything. He loved me, even if he had a difficult time putting what he felt into words.

"If you're not, it's no big deal," I insisted. "I can drive you to the airport if you'd prefer to head back home to Toronto. You don't have to come to Maine. We can wait another month or two."

Maddox turned his head and gave me his molten blue glare, the one that had most people running for cover. But not me. I leaned over and kissed his pouty lips, trying to ease his discomfort.

"Kay."

"Alright?" I asked.

He nodded and suddenly, I was the one who was nervous. I really, really wanted Mad to come home with me. I'd fallen hard for this gorgeous, complicated person and I wouldn't have it any other way.

"Drive."

That was all I needed to hear. I leaned back and turned on the engine, then guiding the truck out of the parking lot. It was a warm spring day, the sun shining high, with the promise of summer in the air. Soon, we'd be in Wells and surrounded by salt breezes, sandy beaches, and the smell of fried seafood. I couldn't wait to share it all with Mad.

It took us over three hours to get from Vermont to Maine. We stopped once to get gas and to fill up on snacks; chips for Maddox, Twizzlers for me, and a gallon of soda to share.

By the time we pulled up to my parents' house, it was nearing on dinnertime. Home was a two-story cape, with white shutters and surrounded by bushes of pink sea roses growing wild all around the property. I turned off the engine and turned to Mad, who had that same determined expression on his face like he did when he was guarding his net.

Before I could say anything, the front door opened and my mom came rushing out.

"You ready?" I asked Maddox.

He nodded, biting his lower lip.

I got out of the truck and ran around the front, opening the passenger door for Maddox.

"What are you—" he started.

I pulled him out of the truck and into my arms, giving him a resounding kiss.

"Aw, you two are so sweet," Mom gushed.

"Has been said about me never," Maddox whispered under his breath, and then politely offered his hand to her. "Nice to meet you Mrs. Melnyk, thank you for inviting me to stay in your home."

My mom waved his hand aside and pulled him in for a long hug.

"None of that formal *Mrs.* stuff. You call me Janie."

Maddox pulled back, his expression stunned, and it made me laugh.

"What's so funny, Kaybear?" Mom asked me.

Maddox finally cracked a smile. "Kaybear?"

"Shut it," I quipped, feeling my cheeks heat.

"That's my line," Maddox replied. "Well, the PG version."

I kissed him again, so happy to be with him, so happy to be home.

"Not anymore."

Maddox

I was ushered into Kayden's family home and greeted like a hockey star carrying the cup.

It wasn't just my boyfriend smiling at me, there were seven more of him...

Seriously, was everyone in this family made of sunshine or something? It was so far beyond my experience of family, or people in general, that I instantly clammed up. I glanced at

Kayden, who knew me too well, and pulled me tight to his side to comfort me.

"Everyone, this is my boyfriend, Maddox," Kayden announced. "Mad, meet my Dad, Janina, Jenna, Reena, Alec, and Rory."

"Wouldn't it be easier if everyone wore name tags?" I quipped.

"We tried that," Janie chuckled. "And we have t-shirts too, but those are only for our family reunions."

"Reunions? How many Melnyks are there?" I blurted out.

I was probably speaking too bluntly. But like Kayden, his family weren't surprised by my statement and laughed instead.

"Hundreds," Alec replied.

"Too many," his father quipped and offered me his hand. "A pleasure to meet you, Maddox. Kayden has told us all about you. In fact, outside of hockey, you're the only thing he talks about."

A rare blush began to creep up my cheeks.

"It's nice to meet you too, sir," I muttered.

"Call me Vic. No formalities in this family."

I nodded.

"Let's get you settled in and then we can all head down to the beach," Janie insisted.

Living with Kayden's family for the summer was kind of daunting when I thought about it, but I was really stoked about being at the ocean. I'd probably become a beach bum and forget about all about hockey.

Nah. Kidding. That was never gonna happen.

"Um, what room is Maddox taking?" Kayden asked as he squeezed my shoulder.

"Your father finished fixing up the unit over the garage. There's even a kitchenette. We thought you two might prefer the privacy."

"That space is for the two of us?" Kayden replied and glanced at me.

I thought we'd have separate bedrooms. A shared space was *living* together. Holy shit.

"Yes, if that's alright?" she replied. "It's like having your own apartment."

"Mad?" Kayden asked hesitantly.

His eyes were hopeful, but his tone said he was wary of my reaction. While a part of me was scared at that level of commitment, the bigger part was excited. We didn't have much privacy in our dorm at school so sharing a place now would be yet another new adventure. A life changing experience and one I only wanted to share with Kayden.

"I think it's awesome," I finally replied, giving Kayden's back a reassuring pat, and then turning back to his mom. "Thank you."

"You're more than welcome. We'll get you moved in and then you can enjoy the rest of the day."

Kayden's brothers and sisters helped us cart our shitload of stuff from the truck to the apartment that would be home for the next three months. The place was nice, a two-bedroom, one bath apartment, complete with a kitchen that overlooked the backyard. Each bedroom had a queen-sized bed, and with the skylights and a cozy living area with a sofa, the place was perfect for the two of us.

Once his siblings headed back downstairs, Kayden took hold of my hand and kissed it.

"You take whatever bedroom you want, boo."

"What do you mean? Aren't we sharing a bed?"

"I didn't want to assume—" Kayden started.

I reached up and kissed his lips, marveling like I always did, at how much my life had changed since meeting Kayden. All for the better.

"I want to sleep beside you every night and wake up to

your smile every morning," I confessed. "And this way, we'll be able to set up the spare room for gaming."

Kayden chuckled and pulled me into his arms. "God, I love you."

"You might not be saying that a week from now," I quipped.

"What about you? I talk in my sleep, remember?"

"I've grown to like it," I confessed. "In fact, I don't sleep well without you."

"Well, we can't have that," Kayden teased and kissed me soundly. "Are you ready?"

"Let the summer adventures begin."

I hope you enjoyed Kayden & Maddox's bonus short! If you want more MM romance, check out my books here.

ABOUT THE AUTHOR

Ava Olsen writes steamy and dreamy MM romance with heartwarming characters, sexy banter, and ALL the romantic feels.

Sign up for my newsletter for the latest updates, cover reveals, and bonus scenes: http://avaolsenauthor.com

FOLLOW ME

ALSO BY AVA OLSEN

Bar Down: MM College Hockey Romance

Rule Breaker

Play Maker

Heart Taker

Stand Alone (enemies to lovers)

Happily Never After

Wayward Lane MM Rockstar Romance

PUNK-IN

B-MINE

4-EVER

Wayward Lane Backstage

Don't Fall For A Rockstar

Don't Fall For A Bodyguard

Don't Fall For A Dreamer

Voyagers Series

Oh Buoy

Starboard

The Cockpit

Endeavor

Nauti or Nice

Stand Alone (Voyagers spin off)

Co-Star

NY Nights

Novel Affair

Troublemaker

Unforgettable You

NY Nights Bodyguard Edition

Hate to Love You

Love Like Yours

Never Knew Love

Stand Alone (novella)

Long Time Coming